Once Again *Forever*

Once Again *Forever*

Patty Wiseman

First edition September 2025

Book Cover and Design copyright © 2025 Shannon Christensen

Library of Congress Control Number Data 2025916375
Patty Wiseman
Once Again Forever / Wiseman Patty
[B&W—Fiction-Romance-Suspense 2. Fiction-Romance-General
3. Drama – Women Authors]
Fiction & Related Items / Romantic Suspense | Fiction & Related
Items / Romance / Modern & Contemporary

ISBN 979-8-9987001-6-3 (paperback)
ISBN 979-8-9987001-7-0 (eBook)

Published by CS Publishing
Marshall, TX
www.countryspunk.com

Dedication

To any woman who ever hesitated to follow her heart—
I wrote this story for you.

Life's paths may often feel obscure, and love might feel like too
much of a risk. But within the heartache lies the chance of
rediscovery.

If you've ever been afraid to trust again, love again, may this story
be a gentle light in the storm—a reminder love lost can be found
once again.

Table of Contents

CHAPTER ONE

Present day – the village of Murphy at the base of the mountain –

USA

Outside the hospital room of the infamous Wolf Kelley, owner of Wolf's Den Lodge, Lady Martha Buford took a deep breath, patted her carefully coiffed hair, and straightened the bodice of her vintage floral dress.

A crazed man identified as Russ Desmond, now in custody, shot Wolf in the back at the Lodge and left him for dead. Thankfully, Desmond botched the execution-style shooting. The bullet went through Wolf's upper right side missing any bones or main arteries; however, loss of blood rendered him weak and in need of nursing to restore his strength.

Martha was ready to provide it.

"Quit lurking in the hall and come on in here," Wolf's gravelly voice called out.

She stepped through the door and glared at him. "I'm not lurking. Just trying to bolster my resolve where your cantankerous mood is concerned."

Wolf scrubbed one calloused hand over his face. "Oh, sorry Martha, I thought you were the nurse wanting to poke more needles in me. Please come on in."

"That's better," she said. "Now...how are you today? I can't tell how pale you are with that blush spreading over your face."

"I feel much better this morning," he said with a lopsided grin. "And I always improve when you come to visit."

Her hands deftly smoothed the blankets. "We'll have none of that, Wolf Kelley. I'm here as a friend, not to rekindle anything we might have had in the past."

He frowned.

She pretended not to notice.

"Have they given you a time of release, yet?" she continued.

"Nope. Since I live alone and haven't any family to care for me, it's a day-by-day situation." He took her hand. "I walked down the hall a ways last night. That's progress, right? By the way, you are beautiful today. How do you do it? Why, you look the same as you did when we first met in Spain. Your hair is still vibrant, still the color of champagne." He sighed deeply. "I've always loved the color of your hair."

She pulled her hand away. "I told you to stop that kind of talk. As far as my hair goes, I've inherited my mother's genes. Never a hint of gray. As for you, Mr. Kelley, your hard living hasn't been kind to you. I'd like to shave that grizzly gray beard off your face. And you've lost weight. Not flattering for a man of your stature. You need more meat on your bones to put a spark in those faded blue eyes."

He fingered his beard. "I'd shave it off if you would do the honors."

She stayed quiet while straightening the covers again.

"Will you, Martha?" He grabbed her hand a second time.

"Well, I might be persuaded. Anything to get rid of it."

"Call the nurse to bring the necessary things."

She hesitated, withdrew her hand slowly, and called back over her shoulder, heading for the door. "Well...if it will make you feel better."

Five minutes later, she returned with a basin of water, a brush, a razor, and shaving cream. Slowly, she lathered his face with the foam and tried not to stare directly at him. Which was impossible.

He kept his eyes on her face. "You're so beautiful, Martha. I love the feel of your hands on my face again."

Her lips pursed.

"What happened to us, Martha?"

She remained silent until the last of the whiskers and foam disappeared from his face. The razor rattled into the basin. "I'll be right back."

When she returned, surprise made her heart flutter. A tear rolled down Wolf's face and he wiped it away with the corner of the bed sheet.

Never has he looked so vulnerable. His six-foot-four frame appears so small and fragile in that bed. Like a little boy who lost his way with his shock of salt and pepper hair all awry. He's very handsome when bare faced.

"Wolf," She sighed while pulling a chair beside the bed. "Don't you remember?"

"No, I don't. I only remember I love you. Have always loved you and always will. Does it matter what happened in the past? We're different people now. Can't we try again?"

A glint of a smile danced on her lips. "But it does matter, Wolf. I'm not sure we can ever pick up where we left off." Her eyes closed as the memory flashed in her mind. "The cantina at the train station in Spain, remember? I was a slip of a girl at nineteen, traveling with my mother on holiday. You walked in, a strapping young man with a jolt of black hair and a smile that lit up the room. You were with your buddies and didn't notice me." A sensuous sigh enhanced her next words. "I was smitten."

Wolf chimed in, "Oh, I noticed you. My buddy, Polecat Robinson, pointed you out. I almost walked over to introduce myself but saw your mother and decided against it."

Her eyes flew open. "Well, Mother didn't notice you and I was glad, as it emboldened me to make an excuse to visit the powder room. Our eyes met when I bumped into you. You said, "excuse me, miss". I smiled and went on my way."

"Except you dropped your pocketbook," Wolf continued, "I waited for your return and handed it back to you."

"Did you know I did it on purpose?" she asked.

The grin that started it all splayed in all its glory on his face. "I had a hunch."

"Well, you cut quite a figure in your uniform, as I recall. Air Force Blue. Really brought out your eyes." She stood and paced the room.

"So glad you noticed." He chuckled.

A frown replaced the previous smile. "Yes, there was an immediate attraction, but little did I know how wrong it would all turn out."

"Come now, Martha. It was perfect for a long time. Once I won your mother over we were good together. The train ride back to England gave us the time we needed to realize ours was one of the greatest love stories of all time. I was mustering out of the service and headed back to the States. But you insisted on going back to England. Your mother liked me so much she arranged a trip for the two of you to come to the U.S."

She ducked her head and whispered, "Yes, I remember... but then the Baron happened."

Silence filled the room as memories of the day at the train station swirled in her head.

CHAPTER TWO

WHERE MEMORIES LINGER LIKE THE SCENT OF A ROSE ~

Spain
The Train Station

The train whistle blew. People jostled each other trying to get aboard. The sun warmed the air and when Martha closed her eyes, she could almost detect the scent of the spicy red carnations and the slight honey-suckle-like scent from the bougainvillea. Spain was adrift in the perfume of various flowers and trees, something she would miss.

"There's the train. I must join my mother. Thank you for returning my pocketbook," she said, reaching for it. "It was clumsy of me."

"You're most welcome. My name is Wolf Kelley. All my friends call me Wolf. May I ask where you're headed?" He still held the purse.

Their hands touched as she retrieved the bag. A tingle rippled through her at the resistance in his grip.

"Good, thank you Wolf. My name is Martha Buford and I'm heading back to England. Holiday is over." She tucked the purse under her arm and turned to go.

His response was quick, anxious. "I'm heading back there myself...to the Air Force Base. My tour of duty is over, heading back to the good old U. S. of A. Back to the mountains."

"How nice for you," she said, tamping down disappointment. Secretly, she hoped he might stay in England. The Air Force base was only an hour and a half from where she lived. "Well, good-bye."

Dame Buford waved at her. "Martha, come now. We must board."

"Yes, Mother." She marched toward the boarding dock where her mother stood. In seconds, the crowd swallowed them up. She tried to look back but couldn't see anything except the throngs of passengers. The brief encounter with Wolf Kelley was over.

The two women found their seats in Economy class and settled in. Mother Buford wanted the window seat which left Martha on the aisle. As the travelers straggled in, she scanned the individuals coming through and secretly hoped Wolf might appear. The two seats directly across from her remained empty as the others filled up. She crossed her fingers under the folds of her dress. But it was not to be. An elderly lady took the adjacent aisle seat and Martha's heart dropped. *Silly me. This is a long train. He's probably in first class or something suitable for the military.*

Never in her young life did she attempt something so bold as dropping her pocketbook to attract a man. The thrill of the deed made her smile. *Why did I do it?*

"Martha, are you listening to me? I've asked you twice," Mrs. Buford said.

A strand of her mother's champagne hued hair peeked out from under the brim of her elegant pearl colored visor hat. Martha lovingly tucked the errant strand back in place, smiling. *Mother would abhor the thought of even one strand being out of order.*

"I'm sorry, Mum. Just thinking. What did you ask?"

"What will you miss most about Spain? Do you want to come back someday?"

"Oh, that's easy. The fragrance of all the beautiful flowers everywhere we went. And yes, I'd love to come back."

The train jerked a bit. She watched out the window as the dock disappeared, people waving their goodbyes, the buildings receding into the background.

"Excuse me, ma'am. I believe you have my seat."

Martha jerked her head toward the familiar voice.

It's him!

Wolf spoke to the elderly lady sitting across the aisle. "I apologize, but my buddy and I have these seats. See? Here is my ticket."

The woman looked up at him, confusion in her eyes. "But..."

He smiled at her. "May I examine your ticket? Maybe I can help sort this out."

The train picked up speed and caused him to wobble a bit in the aisle.

His coat brushed against Martha's hand. She dared a glance at him. The gorgeous black hair, the strong jaw, his straight back sent her stomach into a flip flop.

The white-haired lady produced the ticket.

He studied it, then his face lit up with a grin. "Yes, I see the problem. You are directly behind me." He pointed to the seat. "Just a case of a mistaken number."

"Oh, I'm so sorry. I don't see too well anymore." She struggled with her bag until Wolf reached out and took it gently from her.

"Please, let me help you. The train is liable to catch you off balance." The bag rested in his left hand and with his right he took her elbow.

As she struggled to stand, Polecat Robinson, who stood behind him, retrieved the bag. Free of the suitcase, Wolf placed an arm around her and soon had her settled in the proper seat.

Polecat, a tall, skinny man with red hair, climbed into the seat by the window, but Wolf remained standing beside the woman. "Are you settled now? Comfy?"

"Oh yes. Thank you. I'll be fine."

"You look a bit pale. Can I get you something? A cup of tea, maybe?" he asked.

"I don't want to be any trouble. I think I can manage, although tea does sound good."

Wolf looked around and spotted a young steward. "Young man, can we get this lovely lady a cup of tea? She's rather exhausted and needs a pick-me-up."

"Certainly, sir. Coming right up."

The steward disappeared into the next car.

"Please sit down, young man. I'll be fine," the woman said.

"As soon as you receive your tea. Where are you going, may I ask?"

A sad look spread across her face. "I'm going home to England. My husband passed and wanted to be buried in his beloved Spain. I granted his wish."

Martha studied the woman as she listened to the conversation. *How sad for her.*

"I'm sorry, ma'am. You're traveling alone? No next of kin to help you?" he asked.

"Sadly, no. Our children are in the States and couldn't make the trip."

The steward returned with tea and biscuits on a tray. "I hope this will suffice, sir. It's all they had ready in the kitchen."

Wolf took the small platter, pulled down the tray in front of her and placed the refreshments upon it. "Sugar? Milk?"

"No, I like mine plain, thank you." She picked up the cup and sipped.

"Jam for your biscuit?"

She nodded.

He spread the biscuit with a generous serving of raspberry jam and set it on the plate before her. "There. This should make you feel better in no time. My name is Wolf Kelley if you should need anything else."

"My name is Elizabeth Sterling. You've been most kind, Mr. Kelley."

He smiled and patted her arm. "I'm right in front of you, if you need me."

"Thank you."

Kelley sat down and said something to Polecat Martha didn't catch. She wondered if he even noticed her.

Such care he gave to her. A true gentleman.

While she stared at him, he slowly turned and said, "We meet again, Miss Buford."

Her heart leapt. *He did notice.*

CHAPTER THREE

ONE KISS AND ALL THE WORLD FALLS SILENT ~

"Why yes, so we do," Martha replied, quaking inside at the gravelly, thoroughly male voice.

Dame Buford leaned forward, all smiles, eyelids fluttering her approval. "Your uniform certainly becomes you, sir. Always nice to meet a military man. My name is Dame Buford. Aren't you the young man who spoke to my daughter at the train station?"

"Nice to meet you. My name is Wolf Kelley, and yes, I rescued her handbag. Isn't it nice we are seated so close together?"

"Very pleasant, indeed," Dame Buford responded.

Martha jabbed an elbow deftly into her mother's side who responded with a soft 'oh,' then turned to look at Wolf. "It was lovely what you did for the lady, Mr. Kelley. So gallant."

"Nothing I wouldn't do for my own mother, Ms. Buford. She taught me respect as a boy."

"A good upbringing certainly shows. Will you stay long in England or return to the States immediately?" she asked.

"They tell me I'll be in the UK for about two weeks to wrap up the red tape and such, then back to my mountains as a civilian." His eyes found hers. "I don't suppose I could take you to supper one night before I leave?"

Heat found its way to her cheeks. "I'd like that."

"Martha, dear, don't forget you have an engagement with Baron Chadwick." She leaned over to address Wolf. "He's been courting her, you know. Fine young man, although a trifle older…"

"Mother, please. Mr. Kelley doesn't need the details of my dinner engagements. There is nothing formal between Anthony and I."

Mrs. Buford retorted brusquely, "Just wanted him to know you are well sought after."

Wolf replied, "Well, I will be around for about two weeks. Surely you won't be engaged every night before I leave. Maybe we can find one evening you might have free."

"Of course, Mr. Kelley. Please forgive her impertinence. I'd love to have dinner with you. Will you be bringing your friend as a chaperone?" She looked at Polecat.

"A chaperone…?

She shot him a knowing look.

"Oh," Wolf said. "Yes, I'll bring him along."

"Good, then Mother can have a nice evening to herself," Martha said. A quick glance at Mrs. Buford revealed the matriarch's eyebrows in a knot. "Don't worry, Mother, I'll be in good hands."

The elderly lady behind Wolf coughed and he immediately turned to address her. "Are you okay Mrs. Sterling?

"I'm afraid I got a piece of biscuit caught in my throat and I'm out of tea."

"No worries, I'll get you another cup." He jumped up and headed for the dining car.

While he was gone, Martha turned to her mother. "What are you doing? First you flirt with Mr. Kelley, then you tell him about Anthony. Make up your mind."

The older Buford smiled. "You can't have too many beaus, my dear. I'm just doing what any self-respecting mother might do. Expand your options. I have a feeling Anthony will be at the train station. It might be interesting for him to see another man interested in you. Make him hurry toward a proposal. See what I mean?"

"Mother, you are incorrigible. Will you please leave my love life to me? We aren't in the dark ages anymore."

Mrs. Buford sighed. "A mother has to try."

Before Martha could answer, Wolf returned balancing a cup of tea while the train rumbled on. He delivered it with a bow.

"Thank you, kindly," the woman said.

"Anytime, ma'am," he replied.

He sat down and turned to Martha. "Now, where were we?"

They chatted pleasantly until the steward announced lunch was being served.

Martha hoped he would invite them to share a table.

Instead, Wolf turned to Mrs. Sterling and asked if she would like company for lunch.

She graciously accepted.

Martha tried to shrug off the pang of disappointment.

Polecat allowed Wolf and Mrs. Sterling to go ahead of him, then turned to Martha. "Would you like a companion for lunch? I hate to see two beautiful women eat alone."

Polecat didn't have Wolf's ruggedly handsome looks, but he was a nice looking fellow. Brown eyes, dull red hair. Taller than Wolf, but thinner.

Mrs. Buford answered quickly. "Why yes, young man. We'd love to dine with you."

Martha's disappointment turned to delight when they entered the dining area.

Each table seated four and Mrs. Sterling, already in place, smiled up at them as they entered.

Wolf stood behind the chair across from her. "Mrs. Buford I've saved this seat for you. May I?" He pulled the chair out.

"Well, I always sit with my ..."

Mrs. Sterling cut her off. "I'd love to chat with you, Mrs. Buford. Wolf tells me what an interesting lady you are. Do you mind?"

Dame Buford was the epitome of politeness. She simply had no choice. "Why, of course, Mrs. Sterling. I'd be delighted."

Polecat directed Martha to the table across the walkway, pulled out the aisle chair for her, and took his seat across the table by the window, leaving Wolf to sit directly opposite of her.

I've heard stories about men using friends to meet women. I think they call them wingmen. Is that Polecat's role?

The dining room sported crisp white tablecloths, starched white napkins and light blue China with the train logo in the center. A lovely table lamp gave the ambience an elegant flare.

Martha ordered sliced steak with brown gravy, a garden salad, mashed potatoes, and coffee. She chatted aimlessly while awaiting their meal and couldn't help but see the twinkle in Wolf's eyes at the coup he'd pulled off. They exchanged knowing smiles at the intrigue.

Every once in a while, she glanced at her mother who was thoroughly engrossed in conversation with Mrs. Sterling. She mouthed the words 'thank you' to Wolf who only winked in response.

Polecat joined the conversation, interjecting a joke here, a note about the scenery there, but mostly kept to his meal.

I imagine they do this for each other often. They seem to have it down to a fine science.

They managed to stretch their time in the dining room until the steward announced it closed.

When they went back to their seats, Mrs. Buford elected to sit with Mrs. Sterling. Martha was relieved to have her mother's attention deflected away from her.

Wolf asked her to stroll with him to the back of the rail carriage where they might enjoy the scenery. She'd seen those kinds of scenes in movies, but never actually stood outside in the little hall.

"I'm a little nervous. I know there's a railing here, but what if I lose my footing?" Martha asked.

He took her elbow. "I'd never let anything happen to you, Martha. I'm right here to catch you."

She blushed. "Good to know. It's a bit thrilling to be out here with the wind whistling by; the sounds of the wheels on the track, the scenery whipping by. Almost like a movie."

"There's nothing like experiencing the elements first-hand. Better than being cooped up in the train car." He tightened his grip as the train took a curve. "You're beautiful, you know. Have I told you that before?"

She smiled. "I don't think so. It's nice to hear."

"There is definitely something between us. Can you feel it?"

Her breath became shallow. She could barely say the words as her heart pounded. "I do feel it, but maybe we're just caught up in the moment."

She almost didn't hear his spoken request, his voice only a whisper.

"May I kiss you?"

Words failed her, so she gave a short nod.

He leaned in.

The kiss was soft, tender, but lit a fire inside her.

They parted.

Her face was hot. "Oh!"

He circled his arm around her waist and kissed her again, this time with more passion, more intensity.

She didn't resist, instead melted into him and returned the passion.

"You see, Martha? There is something quite special between us. I can tell you feel it, too."

"Yes, Wolf. I feel it very much."

By the time the train pulled into London, Martha was in love.

CHAPTER FOUR

LO, THE SERPENT JOINS THY GARDEN ~

Baron Anthony Chadwick pulled a silver antique pocket watch from his waistcoat. *I'll have time to arrange a quiet dinner this evening when Martha's train arrives. I wish I could have her all to myself.* He issued a deep sigh. *This chaperone business is a bother. But what can I do? Mrs. Buford is a stickler for propriety.*

To marry the daughter of a wealthy aristocrat was Anthony's sole ambition. His title afforded many luxuries in life, but he found himself at an impasse financially. The estate needed repair, he let quite a few staff go, and merchants questioned his credit. So the hunt for a wealthy wife pushed his interests to the top of the list.

Lady Martha Buford fit the bill exactly.

"I have enough time for a quick tennis game with George," he muttered.

In his room at the main house, he quickly tossed his waistcoat, trousers, and impeccably starched shirt on the bed.

Nothing was out of place in his private quarters. The queen size bed, which fit his six-foot-one frame perfectly, was made up; the large wooden headboard polished to a shine. "Thank goodness I still have Benson."

One maid, one butler, one cook, one gardener. All I can afford.

He shrugged off the depressing thought as he pulled on his tennis whites, recombed his blond hair, and studied himself in the mirror. "Still a handsome devil, old boy! Martha is a little young for my thirty-nine years, but we'll still make a good match."

His best friend, George Beckham, knew of his plan. They did everything together, so it was natural to include him. So far, the task was right on track. George knew Martha through Dame Buford's charity, so an introduction proved an easy accomplishment.

Mrs. Buford took an instant liking to him. Martha, however, turned out to be a bit of a challenge.

She's coming around though. He wrinkled his nose at his next thought. *I'll have to give her a piece of my mother's jewelry to seal the deal. No woman can resist fine jewels. I have to be careful though. Jewelry is my only commodity right now.*

George, who stood in sharp contrast to the Baron with his brown hair, dark eyes, and pale skin, leaned on his racket by the net when Anthony emerged from the side door. "Ready, old man? I feel pretty good today. You might have a tough time keeping up with me."

Anthony chuckled. "That'll be the day. But we'll see what you've got."

They warmed up with a few serves over the net before starting in earnest.

Anthony won the first round with little effort.

George rallied in the second round and beat him soundly.

"I'm parched," Anthony said. "Let's take a break."

On cue, Benson, always properly decked out in perfect butler attire, came through the patio door with a tray of lemonade, his balding head shining in the afternoon sun.

They settled into the wicker chairs and quenched their thirst.

George leaned forward. "Meeting Martha this evening?"

"Yes, I plan on a little dinner to pop the question. I can't wait much longer. I don't want to sell any more jewelry. If only her mother wasn't along."

"Want me to distract her?"

"Could you?"

George smiled. "I'm the master."

Tennis was forgotten as the two conspirators devised their plan.

The train pulled in on time much to Anthony's delight. The jostling crowd filled him with disdain. Usually, he dispatched Benson to pick up friends and family. After all he was a Baron, and this type of chore is beneath a man of his stature. However, today was different. He wanted to make sure Martha perceived him in the right light, a caring, protective man.

"Do you see them, George?" he asked.

"Not yet, I ...wait, there they are just coming down the stairs."

Anthony looked where George indicated. "Yes, I see them." He waved. "Martha!"

She didn't look up; her head bent in conversation with a man he didn't recognize. In fact, her arm was looped through his.

George called out louder than Anthony had. "Lady Buford! Over here."

This time she did look, showed recognition, and waved.

The stranger saw her safely onto the dock, then turned to help her mother down. Another man held the elder lady's elbow, and both men deposited her safely on stable ground.

Martha waited for her mother and the two men before they made their way to Anthony.

Finally, they all converged into a small group and Martha introduced Wolf and Polecat.

Anthony's displeasure caused heat to rise to his face. He nodded at the two men. "Pleased, I'm sure."

George interjected. "Martha, Anthony has the most exciting plans for you both tonight. Dinner at The Savoy! I must say I'll miss the food, but I received two tickets to the ballet for tonight and have no one to accompany me." He turned to Dame Buford. "Will you be so kind as to come along with me? I know how much you love the ballet."

"Me, George? Surely you can find a girl your own age to accompany you," she answered.

"Oh please, Mrs. Buford. I don't want to miss it. It'll be fun since we both like ballet so much."

"But I think it's necessary for me to accompany my daughter."

Anthony bent toward Martha's mother and whispered in her ear. "Not necessary, I plan to propose tonight. I'd like to do that alone. It's done these days, you know."

Dame Buford beamed. "Oh!" She turned to George. "Yes, of course I'll accompany you to the ballet."

Anthony took Martha's elbow and steered her through the crowd without a word to Wolf and Polecat.

George did the same with Martha's mother.

As Anthony helped Martha into the automobile, he said, "You must be more careful who you rub elbows with, my dear. A military man is not suitable company for a woman of your position."

He glanced at her clouded countenance as he maneuvered her toward his pearl blue Astin Martin...and took note of her look back toward Wolf and Polecat who stood staring after her.

CHAPTER FIVE

SOME PROPOSALS SOUND LIKE LOVE, BUT ARE STITCHED WITH LIES ~

Martha turned slowly toward Anthony. "You were very rude. Those two young men are perfect gentlemen who helped me with Mother and another older lady during the trip. You totally misjudge them."

He kept his gaze on the road in front of him. "Nevertheless, one can't be too careful when traveling. Just a bit of a warning, my dear. Don't be angry with me. I'm only looking out for your welfare."

"I'm perfectly capable of watching out for my own welfare. I've always been a good judge of character, as well," she snipped.

"Please darling, let's not quarrel. I have a special evening planned for us. Can we simply enjoy our reunion? I've missed you."

Irritated, but not wanting to spoil his surprise, she sighed, "Yes, of course. Let's enjoy the evening."

They rode in silence until they reached The Savoy.

Anthony paid the valet and opened the door for her.

"I wish I could have freshened up or changed clothes. It was a long trip," she said.

"You look wonderful. You always do."

The hostess guided them to a secluded table.

After their drinks arrived and their order taken, Anthony reached into his pocket and pulled out a red velvet jewelry case. He reached for her hand.

She gasped.

In almost a whisper he said, "Will you be my wife, Martha?" He lifted the lid and revealed a stunning antique radiant cut ruby ring with diamond side accents and yellow gold band.

"Anthony, I don't know what to say. It's beautiful."

"Say yes, darling." He took the ring from the box and reached to place it on her finger.

She pulled back.

"Martha, what's wrong? Is it not grand enough?" he asked.

"Oh no, nothing like that. It's a gorgeous piece," she answered.

"It was my mother's. Then what is wrong? Have I not followed the correct protocol for a proposal? Would your mother object?"

She shook her head. "Oh no. Mother would be over the moon. It's just..."

"What darling? We are a perfect match. Everyone says so."

"Anthony, I'm looking for something specific in a marriage partner. And well... you just don't, well, I simply...don't love you." She sat back against the chair and exhaled.

There, I've said it.

She waited for him to respond.

He didn't. Only sat there with a stunned look in his eyes.

They remained in silence until Anthony started to chuckle. It ended up in a full-blown laugh. "You don't love me? Well, that is something I didn't expect. Romantic love is only one of the elements of a good marriage, my dear. You will learn to love me. Our marriage will produce the power couple of the decade. You have beauty and grace. I bring the aristocracy you desire. Together we'll be a formidable couple.

And then there are children. You do want children, don't you? What great ancestry we can give them. Think about that."

She stared at him. "So you don't love me, either? I haven't heard you say the words."

He made a 'tsk tsk' sound. "Of course I love you, Martha. I fell in love the minute I met you. I'm sorry if I haven't conveyed that to you before. I felt it unnecessary. But I will say it now. I love you. Very much."

Embarrassed, she ducked her head. "Well, a girl likes to hear the words." A steely resolve returned. "But it still doesn't change the fact. I'm not there yet. You'll have to give me time, Anthony."

He snapped the lid closed and took a deep breath. "Certainly. Take all the time you need."

Their food arrived and the remainder of the evening passed in a strained silence.

I've hurt his feelings, but I just can't say yes. He's a fine catch. Any woman would be thrilled to marry a man like him, but meeting Wolf gives me pause.

"Finished?" he asked in a clipped tone.

"Yes, the meal was delicious. Thank you."

His set jaw and rigid timbre in his voice gave an insincere property to his question. "Do you want a cocktail to top it off?"

"No, I'm rather tired. If you don't mind, I'd like to go home."

He nodded, stood, and took the back of her chair in a courteous but stiff manner.

He's furious with me.

The ride home was equally uncomfortable.

He walked her to the door, kissed her on the cheek, and said, "Tomorrow for lunch?"

"Yes, of course. Maybe I'll feel a bit better tomorrow. Good night, Anthony, and thank you for the lovely evening."

He responded with a sharp but courtly bow. "Tomorrow then."

She watched him drive away and wondered if she'd botched the whole thing because of a chance meeting on the train.

<center>~~~*~~~</center>

Anthony arrived promptly at eleven a.m. "I trust you slept well?"

She smiled. "Yes, as a matter of fact, I feel better. Where are we having lunch?"

"At the club, I think. We can watch the tennis matches while we eat. It's a lovely day."

She noticed his countenance brighten with the mention of her restful night.

"I trust your mother and George had a nice evening."

"I really don't know. I didn't hear her come in. I was asleep before my head hit the pillow. I should probably check on her before we go."

Anthony nodded. "Yes, do that. We have plenty of time."

As she hurried up the stairs she wondered if he would propose again. The doorbell rang as she entered her mother's bedroom. *Anthony and the butler can take care of whomever that is.*

Dame Buford sat at her dresser brushing her long hair and tying it up in her signature chignon. "Good morning, Martha!" She turned to face her and declared, "You have something special to tell me I take it?"

"Not exactly Mother. Just that Anthony and I are going to lunch at the club. How was the ballet?"

Mrs. Buford's smile turned into a frown. "What? Why Anthony told me he was going to propose to you. Didn't he?"

"Yes, he did, and I said no."

The elder Buford stared at Martha. "You said what?" her voice screeched like an agitated crow. "Surely you're joking."

"Not exactly no, Mother. A postponement of sorts. I'm just not ready. I really don't love him."

"Love him?" she laughed. "What has love got to do with anything? Why Anthony is a great catch. You'd have status, security, children. You do want children, don't you? The best time for that is while you are in your prime."

"Of course I want children. It's just that...I'm not there yet I need more time."

Mother Buford turned back to the mirror and slammed the brush down, a pinched frown on her face. "How about me? Have you thought about me? I'd like grandchildren. I'd like to see my only daughter safely married. Will you continue to deny me these things in my dotage?"

Martha sighed, then said softly, "I think of you all the time, Mother. But life without love is a hard pill to swallow."

"Do you think I loved your father when I married him? I grew to love him. I married because of convention and so must you."

Her words stung. *She makes me sound so selfish.* She took another breath. "Yes, Mother. He'll ask again. I promise to give it my highest priority."

CHAPTER SIX

FAIR WORDS SPEAKS THE VILLAIN, BUT DARK IS HIS HEART ~

Anthony waved the butler off when the doorbell rang. He could see the blue uniform through the beveled side windows and knew the young military man from yesterday came calling.

He answered the door with a swift motion and a smile. "Good morning, Mr. Kelley. How are you this fine morning?" He noticed a frown form on Kelley's face which amused him immensely.

"It's a fine morning, Baron," Wolf replied.

"What can I do for you?" Anthony asked.

"I've come to see, Martha. I'll be shipping off soon and wish to see her before I go."

"Oh, I'm afraid that is quite impossible. Martha is tending to her mother. But I can give her the message." His smile broadened as he delivered the lie, "Martha and I became engaged last night. I hope you will congratulate us." He held out his hand.

Wolf stared for a moment, then took the offered hand. "Congratulations." He turned to go.

Anthony called after him. "I'll be sure and give Martha your message." A chuckle bubbled to the surface as he closed the door. *That takes care of one nuisance.*

He turned when Martha called from the top of the stairs.

"What's so funny, Anthony?" she asked. "Who was at the door?"

"Oh, no one, dear. Wrong house." He deflected the second question. "How's your mother? Would she like to accompany us to the club?"

"She's well, but no, she doesn't want to join us," Martha answered. "She's tired from last night."

Anthony offered his arm as she landed on the last step. "Shall we go then?"

Martha gave a half smile and nodded, which annoyed Anthony. *She could be a little more enthusiastic. I've got to win her over today. There is no time to spare.*

He opened the door and ushered her outside. "You look lovely today. A good rest has enhanced your beauty, my dear."

"Thank you. I feel much better."

His lapis blue Mercedes Benz sat in front of the house.

As he assisted her into the vehicle, he thought. *She will be mine today and my money problems will be over.*

$$\sim\sim\sim^{*}\sim\sim\sim$$

Wolf's heart sank at the news Anthony shared with him. *Martha is going to marry that stuffed shirt. It's hard to imagine someone as vibrant as her hooked up with someone like Anthony.*

He wandered the streets for a while before heading back to the base. Sadness followed him like a shadow while he meandered through the shops. *I've never met a woman like her before. Beautiful, intelligent. And full of class. But she made her choice. It's too bad. We would have made a great pair.*

Back on the base he ran into Polecat.

"Did you see her? Will she correspond with you? Maybe come to the States? You two make a striking couple." Polecat grinned at his friend.

Wolf sighed. "Nope. She agreed to marry that buffoon who met her at the train. I didn't even get to see her. The Baron met me at the door and handed me the news."

Polecat's jaw dropped. "You're kidding. I thought for sure she took a shine to you. Can't quite see her with that guy. What will you do now?"

"Pal, I'm heading back to the States. Back to my mountain. Reopen my Lodge. The solitary life is what I crave now," Wolf stated.

Polecat remained silent, dipping his head, staring at the ground.

"What's up, pal. You're mustering out too, aren't you?"

"Well, no. What with unrest in so many places...heck, I thought you and Martha were hooking up. I reenlisted. I'll be here for the next few years. God, I'll miss you."

Wolf could only stare. "Stay here? Why I had a place for you at the Lodge. I planned to make you a partner. Why didn't you talk to me?"

"Sorry, thought you..."

"Well, nothing can be done about it now. Gotta go pack up. Leaving on the first flight tomorrow morning."

"Tomorrow? I thought you had another ten days."

"Spoke with the captain about what happened this morning. He pulled some strings. No use staying here now. Have a glass of beer later?"

"Sure, buddy."

They parted and Wolf headed toward the barracks. He packed his duffle bag then sank down on his bunk, dejected, lonely, and disappointed. *She was the one. I know it. Now I have no chance. I can't wait to get back to my mountain and put it behind me.*

He met up with Polecat at a local pub they often frequented. A hole in the wall called Charlie's. Dark and gloomy, just the way he felt. Most military guys hung out here brooding over whatever they left in the States.

"So, you're leavin' in the morning." Polecat's statement came out flat.

"Yep." Wolf kept his gaze on his beer.

Polecat said in a wistful voice, "I'm sorry, man. I'm really gonna miss you." He paused. "You know, you could reenlist."

"Not a chance, man. All I want is the solitude of my mountain. Wish you could come with me. "

Polecat shook his head. "It's just...I was sure you and Martha..."

"Yeah, well. Listen, when you do muster out, there's always a place for you at the Lodge."

"Thanks, man."

Neither had much to say. They sat in silence most of the evening.

Finally, Wolf said he needed to get back to his barracks. They embraced as they parted. Wolf choked back the emotion at leaving his best friend and knowing the woman he fell instantly in love with was out of his reach.

He flew out the next morning, alone, thinking only about his mountain and the peace he desperately needed.

$$\sim\sim\sim^*\sim\sim\sim$$

Martha knew Anthony would ask her to marry him again and dreaded the question. She was sure Wolf would come by and visit and when he didn't, she resolved not to live her life on a chance meeting. Her own home, a husband, children is what mattered now, and Anthony fit the bill. Wolf was an exciting interlude in her life she'd always think on fondly, but that's all it was. He'd fly home to America. *And I will remain in England. My mind is made up.*

Anthony graciously pulled out a chair for her at court side and summoned the waiter.

Much to her chagrin, he ordered for her without asking what she wanted.

"No, Anthony, I want the chicken salad sandwich and a cup of tea." She knew the rebuff would rankle him, but she did it anyway.

A faint flush crept up his face, but he smiled and corrected the order.

I have to show him I won't be run over. I can't lose my independence.

Anthony quickly changed the subject. "Oh look, there's George and his girlfriend on the court." He waved.

George raised his hand to return the greeting and missed the shot she lobbed at him.

Anthony laughed. "He won't let me forget that one. Maybe they can join us after their match. Is that okay?"

"Of course," she answered.

"But first, before they get here, I have to ask you again. Have you considered my proposal?"

She was a little taken aback he'd ask so soon after her refusal. "Yes, I've given it some thought."

He took her hand. "And your verdict, my dear?"

She remained silent for a moment, then looked at him. "Yes, I'll marry you."

He looked stunned at first but then broke out in a grin. "That's wonderful!" He pulled the jewelry box from his pocket, opened it, and presented it to her.

"It's truly beautiful," she said.

He took it from the red velvet case and placed it on her finger.

"Perfect fit," she declared.

"I pay attention to details, my love."

Before she could reply, George and his friend approached.

George razzed Anthony. "You cost me the game."

"You didn't have a chance, George. Lauren is much too good for you. Can you two sit down for a moment? We have some news to share."

Martha felt the heat rise to her face; not sure she wanted to share this yet.

George and Lauren pulled up their chairs.

"So what is this mysterious news, Anthony?" George asked.

Anthony didn't speak. Instead, he lifted Martha's hand to show off the ring.

Lauren squealed, her short blonde hair bobbing and her blue eyes gleaming as she bounced up and down in her chair. "Oh my! How exciting. Congratulations, Martha! Oh you too, Anthony. A wedding!! I can hardly wait. Have you set the date?"

"Slow down, Lauren. It just happened today. We have plenty of time to make plans. Since you and George are my closest friends, I wanted you to know first."

George shook Anthony's hand. "Congratulations, bucko. This is wonderful news. If you need anything, just let me know."

Their lunch arrived, and the rest of the morning passed in a fog for Martha.

What have I done? I should have given it more time. But it's too late now. It's done. Mother will be pleased, at least. This is all I can expect for my life. No excitement, just fitting into the proper slot expected of me. Oh dear.

CHAPTER SEVEN

THOUGH MY HAND BE PLEDGED, MY HEART STILL LINGERS WHERE IT SHOULD NOT ~

The weeks passed in a blur for Martha. Her mother, beside herself with joy, took on the role of overseer for the wedding. Even down to the wedding dress.

Martha showed up for fittings, chose her bridesmaids, etc., but allowed her mother to make most of the decisions. The venue, the caterer, even the date.

The wedding was to be in one month's time. She thought it much too soon. A year would have been preferable, but Anthony insisted, and Dame Buford championed the thought.

When duties for the wedding subsided, she spent her time wandering the shops. Never one to enjoy shopping for shopping's sake, she nevertheless frequented the boutiques on the main thoroughfare. At first, she told herself it was for distraction, but deep down the secret desire to run into Wolf rose to the surface. After all, he'd said he had a few more weeks before going home. She blushed at the thought and even considered it a bit of a betrayal to Anthony, but it didn't stop her from indulging in the fantasy.

However, she *didn't* run into Wolf and knew by this time he was more than likely back in America.

Why do I continue to think of him? It's obvious I was only a dalliance, a short interlude to pass the time on the train. He's forgotten all about me.

The pull of the attraction continued to haunt her. Whenever she saw an Air Force Blue uniform in a crowd, she looked hard to make sure it wasn't Wolf.

Eventually, she shook it off and stepped back into her daily life.

Wolf faded into the background, not entirely, but enough where she could move forward in her life.

Anthony was ever the gentleman. Kind, considerate, everything a woman could ever want in a fiancée. She relaxed, settled in, accepted the inevitable. But at the same time, a light dimmed in her soul as she prepared to step into married life. Emotion took a back seat, and in its place, resignation.

The wedding day dawned. By this time, excitement was not a part of her personality. She only asked herself, "What am I doing?" once. But she brushed it aside and stuffed her mindset back into the box she'd created.

Dame Buford fluttered around the room, adjusting this, fixing that, preening over Martha's very extravagant dress, white organza, low plunged, lace accents. The joy on her face gave Martha pause. *Am I simply spoiled, or expecting too much. Mother was perfectly happy with Father and that wasn't a love match in the beginning. Anthony is a fine man. Do I really think I am such a catch? Am I an immature dreamer wanting a glamourous love story?*

She sighed.

"Are you okay, Martha? Having wedding day jitters?" Dame Buford asked.

"I'm fine, Mother. Let's go down."

Her bridesmaids arranged her train, then moved in front of her to descend the sweeping staircase of Anthony's mansion, happy they decided to hold the ceremony here instead of the church. It was more intimate, more to her liking.

Her mother kissed her on the cheek and followed the bridesmaids down the stairs where an usher escorted her to her place in front of the guests.

Her older brother, tall and handsome Liam, made the trip from Scotland where he lived with his wife and two children to give her away. "Are you ready, sister?"

All she could do was nod. She thought she'd come to terms with this marriage, but now, as she made the descent to her vows, doubt all but choked her. Nevertheless, she took one step at a time until she stood in front of the preacher and her bridegroom.

Anthony beamed...which brought to her mind a vision of the Cheshire Cat.

Woodenly she went through the vows as the pastor presented them. The ceremony didn't take long and before she knew it, the guests were surrounding her and Anthony with congratulations and moving to the great hall where the reception was laid out in grand fashion.

Anthony never left her side, plied her with champagne, shook hands with everyone, and kept a silly grin on his face.

Dame Buford flitted around the room, smiling so big, Martha thought her face would crack. *Well, at least one of us is happy.*

An eternity passed, but finally the guests left one by one.

Only her mother remained. She stood in front of them grinning from ear to ear showing no signs of leaving.

"Mother, it's late. Your driver is waiting patiently outside. Don't you think you should go home and get some rest?" Martha asked.

Mrs. Buford's face fell for an instant. "Oh, why yes, of course. It was such a wonderful party I hate for it to end."

She motioned for Benson to bring her mother's things.

Anthony, always the gentleman, helped her on with her cloak.

They bid her goodnight and watched her drive away.

And then, it was only the two of them.

The bridegroom took her hands in his. "We're finally alone, my dear. I gave Benson the night off. It was a wonderful day, don't you agree?"

"Of course." She pulled her hands free. "I'll just go up and get out of this dress.

Anthony headed for the crystal decanter on the bar. "Yes, I'll be up in a minute. I want to go over our honeymoon trip itinerary. Italy should be splendid this time of year. We leave first thing in the morning!"

She gave him a half smile and climbed the stairs to the master bedroom. Rose petals decorated the bed, the lighting was low, the subtle scent of jasmine floated through the room. To the right, her dressing room door stood open as if to beckon her. She hesitated, her heart pounded but she shook off the doubts and moved forward. The lacy white wedding night negligee lay draped across the chaise lounge. She changed, not comfortable in the revealing gown, but returned to the bedroom, sat on the bed, and waited.

<p style="text-align:center">~~~*~~~</p>

The next morning, she woke still on top of the bedspread with her head on the satin pillow and Anthony, still clothed, snoring loudly beside her.

She sat up and tried to remember what happened. The strong smell of Bourbon and cigar smoke filled her nostrils. *He got drunk... and I fell asleep!*

In a way she was relieved. So many negative thoughts swirled in her head. *I'm obviously not ready and furthermore, I'm not in love. What have I done?*

She slid off the bed and returned to the dressing room, changing into her day dress. After a quick *toilette,* she tiptoed downstairs to find the cook preparing a light breakfast.

"Good morning, madam," Agnes, the cook said, "I trust you slept well."

"Yes, very well, thank you," she replied.

"Will the bridegroom be along directly?"

"He was still sleeping when I left him."

Agnes glanced at the wall clock. "Benson said the Rolls will be ready soon. All your luggage will fit just fine. The Austin is much too small. The ship sails early this morning."

"Yes, I am aware. Might I have a cup of coffee? Then I'll go wake him."

"Certainly, but Benson always rouses Mr. Anthony. Why don't you sit down at the table while you wait. I'll pour the coffee."

Relieved, she didn't have to go back upstairs and face him there; she sighed and sat back in her chair. "Thank you."

The coffee was hot, the aroma restored her foggy brain, and she relaxed. The scenery outside the window revealed a blue sky, a few puffy clouds, and two large dogs bounding across the open field. A serene picture of country life.

"Will you wait to eat with Mr. Anthony, or do you want your eggs now?" The cook asked.

"I'll wait. Maybe just a piece of toast now."

She didn't have to wait long.

Anthony bounded into the room, fully dressed in his fresh traveling clothes. "Good morning, my love!" He issued a quick kiss on her cheek while the cook placed a steaming cup of coffee on the table. "I trust you slept well."

Well, this is interesting. I was sure he'd be upset. I must have already been asleep when he came into the bedroom.

"Yes, I slept well. And you?" she answered.

"Like a baby. I can't wait to start our trip to Italy. We'll have the most glorious honeymoon."

Taken aback by his cavalier attitude she didn't reply at once. *He didn't even mention last night.*

A steaming plate of bacon and eggs with wheat toast, delivered by Benson, garnered his attention. He chattered about Italy while buttering the toast. "I have all sorts of plans for all the excursions we will want to take. Anything in particular you want to see, my dear?"

She raised the cup to her lips and sipped. "Why no, I'm leaving it up to you to surprise me."

He continued to devour breakfast with gusto and managed to talk in between bites. "Well, the Coliseum, of course, and the Pantheon. I'd like to visit a few quaint villages to get the feel of the place. And we won't leave until we visit Venice." Finally, he put the fork down and gazed at her. "You haven't said much, Martha. You *are* excited about this trip aren't you?"

She decided to ignore the elephant in the room for now. "Yes, of course, Anthony. I'm looking forward to it very much."

"Good." He picked up the fork again and finished his breakfast.

After he swallowed the last of his coffee, he instructed Agnes to summon Benson.

Benson arrived stiff and proper as usual. "Yes, sir?"

Anthony didn't glance up, just set his cup down carefully. "Those papers I had you put away yesterday...bring them to me."

"Right away, sir." The butler left hurriedly.

"Papers, Anthony? Something to do with the trip?" she asked.

"Just business, my dear. Having to do with the consolidation of our estates. All legal mumbo jumbo. Nothing to worry your pretty head about. We must have it all in order before we leave the country."

She said nothing, but something cold knotted in her stomach.

The butler returned with a manilla file.

"Good. Now, if you will just sign on the arrows, we can leave right on time. The Rolls Royce is waiting. Time is of the essence if we are to make our ship on time."

"But what is this all about, Anthony? No one said anything to me about any papers to sign."

He sighed dramatically. "My dear. We are married now. Partners in everything. It's just legality really. We leave with everything in order. Nothing to distract us from a marvelous honeymoon. Please, we haven't much time."

Benson placed the papers in front of her.

She glanced at them, but most of it was legal gibberish she didn't understand.

"Please, Martha. We must hurry."

"But…"

"I assume by your consent to marry me you placed your trust in me. I am your husband bound to look after our affairs."

She lifted the pen, even though doubt roiled in her head. Quickly, she signed the papers and gave them back to Benson.

Anthony sat back in his chair, obviously satisfied given the smile on his face. "There, that wasn't so hard, was it?" He clapped his hands together and said, "Let's go! Our future awaits."

CHAPTER EIGHT

IN THE DARK OF SLUMBER, HER VISAGE COMES — WAN AND WEEPING ~

Wolf entered the Lodge, the tension in his shoulders immediately relieved. The trip was grueling, mustering out of the service, arranging travel to get to his beloved lodge high in the mountains. "Home at last!"

His hideaway stood empty, of course. When he left for the military he had to put the opening on hold. He couldn't leave it to anyone else to fulfill his vision. Now he could put all his effort into opening the business.

The duffle bag landed on the dusty floor with a dull thud. "Yep, lots of work ahead, but it feels so good to be back on the mountain."

He made mental notes as he wandered from room to room. In the village at the base of the mountain, he had several friends who would pitch in to get it up to snuff. Then came advertising and getting ready for a grand opening. At the back of the lodge was a garden area he wanted to make accessible to guests during their stay. He wandered out. It was a mess, needed lots of cleaning up. He found the concrete bench he'd placed there before he left to serve his country.

He sat down.

Immediately his mind went to Martha. "Can't seem to get her out of my mind. I bet she'd know what to do with this space." *Well, she made her choice.*

A shout shook him from his thoughts. "Wolf Kelley, you son of a gun. Where are you?"

Pete Grayson!

He jumped to his feet. "Out here you old sasquatch."

Pete barreled through the patio door and grabbed him in a grizzly-like hug. "You're back and it's about time! We've missed you around here. Can't believe you didn't call me. I'd have picked you up from the airport."

Pete, a bear of a man, stands six feet three inches and sports long, unruly, salt and pepper hair. A beard to match hung almost to his knees. He was clad in his signature red flannel shirt and worn-out jeans.

"Aw, Pete, I just wanted a few minutes to enjoy my mountain in peace. Been away too long, wanted to savor it a bit before the chaos begins."

Pete slapped him on the back. "Gotcha!"

"How'd you find out I was home?" Wolf asked.

"The usual way. Victoria Jackson, the biggest gossip in town. Never could figure out how she finds out this stuff."

"No matter," Wolf replied. "Some things never change. How do you feel about helping me get this place whipped into shape?"

"That's why I'm here! Where do we start?"

Wolf chuckled and slapped Pete on the back. "I've just arrived. I could do with a bit of rest. How about you see who's available in the village, then meet me back here in about four hours. I can get a little sleep, then we can plot our course."

"A case of beer, right?"

Wolf grinned. "Ah, you know me well. That'll work."

After Pete left, Wolf picked up the duffle bag and headed to his old room upstairs. He scanned the space. Everything was just as he left it except it was freshly dusted, the curtains pulled back to let the light in, and the bedclothes pulled back as if to welcome him.

"Ah, Victoria, how does she do it?"

The only thing he removed were his boots. He didn't even climb into the sheets, just lay on top of them and fell instantly asleep.

Sleep came quickly, but so did the dream. The train, Martha, her smile, those flashing blue eyes. Her ruby lips begged to be kissed. He leaned forward. Their hands touched. Fire shot through his body. And then...

A knock on the door.

Pete's voice on the other side. "You all right in there? I gave you an extra hour. The guys are here."

Wolf jerked awake with the aroma of Martha's perfume still in his nostrils and the taste of her lips on his. He raked a hand over his face. "Yeah, I'm okay. Be right down."

How five hours passed so quickly was beyond him, but the vivid memory of the dream lingered. To his reflection in the mirror he said, "I gotta quit this. She's gone, married to someone else. The only woman I've ever dreamed about."

The water from the basin revived him. He used the brush left on the sink to tame his unruly hair, then headed downstairs to meet up with the guys.

Several empty beer cans littered the table in the dining room. *Apparently, they started without me.*

Whoops and hollers greeted him as he entered the room. He recognized most of them, but there were a few fresh faces.

Pete popped a beer can open and handed it to him.

"Hey, I haven't eaten in quite a while, I probably shouldn't..."

"Already thought of that. Voila!" Pete stepped aside to reveal a spread of barbeque on the table with all the proper sides. "All you have to do is dig in."

Even though the guys started guzzling beer before he came down, they hadn't touched the feast.

"You guys are the best!"

They ate in amiable comradeship until the last morsel disappeared.

Finally, Peter asked, "So what's first? It's the weekend. We can get quite a bit done."

As Wolf laid out the plans for the restoration, the vivid dream faded from his mind and excitement built as he watched with enthusiasm how his friends pitched in to make his dream a reality.

Days passed and the dream didn't recur. In fact, he hardly thought of her at all while the bustle went on.

Until...

A large bouquet of flowers arrived via the local village florist. The blooms, mostly carnations, triggered his memory of Martha. One of the things they'd talked about was how she'd miss the variety of colorful carnations in Spain.

His heart thumped against his chest.

Could it be? Did she remember...

He hurried to snatch the card from the ribbon and ripped it open.

A quick scan of the handwriting made his heart drop. It wasn't from Martha, but from the Chamber of Commerce welcoming him home. The carnations were just a coincidence.

He didn't know how long he stood there staring at the bouquet, but he couldn't escape the thought something was wrong. Something involving Martha.

Pete's shadow loomed over him, blocking the sunlight. "You gonna stand here all day looking at pretty flowers? The arbor is done in the garden. Excellent job if I do say so myself."

Wolf turned to see Pete's red flannel shirt covered in sawdust. "No, I thought the flowers were from.... Never mind. Let's see the new arbor."

The Lodge came together quickly and before he knew it, Wolf was ready for the grand opening. Wolf hired housekeepers, cooks, and desk clerks. Everything fell into place.

Except, he couldn't shake the feeling Martha was in trouble.

CHAPTER NINE

BENEATH THE GILDED VEIL, MY SPIRIT BREAKS ~

Anthony smirked as he tightened the mandatory black tie while facing the mirror. He winked at himself. *Not bad work old man. Everything fell into place. Martha is none the wiser and I am a rich man.*

He chuckled.

"Did you say something, Anthony?" Martha asked, coming up behind him.

"No, simply sighing with contentment, my love," he replied.

"Need help with the tie?" she asked.

"I think I have it." He turned to face her. "Is it square?"

"Perfect," she answered.

Their eyes met as they paused before going down to dinner, and he reflected on their marriage so far. *She's an adequate lover, even pleasant. Not the best I've had, but tolerable.* The hope of children spurred on his love making. Once he fathered her child, he'd have a permanent tie to the Buford money.

She has no idea what she signed. AND she didn't even read the fine print.

The honeymoon cruise to Italy was a perfect cover. It was rushed, and she had no time to ponder it. *Her mistake! Ah, women, so easily manipulated.*

Upon their return he will be in complete control of her estate. He can pick up his favorite pastime, horse-racing, as he'd done before the financial crunch hit him.

Although everything was ironclad, he made note to be careful not to expose his gambling habit. Right now, she seemed content in the marriage. He needed to keep it that way...at least until a child is born. Which bore the note to make love again this evening.

She must become pregnant on this trip. The sooner the better.

Dinner passed pleasantly enough. Small talk about what sites they would visit topped the conversation. An American band played dinner music and soon people started dancing. After a smattering of applause from the dancers, the band changed pace and played a love song. One he didn't recognize. He watched Martha's face change. A wistful look haunted her eyes; a slight flush stained her cheeks.

What is she thinking about? Not me, I'm supposing. If she were, her gaze would connect with mine. Who then? That Wolf character?

"Do you want to dance, darling?" he asked.

She jerked her head toward him. "What? Oh well, yes, that would be nice."

He held her chair as she rose. On the dance floor she was stiff, gazing at the band.

His glance at the musicians didn't provide any clue to what she was thinking.

"Do you know this song, Martha?"

"Why no, just that it sounds American. It has a lovely lilt to it, don't you think?"

"I hadn't given it a thought. Do you like American music?" he asked.

"Some of it. Why do you ask?"

"I don't know. Just the look in your eyes, how stiffly you hold yourself. Does it remind you of something?"

"Why no. I don't think so. Oh, it's finished."

They stood on the floor and clapped as the band announced a break.

Back at the table, Anthony ordered coffee. "Would you like a piece of pie to top off the meal?"

"Hmm, no. Just coffee."

He ordered a piece of apple pie and a Brandy.

She arched her brow.

"Just a nightcap, my love. No repeat of our wedding night, I assure you."

They hadn't discussed that night. She didn't bring it up, so he left it alone. At the time, he thought he'd need bolstering to make love to her. It was a stupid thing to do. The mistake could have sidelined his whole plan. However, he managed to pull it off anyway.

"What are you smiling about?" she asked.

"Smiling? Oh, I was thinking of what comes next, my dear. You're very fetching tonight." His smile broadened.

She blushed and raised the coffee cup to her lips.

He ate the pie in silence, dabbed the white linen napkin to his lips, and asked, "Ready to go up?"

"Can we take a stroll on the deck for a moment?"

"Anything you wish," he said.

He took her arm and guided her to the promenade deck. They walked a short distance until she stopped at the railing.

She had a far-away look in her eyes.

"What are you thinking about?"

She kept her eyes on the waves before them. "Have you ever been to America?"

The question stunned him. *What was she implying? Was she thinking of the airman?*

"Why, no but I hope to someday. Why are you thinking about America?" Anger rose in his voice.

"Oh no reason," she said dreamily. "Travel is so pleasant. I'd like to see it sometime, that's all."

He took a breath before he said something regrettable. His anger slowed. "We can take a trip there someday if you wish. It might be a while though. I'm hoping children will be in our future soon. Shall we go up?"

He felt her flinch.

"Yes, of course, dear."

Anthony took no time stripping his clothes off. When she returned from her dressing room in a white silky negligee he took no time stripping it off her, as well. He was in a hurry to have his way, determined to wipe any strange thoughts from her head.

The next morning, he apologized. "You looked so beautiful in the moonlight last night; I couldn't help myself. Forgive me?"

She looked across at him from the room service cart, a bruised lip swelling on one side. "Apology accepted. But I do not wish for a repeat performance."

If I can't control my temper, I might blow this. She has to get pregnant soon. I must watch my step.

"You have my promise."

"I hope you understand I will not accompany you to lunch. I abhor gossip. Until the swelling goes down I will stay in the room." She plunked the coffee cup down with a clatter and moved to the dressing room. She turned to face him. "If it's not better by lunch, then I will see you at dinner."

He knew a dismissal when he heard one. She wanted no part of him for a while.

He fashioned a contrite look. "Can I order you an ice pack? I really don't want to spend the day without my bride."

"Yes, that will help. Thank you." With that, she disappeared into the dressing room.

He called room service and placed the order, all the while waffling between remorse and excitement that he might have some time for himself. *Maybe I can find a card game.*

The ice pack arrived. He tipped the attendant and closed the door. "The ice pack is here, darling."

Her muffled voice barely carried through the closed door. "Just leave it on the nightstand."

After he placed it, he called out again. "I'm going downstairs. I'll check in on you at lunch."

She didn't answer.

He closed the door and headed to the casino where card games went on twenty-four seven.

<div style="text-align:center">~~~*~~~</div>

Martha heard the door close as Anthony left the stateroom and sighed in relief. She touched her lip gently and examined it in the mirror. Aloud she said, "I don't know what came over him last night, but I hope this isn't a side of him he's hidden from me. He was an animal."

She finished dressing and returned to the bedroom. The icepack sat in a silver container on the nightstand. The cold stung as she placed it on her lip. *I've made a horrendous mistake.*

CHAPTER TEN

IN FRIENDSHIP'S STEADFAST LIGHT, SECRETS FIND SHELTER ~

Wolf reveled in the grand opening turnout. The whole village wished him well. Bookings were pouring in. For the most part, the staff managed the day-to-day business while he tackled the paperwork. *I should hire an accountant soon. I want to start the survival camps in the near future...the whole purpose of this venture.*

In between greeting guests and running the business, he found time to walk around the property making a check list of things he wanted to change and improve. This was his element. These mountains meant more to him than anything. He thanked his father for that. A skilled woodsman, he'd taught his son everything there was to know about the mountains and living in the wild. He barely remembered his mother. She'd died when he was only five. Since then it was just father and son. The senior Kelley died the year Wolf went into the military, and he missed him every day.

His father's dream, and now his, was to teach people how to survive in the wilderness. He wasn't as much of a loner as his dad had been, but he did like the solitude.

While he looked up at the nearest peak thinking of his father, he heard tires crunch on the gravel parking lot.

A grin spread across his face; the voice of his best friend interrupted the melancholy thoughts.

"Haven't you got some work to do, old man?" Pete called out.

"Taking a break, thinking about what I want to do with the patch of ground up by the river. Might make a good place for a teaching camp," Wolf replied.

"That's why I'm here. You haven't even been fishing since you returned. How about you and I take a hike up there and fish for a couple of days?"

Wolf's heart leapt at the thought. "Nothing I'd like better, but I have a business to run."

"Isn't that why you hired staff? You need a break, man. Let your desk clerk run it for a couple of days. He's a good man, efficient, steady head on his shoulders, fresh out of college. Come on. Let's do this," Pete insisted.

"Well, I dunno…"

Pete veered toward the entry door of the Lodge without saying another word.

Wolf followed wondering what he was up to.

Pete greeted the desk clerk. "Hey Mac, how would you like to run the place for a few days? Wolf and I have some fishin' and plannin' to do."

Mac's youthful face and eager grin displayed the young man's enthusiasm. "Why sure, Mr. Grayson. I can manage things."

Just like that it was settled.

Excitement filled Wolf's heart as he stuffed the backpack with everything he'd need for two days. To get back to nature, shoot the breeze with Pete, catch some trout. *Maybe this is just what I need.*

Pete tugged on his arm as he gave last minute instructions to Mac. "Come on, we're burnin' daylight."

His favorite spot was a good three-hour hike from the Lodge. If they left now they'd have plenty of time to strike camp and fish for a couple of hours. He always had fresh fish on the menu at the Lodge, but nothing could compare with trout caught right out of the river and cooked over a campfire.

They didn't talk much as they traversed the trail. The larger-than-life trees, the sweet smell of the woods, all the nature sounds, calmed him, made him feel truly at home.

And suddenly, they arrived at the small clearing. Across the modest patch was the river and their destination.

They worked silently as they pitched the tent, created the rock fire ring, organized the fishing gear, each knowing what to do.

Wolf was the first to throw in a line. Rewarded with a bite almost immediately, his heart pounded as he reeled in the large rainbow trout. "This is going to taste really good!"

Side by side in companionable silence, they fished until they had enough for dinner.

Together, they'd grown up in these woods; fished in this river more than once. Pete's dad had a cabin about a mile from this spot. Wolf spent many a weekend with the Grayson's. All of them gone now. Pete maintained the cabin but seldom went there. A job in the village kept him too busy.

As the fish sizzled in the skillet, Pete looked across at his friend and said, "Who is she, Wolf?"

"What are you talking about?"

"It's written all over your face. You're pining for someone. Been meaning to talk to you about it but figured the Lodge wasn't the place. So spill. Who is she?"

He didn't speak at first. Pete knew him the best and had no doubt he would wrangle the truth out of him.

Finally, he spoke quietly, eyes focused on the fire. "A woman I met in Spain. Martha."

"Wanna tell me what happened?"

Wolf laid out the whole story including how they parted at the train station in London with Anthony Chadwick whisking her off before they could arrange another meeting. Then the *fait accompli,* how his unannounced visit to her house gave Anthony the opportunity to inform him of their upcoming marriage.

Pete remained quiet for a moment.

The fire crackled, the fish sizzled, and still both men said nothing.

At long last, Pete removed the fish from the fire, placed two on each plate, and said, "So you just left England? You didn't try to see her again?

He shook his head. "I was still wearing the uniform, Pete. Couldn't risk getting reprimanded. You know my temper."

"Doesn't sound like you, Wolf. You always fight for what you want."

"You callin' me a coward?" he spat.

"No, just that you're not telling me everything."

He continued to stare at the fire. "Never met anyone like her before. A real lady. Refined, elegant, beautiful. What am I? Just a rough shod mountain man. What could I give her? She'd never be happy here. I left because I was out of my league."

"There are no leagues when it comes to love."

"What do you know about it? You've never been married. Never even dated a girl that I know of. Did it change when I went away?"

It was Pete's turn to study the fire. "There's a woman. Can't get up my courage to ask her."

"In the village?" Wolf asked.

Pete nodded.

"Who? Do I know her? What's her name?"

Pete finished off his fish and tossed the plate aside. "Never mind that now. We were talking about you. You just gonna pine away for her?"

Pensive now, Wolf answered slowly, wondering how Pete would take what he was about to say next. "I'm having dreams."

"About her?"

"Yep."

"What kind of dreams?"

In the darkness Wolf felt the heat rise to his face. "I smell her perfume, taste her kiss. But at the same time I get this foreboding feeling she's in trouble."

"Sounds as if there's a real connection there. You need to act on your feeling."

"How can I? She's all the way over there and I'm here."

Pete stood up and stretched. "Got any buddies you can contact over there? Maybe they can find out what's going on. Maybe she didn't even get married."

He looked up at his friend and a spark of hope flickered in his brain. "There's Polecat. He's still stationed there. Guess I can contact him."

"There ya go. It's something anyway." Pete stretched again. "I'm turning in. There's a mess of fish waitin' to be caught tomorrow. You coming?"

"Yeah, gonna stoke up the fire so the bears will stay away. See ya in the morning."

The moon lit up the clear night sky as the two men settled in their separate pup tents, but Wolf tossed and turned. He knew he could count on Polecat to find out what was going on with Martha and he could hardly wait to get back to the Lodge.

The day dawned with the sun rising through the trees. After a breakfast of coffee and hardtack, Wolf started throwing his gear into his pack.

"What are you doing?" Pete asked.

"Heading back to the Lodge. I thought a lot about what you said last night. I'm gonna contact Polecat. See what he can find out. What about you?"

Pete frowned. "I'm staying. Got some thinking to do. Got the walkie talkie?"

"Yeah, see you down there."

"Remember, that grizzly is still in this area. Be careful."

Wolf grinned. "He and I are old friends. No problem there."

The trip down went faster than the upward climb yesterday. The Lodge came into view, and he hurried, anxious to make the phone call.

Mac looked disappointed when he saw him.

"Everything okay, Mr. Kelley? I thought you weren't coming back until tomorrow."

Wolf strode toward his office as he answered, "Yes, just remembered a bit of business I need to take care of. Pete's still there. He'll be back tomorrow."

The pack made a thump on the floor as he tossed it in a corner. He knew the base number by heart. When the operator answered he identified himself and asked for Polecat.

The female operator stated in a crisp voice, "I'm sorry, Mr. Kelley. Sargeant Robinson is out on Bivouac. However, I think they are due back this evening."

"Okay, thank you. Will you give him this number? Tell him it's important."

The operator took down the number and assured him she'd pass on the message.

Nothing more to do. Too bad I left Pete up there, but he'll understand.

Mac knocked softly on the door. "Mr. Kelley? Someone here to see you, sir."

"Who is it. I really am too tired to see anyone."

"Victoria Jackson from the village."

Before Wolf could wave Mac off, Victoria burst through the door. "Okay, what have you done with him Wolf Kelley?"

"Done with who?" Wolf answered.

"Pete, of course. He was supposed to take me to the movies last night and I haven't heard anything from him. Now where is he? I know he's here."

Wolf chuckled as it dawned on him. *Pete is in love with Victoria.*

"I left him on the mountain, Vickie,"

"Don't you Vickie me! You hid him away so I couldn't get to him. I'll never forgive you." She stamped her foot.

"Look Victoria, he took me up there because I have woman problems. We talked it out. He'll be back tomorrow. I imagine he forgot all about the date because he was worried about me."

Her face went from anger to curiosity in a split second. "You have woman problems? Who? Do I know her? Tell me, maybe I can help."

Wolf rose from the chair. "Now, Vickie, all is well. I have resolved my problem, and I suggest you go home and be understanding when Pete makes it down the mountain. He's a little gun shy, you know. Let him take the lead. He really likes you."

She blushed. "Really? He said that?"

"He sure did. Now, go and be gorgeous for him when he returns. You won't be sorry."

She blew a kiss to Wolf and hurried out the door.

Mac, who still stood in the doorway, said, "Sorry, Mr. Kelley. I couldn't stop her."

"No one can, Mac. No one can."

CHAPTER ELEVEN

BOUND IN WEDLOCK'S GENTLE CHAIN, SHADOWS LINGER DEEP IN PAIN ~

The swelling on Martha's lip diminished in a few hours, but her ire lingered. When Anthony returned for lunch, she held the ice pack on her mouth and declined his invitation to dine downstairs.

The look of disappointment on his face gave her a strange pleasure. *Let him suffer a bit longer. Maybe he'll think twice before acting like a rutting bull again.*

He asked if she'd like room service, but she shook her head. "I have a few letters to write. You go. I'm sure I'll be fine by dinner."

He hesitated but left with a confused look on his face.

She did want to write to her mother. Thank you notes were also on her agenda. This was a perfect time to accomplish the task.

Their stateroom had a wonderful view of the ocean. The slight swell of the ship soothed her nerves. She poured a cup of tea and sat down, pulled a piece of stationery from the drawer, and tried to begin.

What shall I write to Mother? That Anthony was a perfect brute last night? No, of course not.

Instead of putting ink to paper, she gazed out of the portal and let her mind drift. She touched her lip and remembered the tender kiss she and Wolf shared on the train. *How do I know he wouldn't have turned brutish as well? Are all men like this?*

She shook off the thought and began the letter.

Two hours later, Anthony returned.

"How are you feeling, my love? I brought you a beignet from the dining room. I thought you might be hungry and it's a few hours until dinner."

She licked the envelope of the last thank you note and replied, "How thoughtful of you. I *am* a little hungry."

"Did you get all your letters written?" he asked.

"Just the one to Mother. The rest are thank you notes. But yes, I'm finished."

"And your lip?"

"The swelling is all gone. It feels better."

"Good, then you will dine with me this evening? Everyone asked about you, I only told them you were a bit seasick. I hope that's alright."

She smiled, if only a little. "Yes, that will do fine. I believe I can manage to dine in public this evening."

He sighed. "Wonderful." He reached out and touched her shoulder. "I hope you know how sorry I am. I promise it won't happen again."

True remorse was reflected on his face, and she decided to forgive him. "Thank you, Anthony. We have another two weeks to go on this trip. I hate to spend it with tension between us."

She stood up and pecked him on the cheek.

He encircled his arms around her waist and kissed her forehead. "Our first fight. I'm glad its behind us. Only good things for the rest of the trip."

The remaining days of the honeymoon were pleasant enough, but Martha withdrew a little as time passed. To put a definition on why eluded her, although she suspected she hadn't completely put Wolf out of her mind. A yearning plagued her...for what she didn't know.

Something is missing. Maybe when we get home all will fall into place.

She played the role of a dutiful wife, following what was expected of her, almost like a robot. Italy was beautiful, but somehow her mind kept returning to Spain...to Wolf.

$$\sim\sim\sim*\sim\sim\sim$$

The phone rang late in the night.

Wolf was still in his office, unwilling to retire until he heard from Polecat. He knew he'd call the first time he had the opportunity. He answered on the first ring.

"Wolf? Hey man, is everything okay? I was surprised to hear from you. Sorry I couldn't get back to you sooner."

"Yeah, Polecat, I'm fine. I have a favor to ask." He ran his fingers through his hair, impatient.

"Sure, give it to me. I'll do my best."

"Remember Martha? The girl on the train."

"Of course, how can I forget that. It's the reason I'm still in the military. What about her?"

Wolf barreled ahead, not caring what Polecat might think of his request. "I'm having dreams about her. I need to know if she got married and if she's okay. I can't seem to get her out of mind."

A pause on the line worried Wolf. *Did I just lose the connection?*

"Polecat?" he said into the phone.

"Yeah, I'm here, Wolf."

"Did you hear my question?"

"Yes, I heard you. I can answer your question right now. She did get married, and they're on their honeymoon in Italy. The paper said they'd be gone over two weeks. Sorry, buddy."

Wolf paused a moment. "Okay, I figured she did. But why am I having these dreams? Something is wrong, I can feel it."

"Hey, I want to help. You two had a connection. The electricity was palpable. Look, I know what you're asking me. You want me to check it out, don't you?"

"Is it asking too much? I want to know if she is okay. I simply don't trust that Anthony character. If she's happy, I'll leave it alone. Can you do this for me?" Wolf asked.

"Sure, pal. I'll have to wait until they return from Italy, but as soon as I can I'll call on her. Is that okay?"

Wolf sighed. "Sure. I hate to ask you, but I need to get these dreams out of my head."

"I've got your back, Wolf. You know I'll do my best."

They exchanged pleasantries for a couple of minutes, then hung up.

Wolf sat in the dark for a while feeling a bit guilty for putting Polecat on the spot, but he was crazy with concern. He knew he'd have to wait for any news. They were still in Italy according to Polecat. *I'll just have to keep busy.*

He went to bed early that night, knowing the dream might invade his mind again,

The next morning dawned with his head throbbing from tossing and turning.

As he went about his business, he found himself watching the entrance. *Pete should be back soon.*

He and Mac were going over the reservations around noon when Pete strolled in the front door.

"Oh good, you're back," Wolf said.

Pete frowned. "No thanks to you, friend. I hope it was worth it. Did you make the call?"

Wolf motioned him to follow him to the office. "I did."

"Hey, I'm starved and thirsty. Got something for a weary traveler?"

Wolf looked at Mac. "Send something to my office for this old grizzly."

Mac nodded and headed toward the kitchen.

Pete dropped his pack and sat down with a grunt. "Man, I forget how long a hike that is when you're by yourself."

"Ah, it wasn't so bad. You're just getting' old."

"So." Pete said. "What did you find out? Is she married?"

"Yep, and on her honeymoon in Italy. So all this was just a waste of time."

"You never know. You're having dreams, a bad feeling. Maybe something isn't right about the whole thing."

Mac interrupted with a tray of barbeque sandwiches and a couple of beers.

"Thanks Mac, put them on the desk."

"Sure, Mr. Kelley. Glad to help. Happy to see you back, Mr. Grayson."

Pete nodded and watched the young man shut the door behind him. "So what's the next step? There is a next step, right?"

"Well, Polecat is checking into when she returns from Italy, then he's gonna scout it out and see if he can catch her without her husband so he can talk to her. It'll be a while though."

Pete picked up a sandwich. "Well, it's something." He took a huge bite and then popped open a beer.

Wolf helped himself to a beer and studied Pete. "I had a visitor yesterday."

His mouth still full of barbeque, he mumbled, "Oh, who?"

"Victoria."

Pete stopped chewing, his face the color of crimson. "Victoria? Why?"

"You know why, Pete. You were supposed to take her out. You just left without a word. She was furious. Thought it was all my fault."

Pete set the beer down on the desk. "What did you tell her?"

Wolf chuckled. "I told her the truth. You thought I was pining away for a woman and figured you needed to get me out of here and up the mountain, you know, for man talk."

"She bought it?"

"Sure, it's the truth. You should have seen her face. Wanted to know who, what and where in classic Victoria fashion. I told her I had it handled, and you would be back today."

Pete groaned.

"Why didn't you tell me it was Victoria?" Wolf asked.

"I thought you'd laugh at me. I mean...it *is* Victoria, after all."

"Look, Pete, She's a nice gal. Pretty, too. What she wants with a weather-beaten mountain man like you, beats me. But she does."

Pete looked up sharply. "She does?"

Wolf nodded. "I told her to get all gussied up and be ready for you when you get back. What's the matter? I thought you liked her?"

Pete picked up another sandwich and took a huge bite. Mumbling as he chewed, he said, "I do, it's just that, well, I...just don't know how to act around her."

"Well, other than polishing your table manners, I'd say simply be yourself. That's what attracted her in the first place."

Pete wiped his mouth on the back of his sleeve, then looked sheepishly at Wolf. "Sorry, too much time in the woods. Yeah, I'll have to work on that."

Wolf grinned. "She's waitin', man. Times a wastin'."

Pete swallowed hard and took another swig of beer. "You're right. I should go home and clean up."

"And don't chicken out this time."

"What about you? Are you okay?" Pete asked.

"It'll be a week or more before I hear anything. I have plenty to keep me busy. Now go."

Pete hurried to the door but turned to look back at his friend. "Thanks, man."

He waved Pete off and grinned as the door shut with a slam.

The smile faded, however. It would be the better part of a week before he could expect any news from Polecat.

He only hoped the dream wouldn't come back.

CHAPTER TWELVE

LOVE HAS FLED, A SHADOW NEVER REAL ~

Anthony stood on the deck as the ship entered the harbor. Martha settled beside him, a wistful look on her face. Can't wait to get back to my regular life. This has been the most difficult two weeks I've ever spent. Wooing Martha isn't my idea of a good time. She seems distant, preoccupied.

"One more night in Italy, then we fly home." He reached for her hand. "Will you be glad to get back?" Ever so slowly, she withdrew from his touch.

He almost flinched every time she did. And the withdrawal happened more frequently now.

"I will actually be happy to be home. This has all been lovely, but I've missed Mother." She drew a white lace shawl closer around her as if she were cold.

"I know how close you two are. She'll be glad to have you home, as well," he answered.

She didn't reply, only gazed at the shoreline.

"I suppose we should ready ourselves to disembark," he stated.

$$\sim\sim\sim*\sim\sim\sim$$

The flight home was equally frosty. She hardly said two words to him. He attributed her silence to exhaustion and was convinced she'd bounce back once she immersed herself in her new role as Lady of the Manor.

Benson met them at the airport and inquired about their trip with polite diplomacy.

Anthony gave his butler a thumbnail sketch of their travels as they drove along.

The few staff still in his employ greeted them heartily when they arrived.

"I'd like to lie down before dinner, Anthony, if you don't mind," Martha said.

"Certainly, dear. I have a few business things to take care of, so I'll be out for a couple of hours. Should I run by and invite your mother to dine with us?"

"Oh that would be lovely. Thank you."

He pecked her on the cheek, grabbed his briefcase, and headed for the sports car.

Benson called after him. "Would you like me to drive you, sir?"

"No, no. I'm taking the Austin. I need to take care of some business. No need for you to come."

"Yes, sir," Benson replied.

Anthony slipped behind the wheel and headed straight for the racetrack. Finally, freedom!

Several of his old cronies stood against the rail waiting for the next race.

He waved off their greetings and asked about the horses.

One older gentleman said, "We thought you'd be cozied up at your house with your new bride."

"She's resting. I took the opportunity to play a bit. Only have a couple of hours."

An hour and a half later, he came up empty on two races and remembered he needed to see Martha's mother.

Must keep the old crone happy so she doesn't suspect anything. Oh the tribulations I must endure!

Martha entered her chamber happy to have some time alone. She settled at the vanity and let her hair down while gazing at her reflection. *I should have reveled in the sights we saw, but all I could think of was getting home. Things are not right between Anthony and me. He's keeping something from me, but what?*

She rose and changed into a dressing gown. Lying down on the soft comforter soothed her nerves. Eventually, she fell asleep but woke with a start an hour later from a dream. "Wolf," she murmured. The image in her mind was of the kiss they shared on the train in Spain. *Why can't I get him out of my mind?*

The house was quiet. She knew Anthony wouldn't return for another hour after she glanced at the clock. So, she lay there trying to conjure the dream again. The wind gently tousling his hair, the movement of the train beneath their feet. The kiss, soft and sweet, yet sensual.

She sat up abruptly. In a soft voice she said, "How can I remember each tender moment of that kiss, but can recall almost nothing of my honeymoon?"

Afraid to try to sleep anymore, she settled into a chair by the window and surveyed the garden outside. Butterflies danced between the flowers, birds sang their sweet songs, and she let a smile form on her lips. *This is a beautiful place. I should be very happy here. I have a husband who dotes on me, a gorgeous house, everything a woman yearns for.*

Reality wormed its way into her thoughts. *I'm not in love. That is the problem in a nutshell. But what am I to do about it now?*

The next hour passed slowly, with tears blurring her vision as she watched the wildlife in the courtyard outside the room. Finally, she stood to dress for dinner.

Anthony will be home soon with Mother. I need to shake off this melancholia and put on a happy face. I'll figure all this out later.

$$\sim\sim\sim\!{}^{*}\!\sim\sim\sim$$

Dame Buford, full of questions about the honeymoon, kept the conversation lively during dinner. Anthony answered most of the questions.

Martha barely touched her food.

"You look a little pale, daughter. Are you feeling alright?"

"I'm fine, Mother, a little tired from the trip. I'll be okay tomorrow."

Anthony looked over his wine glass at her. "It was a long and busy trip. I'm sure you'll feel restored after a good night's rest."

"Yes, I simply need to regain my balance at being home," she replied.

"Would you like to lunch in the village tomorrow?" her mother asked. "It might do you good to see familiar places."

"Actually, no. I want to stay home. How about I have Agnes prepare a nice lunch. We can eat in the garden. Will you be joining us, Anthony?"

He shook his head. "I'm afraid not. Business beckons, but you two enjoy your day together. I'll probably be out until late afternoon."

Martha hoped the relief of his absence didn't show on her face. She looked forward to talking alone with her mother.

After dinner they retired to the parlor for a nightcap.

As the clock struck eight, Benson poked his head in the doorway. "The car is ready for you, Dame Buford."

"Yes, yes, of course. I'll leave you two love birds alone. I know how tired you both are. Thank you for including me in your welcome home dinner. I'll see you tomorrow, Martha. Good night, Anthony."

They walked her to the door and gave her a peck on the cheek and then, she was gone.

"You look very tired, Martha. I hope you aren't coming down with something. I'll sleep in my room tonight and give you a little peace."

"Thank you, Anthony. I'm sure I'll be fine tomorrow."

But she wasn't fine.

Disconnected dreams kept her in a fitful state, and she awoke with a major headache. She listened at the door to see if she could hear Anthony, but no sound came from his room.

After dressing, she sauntered downstairs to the breakfast room, not really hungry, but knew she should eat something. The sunlight streaming through the sheer curtains did little to lighten her mood.

Benson informed her Anthony left earlier to tend to business at the office.

Relief flooded her being. *Maybe with him out of the way I can shake this mood.*

Between breakfast and lunch she went over the household duties with the housemaid. She liked Ella. Young and eager, she took her job seriously. From experience, Martha knew when one servant had run the household for a while, they became territorial and resented handing over the power to anyone new. But Ella seemed pleased Martha was there.

They chatted amiably and soon it was time for lunch.

Dame Buford arrived early, as was her habit, and greeted her daughter with a quick kiss on the cheek.

The women talked in generalities, how perfect the weather turned out for lunch in the garden, the latest gossip in town, the new boutique with the latest fashions.

They enjoyed coffee after the meal, and finally, Mrs. Buford asked about the more intimate aspects of the honeymoon.

"So, you are happy both physically and emotionally, Martha?"

"Mother! What a question. Of course I am."

Mrs. Buford peered over the China coffee cup. "Well, you don't look happy. You look absolutely miserable. Is Anthony a bad lover? If so, then you need to tell him what you want and need. Men must be taught, you know."

Martha stood up with the cup still clutched in her hands. "I refuse to have this conversation with you, Mother. I'm not a child, and frankly, it's none of your business."

"I'm sorry, Martha. I'm only concerned as a mother. Please don't be angry."

She set the cup down with a bang. "I've had a busy morning. I think I'll rest in my room. Benson will see you out."

She fled the garden and took refuge in her bedroom close to tears. *I know I shouldn't yell at my own mother, but she is hitting close to home. I'm miserable and don't know what to do about it.*

CHAPTER THIRTEEN

AGAIN I SEE YOU, MY OLD FRIEND ~

As the days wore on, Martha tried to immerse herself in the household duties. The house ran smoothly, but it didn't escape her notice on how short staffed they were.

Ella always had dark circles under her eyes. Agnes looked frazzled half the time. Benson scurried from room to room tending to mundane duties which should be relegated to someone else.

She decided to ask Anthony about it.

"Of course, we can hire more staff, darling. When it was only me, I really didn't need more than we have, but I can see where it will benefit everyone to add a couple more. Ella does need help. It's a big house. And Agnes needs a prep assistant. I'll take care of it right away," he replied to her question.

"Actually, I was thinking of doing that myself. There's an agency downtown. I can go there to inquire. It's part of my duties, after all."

"Certainly, as you wish."

She looked forward to an afternoon out of the house alone. Benson drove her and as they arrived at the agency, she said, "Don't wait, Benson. After I conclude my business, I want to walk around the shops. Give me about two hours and I'll meet you here."

She concluded her business with the agency much sooner than expected and looked forward to the interviews with the prospects the next day.

Her spirits lifted as she walked around the little village shopping center, drifting into one shop and another. She made no purchases, but it was fun to look at the latest fashions displayed at the new boutique. After glancing at her watch she concluded there was time for a scoop of ice cream at the soda shop. She placed the order and settled at an outdoor table.

The sun warmed her face, the breeze cooled her skin, and for a few minutes contentment filled her soul.

Until a voice spoke behind her.

"Hello, Martha. Do you remember me?"

She whirled around at the familiar voice and gasped at the tall man in the Air Force blue uniform. "Polecat! What are you doing here? Why are you still in uniform? I thought you'd mustered out like Wolf."

He pointed to the opposite chair. "May I?"

"Yes, yes, please sit."

As he settled in the chair, he explained, "I would have mustered out, but I thought you and Wolf were getting together and decided to stay in. Then I heard you got married to someone else."

She blushed, the pounding in her chest intensified as the meeting on the train came rushing back.

"I'll come right to the point. Wolf called me. He's back in the States, you know. Back at his mountain lodge. But he's been having dreams. Disturbing dreams...about you."

"About me? I don't understand."

"He thinks you are in trouble and simply can't get you out of his mind. Wanted me to check on you, make sure you're okay and happy."

She remained silent as the waiter brought her order.

"Can I get you something, sir?" the young waiter asked.

"Yes, a coffee, please."

"Right away."

"So, Martha. Are you happy, healthy, moving on with your life?" Polecat continued.

"I...I don't know what to say." She ducked her head.

"Then the marriage isn't going well? I'm your friend, Martha. I only want to help," he said.

A tear fell on her cheek. "Oh, Polecat. I'm so unhappy. I shouldn't confide this to you. You're practically a stranger, but I feel I've made a horrible mistake."

"I'm sorry to hear that. What can you do about it? An annulment maybe?"

"No, no. I can't do that to my mother. She's so happy with the match I've made. I don't want to disappoint her." She hastily wiped away the tear.

"So you intend to live in misery for the rest of your life? This isn't medieval times. You have a choice, you know." He paused, then asked, "Do you ever think about Wolf?"

"You said he has dreams about me. Well, I have them too, but they are sweet, nothing bad." She paused. "There was such a connection between us. If only he had come by the house before he left, I might have turned Anthony down. When he didn't show up, I thought the connection wasn't as strong for him. I felt trapped, like I had no alternative but to marry Anthony."

Polecat reached across the table and placed his hand over hers. "But he did come by. The very next day. Anthony met him at the door and told him you and he were engaged to be married. He said you were tending your sick mother, and he would give you the message that he'd stopped by."

Martha could only stare at him. When she finally found her voice, she said, "The very next day?"

"Yes, that morning."

"But...but we *weren't* engaged. I'd turned him down. Anthony lied to him. He lied to *me*. I asked him who was at the front door. He said someone looking for another house. He'd set him straight; told him he was looking for the house next door." Her breath caught in her throat. "It was...Wolf?"

He nodded. "Wolf was devastated. He left the very next day. This is the first I've heard from him. He sounded tired, depressed, and worried. That's not the Wolf I know. He is always happy-go-lucky, always in good spirits. He's got it bad for you."

She wiped away another tear. "But there's nothing to be done. I'm married."

They sat in silence for a while.

The waiter brought his coffee.

 He sipped at it but didn't speak.

The ice cream melted in the bowl. She couldn't bring herself to enjoy it.

Finally, she said, "You can't tell him, Polecat. You simply can't. There's nothing I can do about this now. He needs to move on. Forget about me. Find someone else."

"You want me to lie to him then?" Polecat answered.

Her fist clenched on the table. "No, just be noncommittal. Tell him, yes, I'm married, but don't let on how miserable I am."

"Why don't you tell him? I have his number. I'm not a convincing liar. He'll know."

She watched Polecat write down the number on a scrap of paper.

He handed it to her.

She hesitated and drew back. The thought of having the vehicle in which to hear his voice was overwhelming. One phone call will crash her world.

"No, I can't. I mustn't."

Polecat reached for her hand and pressed the note into her palm. "It's up to you, not me. I'm only the messenger. He deserves to hear from you, Martha. One way or the other."

Polecat rose and bent down to fold her fingers over the note, kissed the closed fist gently and left.

She watched him melt into the crowded street until she could see him no more. The paper tingled in the palm of her hand. Her fingers tightened around it as she fought the temptation to examine it. A direct connection to Wolf. *It's too much. I can't betray my marriage.* She stuffed it in her purse and hurried to meet Benson.

Days went by and still she didn't look at the note because to see the numbers which could connect her with Wolf would cross a line she didn't think she had the strength to come back from.

Two new staff members joined the household, and she busied herself with training them in order to push the meeting with Polecat from her mind.

Agnes enjoyed the extra help young Elsie brought to the household. Barely eighteen, her first job, she added exuberance to the otherwise dull kitchen. Martha, pleased to hire her as an apprentice sous chef, saw the difference in Agnes who showed her the ropes while grinning from ear to ear.

She hired Ivy on the spot when the girl proudly displayed a Level 2 Certificate in Hospitality and Catering Principles. Several years older than Elsie, she fit in immediately and Ella was glad for the extra help.

Once Ella and Agnes took the new girls under their wings, Martha once again found time on her hands with nothing much to do.

At night when the silence allowed thoughts to invade her consciousness, the temptation to look at the note Polecat pressed into her hand almost made her waver.

Anthony visited her room a few times, and she let him, but she remained aloof and distant. He'd ask about her monthly visitor, expressing his desire to have a child. It did not happen, and she was glad.

Even her mother made pointed suggestions about grandchildren. Martha brushed them off. Things remained strained between them.

The only pleasure she enjoyed was friendly chit-chat with staff. She often found herself sitting in the kitchen with a cup of tea catching up on all the gossip.

The rhythm of life lulled her into complacency, as the months passed. The dreams abated and she came to accept the lot life threw at her.

Until one day, while in the kitchen with Ivy and Agnes, the wall phone rang.

Ivy answered and listened intently. "Long distance for Martha Chadwick? One moment, please." Ivy looked at her employer. "It's a man for you, Mrs. Chadwick."

Martha froze. "Long distance?"

"Yes, ma'am."

Oh my God, it can't be. Not here. Not at my home. Polecat must have betrayed me!

Chapter Fourteen

To ease his ache, she silenced her own ~

Wolf had waited several days for a return call from Polecat. Finally, he lost patience and dialed the base in England. The operator said she'd give him the message to call him.

Wolf sat late in his office waiting, wondering why Polecat didn't call him back.

At one o'clock in the morning the phone rang. He'd fallen asleep with his head on the desk but jerked upright at the jangle of the telephone.

"Yes, hello? Polecat is that you?"

"Yeah, it's me. Sorry, I know it's late there."

Wolf rubbed a hand over his eyes. "Never mind that. Did you find her?"

"Yes."

"And?"

"I hoped she'd reach out herself. That's why I haven't called you."

"Is she all right? Is she happy?"

The silence on the other end struck panic in Wolf's heart. "Answer me, man."

"Look, she's married. There's nothing to be done now. I'm afraid you need to leave it alone and move on."

"She said that?"

"In so many words, yes," Polecat answered.

"Does she know I came by the next morning?"

"She knows."

"I don't understand. How could she become engaged so quickly? We'd just been on the train the day before. We kissed."

"She wasn't engaged. Anthony lied to you. He never told her you came by. She thought you didn't care."

Wolf almost dropped the phone. He...lied?"

"Look man, it's too late. She was upset. *Very* upset, but it changes nothing. Anthony eventually persuaded her to marry him, and she did. End of story. She made it clear she is staying with the marriage. I gave her your number. It's in her hands now."

Wolf shook his head in agony. "The creep lied. It's all my fault, I should have been more persistent, come back in the afternoon or the next morning. I didn't try hard enough and now she's trapped in a marriage she doesn't want."

"Wolf, it's not your fault. It's Anthony's. He manipulated the situation. Unless she changes her mind, you need to let this go."

His voice cracked; despair filled him. "I can't Polecat. She's unhappy. I have to do something about it."

The phone dropped into the cradle as he laid his head on his folded arms and wept.

<div align="center">~~~*~~~</div>

Polecat heard the disconnect on the other end and worried. He'd never heard Wolf so distraught in all the years he'd known him. *Poor guy. He's got it bad. I need to do something about it. But what? I don't want to meddle in Martha's life. She made it clear where she stood. But he sounded so bad.*

He let several months go by, trying to figure out a way to solve this dilemma for his friend. A few trips downtown proved futile. He hoped to run into Martha again, but it didn't happen.

One day, he walked by a phone booth downtown, stepped into it, and looked up her number. He copied it and stuck it in his pocket. *I shouldn't interfere. This is between them, but I hate to see Wolf suffer so much.*

More time passed, and he couldn't shake the feeling he should do something. He pulled out the number from his wallet and dialed it.

A young woman answered.

He listened as she told Martha it was long distance from a man...and waited.

After what seemed an eternity, Martha's voice answered, soft and shaken. "Hello?"

"Martha, it's me, Polecat. I need to talk to you. Please, can we meet downtown for lunch?"

He heard the audible exhale from Martha and immediately flushed with guilt. *She thought I was Wolf!*

"I don't know if I can, but I'll try," she responded.

"The soda shop, eleven thirty then?" he asked. "Yes, okay."

Polecat hung up the phone and scratched his head. *I have no idea what I will say to her. I'm out of my league, but Wolf's friendship means the world to me.*

~~~*~~~

Martha settled the phone back in its receptacle slowly and stood staring at it.

"Madame, are you okay?" Ivy asked.

"What? Why yes, I'm fine," she replied. She left the kitchen in a hurry and went to her bedroom.

What am I to do? I know Polecat has something important to tell me about Wolf. It's wrong, but I have to know if he's okay.

She looked at the clock. *An hour. What excuse can I make?*
~~~

After a minute to think she decided to meet Polecat. She changed her dress, went downstairs and summoned Benson.

"I need to take care of some business in town. Can you drive me?"

Benson answered in his polite, professional manner. "Of course."

Her mind raced as Benson maneuvered through the traffic. *What is this news? I hope it isn't bad. What am I to do about Benson?*

She tapped him on the shoulder. "Leave me at the agency. Come back in two hours."

He nodded and pulled into the parking space, exited the car and walked around to open the door for her.

To make her trip more convincing, she went into the building. A young woman greeted her.

"Yes, ma'am, may we help you?"

"Yes, I'd like to speak to your supervisor," Martha answered.

A voice behind her said, "Yes, I'm the supervisor. What can I do for you?"

"Hello, I simply wanted to come by and tell you I am very satisfied with the employees I was able to hire through you. You've done a great job vetting your people. If I have need of your services again, I will surely seek your business."

The supervisor revealed straight white teeth in a broad smile. "Why, thank you, ma'am. You are Mrs. Chadwick, aren't you?"

"Yes, I am. Well, that's all I wanted. I'll be on my way."

She glanced through the door to make sure Benson had left. Satisfied she killed enough time; she made her exit and headed to the soda shop.

The time was eleven fifteen. *I'm early.*

She took the time to survey the little crowd, hoping she wouldn't see anyone she knew. The waiter appeared and she ordered a coffee. Ice cream wouldn't do this time.

"It's a warm day, ma'am. May I suggest an ice coffee?"

"Why yes, that would be lovely."

Her order appeared and as she took her first sip, a flash of Air Force blue caught her eye.

Polecat walked steadily toward her, a grim look on his face.

"May I?" he said, indicating the chair opposite her.

"Certainly," she replied and set the coffee on the table.

The waiter returned and asked for his order.

"Nothing for me at the moment."

Once the waiter left, Martha leaned forward. "What is it? What has happened?"

Polecat answered softly, "I spoke to Wolf a while back. He was devastated. I've never heard him like that. I should have called again, but I've put it off."

She didn't speak, only stared at him. Finally, she found the words. "You told him Anthony lied?"

Polecat nodded.

"But you did tell him I can't change anything now."

"I did."

"But, he has to understand there is nothing I can do."

Polecat leaned back in his chair and sighed. "That doesn't make it any easier for him. He fell for you, and he fell hard. He never was much of a ladies man. Talked mostly about his mountains. Couldn't wait to get back to them. Don't get me wrong, he loved serving his country, but his heart was always back at his mountain."

"Why are you telling me this, Polecat. What do you expect me to do?"

He shook his head. "I don't know. Just thought you should know. I'm worried about him."

She didn't speak. The ice coffee slid down her throat soothing the raw onset of tears.

They both sat in silence for a while.

The waiter returned to ask if they needed anything.

Polecat ordered a coffee.

"Iced?"

"Sure, I'll try one."

When the waiter left Polecat asked, "Do you still have his number?"

Her face flushed with guilt. "Yes, I do."

"I don't suppose you will call him?"

"What good will it do?"

"I think he might let it go if he heard from you personally."

She squirmed in her chair. "I can't. It will be betrayal."

The waiter brought his coffee.

He sipped but kept his eyes on her.

She whispered, "I'll think about it."

"That's all I ask, Martha."

She looked up at him. "We hardly know each other. How can I be sure it was real?"

"Sometimes things just are, Martha. You have to trust it. I'm not saying you have to get out of your marriage, but Wolf deserves an answer. That you care. Let him know you were duped just like he was."

"I don't want him to be in pain. He deserves more in life," she said.

"Anthony lied. That's grounds for an annulment."

She looked up sharply. "It is?"

Polecat nodded. "It is in the States. I'm not sure about here. You could check."

She shook her head. "I don't know...there's Mother to consider. It would break her heart. Plus, there's the possibility I am pregnant."

Polecat stared at her. "I see. Well, it is your decision." He stood up and bid her goodbye. "I'm due at the base. Think about giving Wolf a little peace."

She nodded and watched him go. Two hours passed swiftly, and she hurried to meet Benson.

He waited where he'd left her and opened the car door.

"I went shopping for a bit."

He merely nodded.

She wrestled with the decision. *Should I call him or not?*

As the pastoral parks and trees passed by, she let the memories of the train, the kiss, the connection they shared wash over her. Tears moistened her eyes, and she hoped Benson couldn't see them in the mirror. Guilt choked her, but the more she thought about the tenderness in Wolf's kiss, the more she wanted to ease his pain.

She set her jaw, opened her purse, and wrapped her fingers around the scrap of paper with Wolf's number written on it.

The decision was made.

CHAPTER FIFTEEN

JUSTICE THOUGH LATE, STRIKES WITH A THUNDEROUS END ~

Anthony cleared his throat during the mundane business meeting. This morning it felt like he'd swallowed a prickly pear cactus. Add a slight flush to his face and he knew he'd caught something.

"Did you want to say something, Anthony?" one of his colleagues asked.

He reached for a glass of water and shook his head. After a quick sip, he said, "Frog in my throat. Sorry."

The meeting dragged on.

The symptoms worsened. He knew exactly where he caught the bug. At the race track a week ago. So many people coughing and sneezing. It filled the air. *Well, Martha is a good nurse. She'll know what to do.*

He made his excuses and headed for home.

Benson pulled in ahead of him in the garage.

He was a bit surprised when Martha exited the vehicle. "Where have you been?"

She raised her eyebrows at the forcefulness of his question. "Out running errands. You look pale. Is something wrong?"

He pursed his lips, then spoke hoarsely, "My throat is sore. I think I have a fever, and I feel weak."

Immediately, Martha grabbed Benson's arm. "Help him upstairs. I'll get a wet cloth and some honeyed tea."

Benson put his arm around Anthony's waist and guided him into the house. After slogging up the stairs one step at a time, Benson finally got him in fresh pajama's and settled him in bed. "Is there anything more I can do for you, sir?"

The strength ebbed from his body and all he could do was shake his head.

Martha entered as the butler turned to leave. "Thank you, Benson. Stay close by. We may need the doctor."

"Yes, madam." The door closed quietly behind him.

"When did this start, Anthony?"

"This morning," he croaked. "I woke up with a sore throat. Thought I could shake it off, but it's hit me like a freight train."

She placed the cold cloth on his forehead and asked, "Would you like a sip of this honeyed tea? It might make your throat better."

He shook his head. "Can't swallow."

She set the cup aside.

Ella brought a pitcher of cold water, and a basin, along with fresh cloths.

"Benson told me to bring these up," the maid explained.

"Thank you, Ella."

The young woman nodded and quietly left the room.

As Martha removed the first cloth to apply a fresh one, Anthony noticed a shocked look as she stared at his face.

"What is it?" he whispered. "Why are you looking at me like that?"

She hesitated. "Have you ever had the measles?"

"Not that I know of. Why?" he rasped.

"Were you vaccinated as a child?"

"I honestly don't know. If I was I don't remember. Will you tell me why you're looking so horrified?"

She placed a hand on his chest. "I think you have the measles. Your face is blotchy. I think a doctor is warranted.

Measles in adults is serious. Would Benson know if you were vaccinated as a child?"

He shook his head. "No, he came into my employ after my parents died."

"Let me get him to call the doctor. I'll be right back. Close your eyes and rest."

Measles? That's preposterous. How can I have measles.

The fever claimed him; and he fell into a fitful sleep.

When he awoke in sweat, the doctor stood over him.

"Hello, Anthony. Looks like you're in a bit of a pickle. It's definitely measles. We can't take any chances. We must get you to the hospital."

Anthony saw the doctor's lips moving, but the words muddled in his brain. The only one he deciphered was 'hospital'.

Martha moved to his side and murmured, "You'll be fine, Anthony. I'll be with you."

The words gave him comfort.

$$\sim\sim\sim^*\sim\sim\sim$$

Martha had never seen a case of measles in an adult, and it was terrifying. As the days marched by, he developed pneumonia. She sat by his bedside day and night, slept in a chair by the bed, only left his side to take a meal or two in the cafeteria.

Ella or Ivy brought her fresh clothes and toiletries.

Benson stood vigil outside the room. She couldn't persuade him to leave.

Her mother came once or twice, but Martha suggested she not come anymore. It was too hard to see Anthony suffering.

The doctors remained grim. If they couldn't eliminate the pneumonia he would die.

Anthony talked out of his head and only calmed when Martha spoke softly to him and smoothed his hair.

Two weeks went by. Anthony didn't rally. He was gaunt like a skeleton. The blotches had receded, but his skin was pale, and he struggled to breathe, each day worse than the day before.

The doctors gave him little hope.

"We seldom see cases like this, Mrs. Chadwick. We've done all we can do. The fight is up to him. We'll keep the oxygen tent over him, but I'm afraid there is little more we can do. Only wait to see if he improves."

The days dragged by with no thought of Wolf or the phone number she'd stuffed in her purse. Her husband was dying, she could only think of him, now.

Benson maintained his vigil outside the door, only poking his head in to attend to any request she might have. Grateful for his steadying presence, she leaned on him more and more.

Fifteen days into the ordeal, she raised her head from Anthony's bed. She'd fallen asleep holding his hand. He was cold. No sound came from the plastic tent.

Terror gripped her.

She looked at his chest. It wasn't moving.

In a panic, she pushed the chair back and summoned Benson. "I think he's gone! Get the doctor."

Benson hurried down the hall.

She realized the call button was beside Anthony, and she pushed it over and over.

After what seemed an eternity, the head nurse entered. A crash cart was wheeled in and Martha stood back in horror as they worked on him.

The on-call doctor entered and took over.

Finally, the doctor turned to her and shook his head. "I'm sorry Mrs. Chadwick."

She screamed at him. "How can this be? Don't you monitor from your station? This is negligence."

Benson entered the room and put his arm around her, holding her up.

"He only died a few minutes ago, Mrs. Chadwick. The alarm went off about the same time you found him. I'm very sorry. His immune system wasn't strong enough."

The butler took over and ushered her out of the room.

She fought him at first, but then collapsed in his arms, sobbing over and over, "I didn't want him dead."

Benson consoled her, "I know, ma'am, I know. Please let me take you home."

She shook her head. "I can't leave, I just can't."

The doctor came out. "Mrs. Chadwick, you should go home. The hospital will take care of things until you make plans." He looked at Benson. "I'll give her something to sleep."

He nodded and gently helped her down the hall.

She looked back at Anthony's room and hesitated, but Benson urged her on.

CHAPTER SIXTEEN

THE MAN SHE ONCE LOVED RETURNS AS THE GHOST WHO NEVER LET HER GO ~

The days went by in a blur. Martha was vaguely aware of her mother coming and going; Anthony's business partners, other friends and neighbors paying calls of condolence.

Benson took care of everything.

She was numb.

After the funeral, she wandered around the house, touching this, opening drawers and closing them again. She couldn't put her mind to anything just yet.

The garden became a sanctuary as the anniversary of their marriage approached. *Not even a year of marriage and I am a widow.*

As she strolled to her favorite bench, she heard sobbing. She turned the corner and found Benson on a bench, bent over, face in hands.

A light touch on his shoulder made him stand straight up, his face red.

"Benson, what is wrong?" she asked.

"Nothing, madame."

"How awful of me. I totally dismissed how much you cared for him. Completely ignored your grief. I am so sorry."

"No matter, ma'am. I'll be fine." He turned to leave.

"Wait," she said. "Will you talk with me?"

He hesitated at first but nodded.

"Please sit." She sat on the bench and motioned for him to join her.

"We must find a way through this. I'll need your help."

"Whatever I can do, I'm happy to oblige," he answered.

"I want to ask you about those papers Anthony had me sign before we left on honeymoon. I glanced at them, but he was so insistent and in a hurry. What were they about? We must get all this settled. Too much time has passed since his death."

Benson's face flushed again. "I don't think it's my place to say, ma'am. I did his bidding. I have no opinion when it comes to those matters."

"I'm not asking for your opinion. Surely, you knew what was in them. Please, it's imperative I understand what his death means for my future."

He hesitated but finally turned to face her. "The papers referenced his heir. If you were to have a child all property, money, and possessions would go to the child with a guardian until the child was of age. It included all you brought to the marriage, as well."

She stared at him in disbelief. "You mean I was to be pushed out? He would control everything?"

He nodded. "I'm afraid so, madame."

The shock rendered her speechless.

"I must go," Benson said.

She reached out to stop him. "No, I must decide what to do now. You must help me. You're all I have. I do not have a child. I'm not pregnant. So what happens now?"

"According to law, you are the heir. It should be no problem for everything to go to you, now."

"You knew this, and you didn't tell me?"

He hung his head. "Mrs. Chadwick, I am no longer a young man. Mr. Chadwick gave me a job when no other would... in return for my absolute loyalty. I had to look to the future." He looked at her with sorrow in his eyes. "I pray you will forgive me."

She sighed. "It's not your fault, Benson. I should have insisted on reading those papers. He manipulated me from the beginning. All for my money. He'd have kicked me to the curb if I'd a child. I'm thankful there is not." She placed her hand on his. "Will you help me, now? I promise to continue your employment here. You need not fear. I desperately need someone to help me navigate all the legalities."

Light glimmered in his eyes. "Oh yes, madame. I'll be happy to stay on and help you. Thank you. I prepared for dismissal. The future is bleak for me outside of service." He paused. "What of Cook, Ella, Elise, and Ivy?"

She smiled. "They stay on, too. We'll work around any problem as it comes. Thank you, Benson. Oh, will you please retrieve those papers, and anything else you deem necessary to settle all this? I can't bear to even look at them. The betrayal runs too deep."

"Certainly. I will take care of everything for you." He turned to go but looked back. "I am grateful, madame. I will not fail you."

Benson, true to his word, arranged all the legalities and soon, she saw the true scope of Anthony's betrayal. The gambling debts, the shady business practices. One by one, she dealt with the aftermath of his death. Funds were tight, but she had no doubt with a little frugality, she would put the ship aright. The loyalty of her staff buoyed her through the worst of it.

Six months after the first anniversary of her marriage to Anthony, she sat in the parlor, paying bills, when Benson entered.

"You have a visitor, ma'am."

"Oh, who?" she asked.

"A Mr. Polecat?" The words sounded awkward on his tongue.

"Of course, send him in."

She stood to greet him; her heart almost stopped at the site of him in his Air Force blue. "Polecat, it's been a long time. What brings you by?"

"I tried to wait for the period of mourning to pass. I hope I'm not intruding."

She gestured for him to sit down. "Benson, have Ivy bring tea and biscuits, please."

He nodded and left.

"Why have you come?" she asked.

"It's Wolf, Mrs. Chadwick. He's asking about you. He heard you are widowed. I don't know what to tell him, so I thought I'd make a visit and find out for myself."

"How is he?" she whispered; her eyes downcast.

"It's a day-by-day thing with him. He has the Lodge..." His voice broke off and he shrugged his shoulders.

She didn't answer right away, only turned to gaze out the window as if remembering.

Ivy brought in the refreshments, asked if they needed anything else, and left quickly when Martha shook her head.

"Please, Polecat, help yourself." She poured a cup of tea. "Cream or sugar?"

"Plain, thanks," he stated as he reached for a lemon cookie.

"What do want me to do, Polecat? Run to him after my bereavement? I've tried not to think about him, to tell the truth." The teacup clattered on the saucer as she handed it to him.

"So, you never called him after we last spoke?"

"No, that very day is when Anthony fell ill. All else was pushed to the background."

Polecat took a sip from the cup. "It's in your hands now, Martha. I won't bother you again. You can choose to stay here and play the wounded widow, or you can start fresh in the United States with a man who utterly adores you."

Shock jolted her upright. "Wounded widow? Those are harsh words. You know more than anyone I didn't love

Anthony. But to bolt to America seems a bit callous to his memory. What will people think if I run off like that?"

He looked awkward at her sharp retort with the teacup held delicately in his big hand. "You can stand on propriety for all your friends to see or you can follow your heart and find happiness with the man who cherishes you."

"I don't know...I'm a creature of propriety, Polecat. It's how I was raised. Can I change so completely to become someone I don't recognize?"

He set the cup down. "I don't know, Martha. Only you can answer that question. This will be my last visit. I will always be available if you need me, but it must be you who initiates the communication. I've done all I will do now."

He rose to leave. "Do you still have his number?"

"Yes," she answered in a whisper.

"Then, I bid you good day, my friend." He turned and left the room.

She heard the front door close.

Benson came in and asked, "Did your visitor leave, madame? I would have shown him to the door. I apologize."

"Quite alright. No need." She excused herself and hurried to her room, tears scalding her eyes.

CHAPTER SEVENTEEN

A MAN'S ANGUISHED HEART, A WOMAN'S UNEXPECTED DECISION ~

Wolf stared out the window of his office. Concentration eluded him now. Ever since he heard about the death of Anthony Chadwick, Martha filled his thoughts, relentlessly.

She's alone. Should I go to her? Is it too soon?

He talked to Polecat a couple of times, but he was reluctant to keep pestering Martha. Polecat's friendship meant a lot to him, and he didn't want to pressure him as his go-between.

Several months passed since Chadwick's death, but he wasn't sure what the appropriate amount of time was for mourning. Meanwhile, he tried to immerse himself in the day to day of running the Lodge.

Pete and Victoria were officially an item now. Wolf was happy for them but seeing them together brought back painful memories. He'd agreed to be Pete's Best Man. The wedding, not scheduled for a few months, only heightened the awareness of Martha's absence in his life.

He sighed and reached down to pet the silky ears of his fawn-colored wolfhound, Lobo. "No use to dwell on things I can't control, aye bud?"

The dog looked up at him and wagged his tail.

Pete surprised him with the pup a few months ago. He wasn't quite a year old, but trained really well, and the canine restored a sense of purpose, a great distraction.

Mac poked his head in the door. "New customers, sir. Want me to initiate them for the hike up to the lake?"

He shook his head. "No, I'll do it. Lobo needs a run."

A group of about twelve men and women gathered in the foyer chatting. waiting to start on their hike.

"Good morning everyone," Wolf boomed at the novice group.

All responded with enthusiasm, gathering around him to receive instruction.

This was his favorite part. Taking greenhorns up to the lake for their first experience with hiking and fishing, and basic survival. Either they loved it and will return for more, or they will find out it isn't their cup of tea. Either way he enjoyed the conquest to convert them into seasoned survivalists.

I really must hire someone to take this over for me, as much as I hate the thought. If these excursions keep growing I'll need some help.

Lobo trotted along beside him as he led the newbies up the steep trail. At least these trips distracted his mind from thinking of Martha. He must decide soon if he should contact her or not.

The trip progressed smoothly. He finished tent pitching instructions, gave a demonstration on baiting a fishing line, and encouraged his students to try their new skills. Everyone found a spot around the lake to practice. He walked from one new recruit to the next giving advice, praising them, and showing patience when necessary.

The evening fish fry always tickled him with the excitement the group showed after a successful day. But Wolf soon tired of the conversation. He and Lobo retired to his tent, smiling at the enthusiasm of the group who were reluctant to end the evening.

Three days later, he led the group back down to the Lodge. Everyone enthusiastically bid him goodbye and assured him they will be back.

Per his habit, he sought out Mac and asked him if anything significant happened in his absence.

"Nothing big, but you received a phone call from Polecat. I explained you were on an excursion." Mac shifted through a few pages. "Here's his phone number."

Wolf snapped a caustic answer, "I already have it."

Mac's eyes widened. "Sure, ok, sorry."

Wolf flushed. "Sorry, I'm just tired." He walked briskly to his office, Lobo on his heels.

He picked up the phone and dialed. The operator said she'd page Polecat. He thanked her and returned the phone to its cradle.

"Now we wait," he said to the dog.

Lobo's tail thumped his agreement on the floor.

Half an hour later the phone rang. Wolf listened as Polecat described his last visit with Martha. "So she has my number and decided not to reach out to me. I guess that's my answer, right pal?"

He bristled at his friend's suggestion he should give up the quest and move on with his life. "Easier said than done, but maybe you're right."

Lobo licked his hand as Wolf ended the call. "Yeah, buddy, looks like it's over for any chance to connect with Martha."

The dog whined and licked his hand again.

As the days rolled by, Martha thought more and more of the last conversation between her and Polecat. The label 'wounded widow' stuck in her craw. All her life she did the bidding of others for the sake of propriety or to please her mother. *But what of my happiness? Does it not matter? Who am I living for anyway? Them? Is that my legacy? Will my epitaph read 'She did what they wanted'?*

The garden became her refuge. A place to think, to mull over the future. More and more she put off her mother's visits, wanting to think things over for herself. She'd caught the not-so-subtle suggestions Dame Buford put forth occasionally.

"You must think about acquiring a new husband. You aren't getting any younger, and I want grandchildren."

Martha answered her rudely and on more than one occasion asked her to leave.

I won't be bullied. Time to make up my own mind.

Benson found her in the garden one day. "Ma'am, your mother is on the telephone. Will you take her call?"

"No, tell her I'm busy."

He turned to go.

"Wait, Benson. After you hang up with Mother, please come back here. I need to run something by you."

"Certainly, ma'am."

She waited patiently, plucking the petals from a red rose she'd snapped from the trestle, silently reciting the age-old verse, 'he loves me, he loves me not'.

Benson returned as she discarded the last petal.

"Your mother wasn't happy, but I assured her you will talk with her soon."

"Thank you, Benson. I'd like you to sit." She motioned to the wrought iron chair across from her.

He gave a slight bow and sat down.

She cleared her throat and began, "First off, I'm going to change my last name back to my maiden name. I want to shake off any attachment to Anthony. The marriage was a sham, and I want to be rid of it."

He blinked but nodded.

"Can you arrange this for me? I don't know where to begin."

"Of course, ma'am. I'll see to it right away."

She looked him directly in the eye. "I'm not going to beat around the bush. How do you feel about moving to America?"

His jaw dropped; his face drained of color. Speech left him for a moment until he finally croaked, "America?"

"Yes, that's what I said."

"But why, ma'am?" he asked.

Her jaw jutted slightly. "I want to start a business there. A tea house. Something out of the ordinary in that country.

There are too many of them here. I must find a way to elevate my existence, and I think America will be perfect."

"Have you thought of a destination?" he pursued.

"Yes, a little town called Murphy in the Rocky Mountains."

"That's very specific. Is there a reason?" he continued.

"Yes, there is, but it is of no concern to you. I'll need your help. Are you willing?"

He leaned forward. "This is sudden. I'm not sure what to think. My position here is probably the only one I will have because of my age." He paused, then continued, "Yes, if you'll have me, I will go. What of the rest of the staff? Are their jobs in jeopardy?"

"They will come, of course. I'll need help with the tea house. It'll be a real adventure for us all." She stood up. "Go and gather them all in the dining room. I'll explain to everyone. Oh, and I leave the arrangements to you. We'll have to sell the house. That might take time. There will be travel arrangements."

"What of a place to live, ma'am? Shall I inquire about an abode?"

"We will start at Wolf's Den Lodge, then take a bit of time to find the perfect place in Murphy. Now go."

He bowed and hurried toward the kitchen.

~ ~ ~ * ~ ~ ~

Almost two years to the day from when she first met Wolf, her entourage made quite a spectacle as they boarded their plane. For the first time in forever she felt free. She sold Anthony's house and funded the trip with the proceeds. Benson made all the arrangements. Everything fell into place perfectly.

Her mother made her disapproval clear when Martha told her about the name change. "But the Chadwick name is respected here. It's an honor to carry the name."

Her reply was steadfast, "So is the Buford name. Anthony ruined any respect his family name carried. I want to go back to Buford, and I shall."

When her mother tried to protest again, she stopped her abruptly. "I will hear no more about it."

She thought about warning Wolf of her arrival but decided to surprise him. After all, Polecat insisted he still pined away for her.

Her mother was distraught. Martha invited her to come along, but Dame Buford was too entrenched in her way of life for such an upheaval. Martha assured her there would be visits.

After several flight changes, they finally landed at their destination. Benson found transportation to the Lodge and a storage facility to house most of their belongings until they found a place in Murphy.

Martha's heart fluttered at the thought of seeing Wolf's face again as the women chattered away in the back of the van Benson acquired. She watched the butler with amusement. He sat ramrod straight drinking in the scenery as they passed by. Somehow he looked younger, more vigorous. There was color in his otherwise pallid complexion.

She smiled. *I made the right decision. We all feel more alive with this adventure before us. I can't wait to find the perfect place for the tea house.*

The scenery took her breath away. A thick forest, huge mountain peaks, blue sky all bigger than life. For all of her existence city life claimed her soul. Trips to Spain expanded her horizons with lovely views of the countryside, but nothing compared to these American mountains. Understanding of Wolf's love of this place settled over her. *No wonder he was so anxious to come back here.*

The winding road continued for miles, and she wondered if they'd ever arrive. Finally, the Lodge came into view, and it took her breath away. Large and rustic, the Lodge settled in a clearing surrounded by a thick population of evergreen trees. A large snow-covered mountain provided the backdrop and dwarfed everything else. The Lodge, a two-story building built with treated logs, sported a large wrap-around porch. A few people sat in chairs made of twisted branches from the natural habitat.

Her heart pounded and her face flushed at the thought of seeing Wolf again.

The women ceased their chatter, and Benson leaned forward for a better view.

The driver parked the van deftly in a space next to the main entrance. "Here we are! So you plan to stay the night, or shall I stay for your return trip?"

"If you can wait for a moment so we can make sure they have rooms available I'd appreciate it. I'll send Benson back to let you know," she said.

"Certainly," the driver tipped his hat.

They exited the vehicle one by one and stood gazing at the huge building.

A man came out of the front door. Martha's heart leapt, but she soon realized it wasn't Wolf.

"Good morning!" the man greeted them with a smile. "My name is Mac. Do you have reservations?"

"I'm afraid not," Martha answered. "I hoped to surprise the owner. Do you have rooms available for my group? I need to send the driver on his way, or we need to go back with him to Murphy."

Mac nodded. "We have plenty of room. So, you know Wolf?"

"Yes, we met in England when he was stationed there," she stated.

She nodded to Benson to pay the driver and watched him drive away with a knot in her throat hoping she'd done the right thing.

Mac continued, "I noticed your accent. He'll be glad to see you I'm sure."

At that moment, the front door of the Lodge opened, and this time, Martha's heart skipped a beat.

Wolf's easy gait halted in mid-stride as he stared at her.

Neither one spoke for a full minute.

Finally, Mac broke the tension. "Let me lead this little group inside. I'll send a bell- boy to gather the luggage."

Benson and the women discreetly followed Mac inside leaving Wolf and Martha still staring at each other.

Wolf took a step toward her and whispered, "Martha?"

She ventured forward and reached out a hand. "Wolf. I hope you're not upset that I've come."

His eyes glazed over with tears, but he swiftly wiped them away. "How can I be upset, Martha? I must say I'm dumbfounded. Why didn't you tell me you were coming? I could have made special accommodations for you."

"I have so much to tell you. Too much to tell on the phone." She looked him up and down. "This mountain air must be doing you good. You look wonderful."

"And you are as gorgeous as I remember." He blushed. "Forgive me, where are my manners. Please come inside and rest. I'll order some refreshments. I see you brought your entire staff. Have you left England for good?"

"I'll tell you all about it. Let's go inside."

He led the way and ushered her into the great room.

She gazed in awe at the beautiful décor. Rustic hanging chandeliers made of animal horns, a huge rock fireplace, chairs matching the ones outside, animal hides for rugs.

"Wolf, it's amazing. You've done a wonderful job here."

"Thank you, Martha. Your approval means so much to me. Please come this way." He led her into his office. "Make yourself comfortable. I'll be right back."

She found a chair across from his desk and waited.

He came back with a bottle of his finest wine. "I've given Mac instructions to settle your staff in their rooms and escort them to the dining room for refreshment. I hope you don't mind; Mac is bringing our food to us. I want you all to myself."

She chuckled. "Perfect. Thank you for taking care of Benson and the others."

He grabbed two wine glasses from the glass cupboard and poured. "I want to know everything." He laughed. "I still can't believe you're here. It's like a dream."

"I was terrified you'd reject me. I treated you badly, I know. But what I didn't know is that you came by the next day and Anthony lied."

Wolf engulfed her delicate hand with his meaty paw. "It doesn't matter now. You are here."

CHAPTER EIGHTEEN

NEW BEGINNINGS RESULT IN RESTRAINED PASSION UPON UNCHARTED WATERS ~

Martha and Wolf talked well into the night until she tried to stifle a yawn.

"Oh for gosh sakes, what's the matter with me?" Wolf exclaimed. "You're exhausted and I keep chattering on. I still can't believe you're actually here. Please forgive me."

She managed a slight smile. "I *am* tired. The trip was a long one, but we had so much to catch up on. I'm fine, really. Nothing a good night's sleep won't cure. If you will show me to my room, please.",

"Of course." He took her hand and led her through the empty common room and up the stairs. At the door he hesitated.

She looked into his eyes. "It's too soon, Wolf. A peck on the cheek will have to suffice. Let's recapture what happened in Spain when we're both clear headed."

His face turned the shade of an over ripe apple. "You're right. Until tomorrow." He leaned in slowly and lightly brushed his lips across her cheek.

She grabbed his arm as he turned to go, smiled, and planted a solid kiss on *his* cheek. "Yes, until tomorrow."

He touched the spot where she kissed him, and her heart swelled at the sweet gesture, his simple sentimentality not lost on her.

She closed the door and leaned against it savoring the moment. *I'm actually here and he's glad.* The sparkle in the deep blue of his eyes sent a shiver through her tired body and she almost opened the door and called after him. She held the cool metal doorknob in her hand but slowly withdrew it. *Time enough for us to follow our hearts.*

The rustic room fit the décor of the Lodge, but it didn't escape her notice the lace curtains on the windows, the red rose embroidered coverlet on the bed. On the dresser top sat a pitcher and basin, the wonderful pattern of roses made her smile. All around the room vases of red roses adorned each available space. Her heart beat fast in her chest knowing the meaning of the color red, and knowing Wolf planned the whole décor, even the single red carnation on her nightstand. She took it all in. *How did he pull this off? He must have given Mac instructions while I waited in his office.*

Finally, she sat down in front of the mirrored dresser and noticed the tinge of pink dotting both cheeks. She sighed. *I made the right choice in coming here.*

The rhythmic motion of the brush through her hair settled her excitement and sleep beckoned.

The last thought in her mind as she shut her eyes was the sweet kiss Wolf placed on her cheek.

$\sim\sim\sim^*\sim\sim\sim$

Wolf took his time down the stairs. The feel of Martha's kiss lingered. He reached to touch the place several times still feeling the sensation. His heart swelled with love for this woman he'd waited for all this time.

Even though the quiet beckoned sleep, he knew he couldn't just yet. He went to his office, reached for a decanter of bourbon, but thought better of it. *No, I've had enough for tonight. I must be in good form tomorrow.*

The darkness enfolded him, giving comfort and peace. *Is she really here? Just upstairs? Will I wake up tomorrow and find it was all a dream?*

He didn't know how long he sat there reveling in his good fortune, but finally he rose to make his way to his room. The temptation to tread back up the stairs and knock on Martha's door almost overwhelmed him, but he stopped himself and changed direction.

He closed the door softly and sat on his bed hoping she knew the meaning of the roses he placed in her room, a symbol of his love, *and* the carnation on her nightstand. Morning couldn't come fast enough.

~~~*~~~

</div>

Wolf woke before dawn and hurried dressing, taking extra care with his almost unmanageable salt and pepper mane, checking his freshly brushed breath.

In the kitchen, he noticed Chef Otis already busy at the stove.

"You remember what I asked for on the hotcakes this morning?" he asked.

"Of course, a rose design on top. Got it!" the chef answered cheerfully.

"Good. Is the orange juice fresh squeezed, the eggs gathered this morning?"

Otis grinned. "This really must be someone special. You never come into the kitchen. I promise, everything is as you ordered, Mr. Kelley."

Wolf felt the heat rise to his face, then gave Otis a lopsided smile. "Actually, yes, she's very important."

The chef winked and said softly, "All is ready, don't worry."

Wolf nodded and retreated to the dining room. As directed, a special place-setting accompanied a single red carnation in a crystal vase. He hoped she recognized the meaning.
~~~

The table accommodated the rest of the guests, of course, but he wanted Martha to have the place of honor.

Benson was the first to arrive, dressed, as always, in his very proper butler attire.

Wolf greeted him warmly, "I trust you slept well after your long trip, Benson."

The butler displayed a slight bow and replied, "Very well, Mr. Kelley."

"Please, let's dispense with the formalities. Call me Wolf. You are in America now."

Benson's face took on a quizzical expression. "Old habits are hard to break, sir, But I will try."

Before either could say more, Ella and Elise made their entrance.

"Good morning, ladies, please join us. Did you sleep well?" Wolf asked.

Elise hung behind Ella.

The usually self-assured domestic servant looked from Wolf to Benson and back again. A quick nod from her co-worker helped her find her tongue. "Very well, sir. Thank you. You have lovely accommodations here."

"Thank you," Wolf answered.

Ella continued, "If you will show us where the servant's scullery is, I'll make sure our group is properly fed. Agnes should be down directly and Ivy."

"No need!" Wolf replied, a big smile spreading across his face. "You all are my special guests and as such, will dine in the main hall. Your places are already set, so please sit down. Breakfast will be served shortly. There is coffee on the sideboard and juice at your plates."

Ella's eyes grew round as she struggled to answer. "Oh no, sir, that is not proper. I, we couldn't…"

Wolf waved his hand at her comment. "I insist. You are on equal ground here." He indicated the place settings on the table and said, "Please find your places."

At that precise moment Martha, trailed by Ivy and Agnes, entered the dining hall.

"What is this? Mutiny?" She laughed. "You heard what Wolf said. We will all eat together." She gave him a warm smile. "Thank you, Wolf."

Trying hard to hide the blush he knew spread across his face, he moved to Martha's place and pulled the chair out for her.

Benson did the honors for the remaining ladies, then waited until Wolf sat beside Martha and settled himself in his chair.

Otis came through the swinging door laden with a huge platter of hotcakes, butter, syrup, bacon, and eggs. He set it down in front of Wolf. "As you requested, boss."

Wolf gazed at the two stacks of hotcakes and smiled at the rose appliques on top. "Good work."

As Otis returned to the kitchen, Wolf asked for Martha's plate and served her the topmost hotcake making hers the one with the rose. He followed with the rest of the sumptuous feast. One by one, he played host and served his guests until all plates were full. Then he went to the sideboard, grabbed the coffee pot, and made the rounds for those who wanted to partake.

When he finally sat down, Martha said, "This is over and above, Wolf. Such a warm welcome for us all."

The others all nodded; their mouths full of the melt-in-your-mouth hotcakes.

"My pleasure," he answered. "I want you all to feel welcome."

As they enjoyed their breakfast the conversation drifted to the future.

"So, you want to open a tea house in town?" Wolf began. "I can hook you up with a realtor if you wish."

Martha set her coffee down. "Actually, Benson is in charge of all that. I'm not up to such tasks. Yet. One of the reasons I brought them all with me. I know I can't do this alone."

"Of course. But, if you do need any assistance I offer mine," he said. "You have rooms here, of course, so one problem is solved."

Martha pursed her lips. "I appreciate it and will take advantage until accommodations can be found in town."

Wolf paused with the fork halfway to his mouth. "You want to live in town?"

"Well, yes. I can't very well run a tea house from here, can I?"

"But you have Benson and the ladies..."

"Wolf, this is my project. I need to be hands-on. Besides, it's not proper for me to stay here permanently."

"Well, I simply thought..."

Benson stood up and motioned for Ella and the others to follow. "Thank you so much for the fine breakfast, Mr., er, I mean Wolf. We have much to do. Will you excuse us?"

Wolf nodded.

After they left, he turned to Martha. "Have I assumed too much? I thought we understood one another."

She placed her hand over his on the table. "I'm here now. We barely know each other. It's too soon for a commitment of any kind. I made that mistake once; I won't make it again. Give me this, Wolf."

He covered her hand with his free one and gazed into her eyes. What he saw there was pain, hope, confusion, all rolled into one and knew he must give her the space she asked for, no matter how difficult it was for him. "Of course, my dear. Anything you want."

CHAPTER NINETEEN

THE FELLOWSHIP BEHIND CUPID'S AIM ~

Benson, Ella, Elise, Cook, and Ivy converged in the upstairs hallway.

"What do we do now, Benson?" asked Ella fidgeting with a loose thread on her sleeve. "It's clear Lady Buford is conflicted. Have we made a mistake by coming here?"

He shook his head. "No, not at all. Stay calm. She needs time to adjust is all. We need to continue with her initial plans. Once we procure a place of business all will fall into place. I will begin talking to realtors. I feel if we can find the right building for the tea house, Lady Buford will turn from any doubts she's fostering now. I noticed a clerk behind the desk downstairs. I'll start with him. We must make sure our lady is well cared for...her clothes, her comforts, etc. Ella and Elise, I leave that to you. Agnes and Ivy, maybe you can get to know the cook. Let him know some of her favorite dishes, assist him in some way."

"But Mr. Kelley said he would help you with the realtors," Ella said.

Benson frowned. "I know, but I'd rather not pull him away from our lady at the moment. I'm sure the clerk will be very helpful."

Ivy nodded in agreement. "Anyone else shocked at eating at the same table? It was awkward, at first."

Benson's concerned look turned into a chuckle. "This is America, Ivy. We need to adjust to these things. Mr. Kelley welcomed us rather gallantly. I doubt it will be an everyday occurrence. Now everyone quit worrying. We are a team, and I intend to take care of all of you." He clapped his hands. "Go now, keep busy and out of their way. They need time to reacquaint."

Ella and Elise headed toward Martha's room.

Agnes and Ivy retreated down the stairs to find the cook.

Benson peered over the rustic, but polished banister and observed Wolf and Martha walking arm in arm toward the garden. When they disappeared, he made his way downstairs to the clerk behind the desk. "Greetings, my good man. I wonder if you can assist me."

The clerk looked up from the paperwork spread before him. "Call me Mac. Everyone does. What can I help you with?"

"Yes, of course, Mac then. And please address me as Benson. I'm looking for a list of realtors in Murphy. Someone suitable to show business properties. Can you provide me with such a list?"

"No problem, Benson. There is only one realtor in Murphy. Victoria Jackson. If anyone can help you it will be her." He wrote down the phone number and handed it to him.

Benson blinked as he took the paper. "Only one? How unusual. But thank you. I'll call her now."

"Any time," Mac said. "How about a beer after my shift? I'd love to hear about where you come from."

Benson blinked several times. "A beer? Although it's highly irregular, I find I might enjoy a little conversation. What time is your shift over?"

"Eight o'clock. By then everyone is back from excursions and dinner, and I leave it to Wolf."

"Eight o'clock, it is. Good day." Benson headed for the stairs with Victoria's number clutched in his hand.

He muttered aloud as he climbed the stairs to his room. "These American customs will take some getting used to."

Victoria answered the phone on the first ring, her voice shrill, but professional. "Jackson Realtors, what may I help you with?"

"Good morning, my name is Benson. Mac from the Lodge gave me your number. I'm here from England with my employer, Lady Buford. She is looking to open a tea house in Murphy. We'd be interested in any business property you can recommend."

Victoria's voice elevated a notch. "Lady Buford? From England? Oh my goodness, Wolf's Martha?"

Benson stumbled over the impertinent question. "Why, er, yes. Martha Buford. Do you have any properties she can assess?"

Victoria recovered from the surprise bit of gossip she loved so much. "Yes, yes, of course. I assume you are staying at the Lodge. When can you come to town?"

"We are indeed at the Lodge. I'm not sure about transportation. I suppose Mr. Kelley will provide something for us."

"No, I'll send a car for you. Tomorrow morning. Early, say nine o'clock?" Her voice quavered with excitement."

"Well, I suppose that will be acceptable."

"Good. Tomorrow morning then."

The telephone clicked in his ear. "What a strange way to do business." He said aloud.

The rest of the day stretched before him, so he decided to check in on Ella and Elise. He found them giggling together while peering out of the window.

With practiced stealth, he moved behind them and cleared his throat.

The women jumped guiltily and turned to face him.

"Just what are you doing, ladies?" He asked, a disapproving frown etched on his face.

Ella stumbled over her words. "Er, we, uh, we noticed the view and decided to take a gander."

Elise nodded vigorously.

Benson moved them aside gently and glanced out of the window where he saw Wolf and Martha, heads together, on a bench in the garden. "Spying? I thought I trained you better."

Ella ducked her head. "Sorry Benson. Got caught up in the moment. It's so romantic."

Elise retreated to the closet where she moved hangers around and reached for another garment.

Benson scowled at them. "I hope this is the last time I see behavior such as this. I specifically said they need privacy. If it happens, again, I'll pack you both up and send you back to England with no references. Understood?"

Elise dropped a curtsy and Ella whispered softly while gazing at her shoes. "Yes sir. Understood." He turned to go but stopped. "By the way, I'll be heading to Murphy early in the morning to look at properties. I might see you at breakfast, but if I don't please be on your best behavior until I return."

He hurried downstairs to tell Mac of his appointment in the morning and to thank him, but the clerk wasn't there. Instead, he walked toward the kitchen to check on Agnes to see if she made any inroads with the chef in residence.

Voices carried through the swinging door. He hesitated and listened.

The chef sounded delighted with the information Agnes gave him. "Why of course, Miss Agnes, I'd be happy to include those dishes. Will you assist me? I believe together we can accommodate both Wolf and Lady Buford. I'm a die-hard romantic, so anything that will help secure their reunion is most welcome."

Benson could almost see the blush spread across Agnes's face as he heard a sound he'd never heard before. Agnes giggling.

He rolled his eyes. *Oh no, it seems I will need to keep my eyes on Agnes, as well.*

As he entered the kitchen, Agnes's face blazed with the blush he'd imagined.

Ivy stood to one side, smiling.

"I trust our Agnes is not keeping you from your work," he addressed the chef.

Otis beamed a brilliant smile. "Most certainly not, sir. She is most helpful in enlightening me on a few dishes Lady Buford might enjoy. I pray you will allow her to assist me. Some of these recipes are unfamiliar."

Agnes wrung her hands and gave Benson an imploring look.

"I'd be more than happy to entrust her into your care, sir." He then addressed Agnes. "A word, Agnes?"

She followed Benson into the dining room.

"I trust you are acting in a manner which befits your station, Agnes."

"Why, of course, Benson. You asked me to see if I could assist the chef, and as you see, he is more than willing to allow me access."

"Don't try to fool me. I heard you giggling. Most unbecoming."

Agnes's face once again wore a blush. "Sorry, sir. It won't happen again."

"I just found Ella and Elise peering out the window of Martha's room spying on the couple. Even though I said we need to adapt to American ways, it does not mean we act unprofessionally. I am entrusting the girls to your care while I travel to Murphy to look at properties. Can I count on you to keep order?"

Agnes raised her chin. "Certainly. I'll look after them. Does this mean we will be able to find a proper building for the tea house soon? How many realtors will you be meeting with?"

"Only one. Murphy is a small town so it shouldn't be long before we find the right fit. See you all act in a manner that will do our mistress proud."

Agnes looked toward the kitchen and blushed again. "You can count on me."

CHAPTER TWENTY

THE HEART WANTS WHAT IT WANTS AND COMPLICATIONS ABOUND ~

The garden's fragrance almost overwhelmed her as they strolled through the arbor, followed by the ever-present Lobo. The perfume of honeysuckle, roses, and mountain laurel surrounded her, reminding her of the time she met Wolf in Spain.

"I can't believe how wonderful this garden is. Reminds me of our English gardens. Most of all, I feel transported back to where we met."

He squeezed her hand. "I created it with you in mind, Martha, and hired the most experienced Master Gardeners. Secretly, I wished some day you would see it. And here you are!"

The trill of an oriole caused them to stop and listen, and Lobo's ears pricked upward at the sound, as well. The coo of a mourning dove added to the sweet sounds, a paradise all their own. They basked in its glory.

"It's perfect."

He guided her to a concrete bench adorned with a tufted dark red cushion nestled into a greenery alcove. "Let's sit here and catch up."

Lobo settled at his master's feet, his head resting on one of Wolf's boots.

Wolf and Martha made an odd couple. She wore a salmon-colored day frock with full skirt and cap sleeves, dainty black patent leather pumps, and the only jewelry were tiny pearl earrings. Very lady like and proper.

Wolf sported his signature red and black flannel, lumberjack shirt and denim jeans, rugged and all man. Somehow they made it seem natural.

She smoothed her skirt and said, "You've done a wonderful job with the Lodge, Wolf. I used to picture it in my mind as you described it to me. I must say this exceeds any expectations I ever had."

"You are the inspiration for all of it, Martha. This is your special garden. There's a gazebo around the corner with a table and chairs. A great place for tea and crumpets. We can relax here every day and enjoy our time together."

She was silent, unable to break the spell of their reunion.

Wolf searched her face. "What is it, Martha? Did I say something wrong?"

Softly, she answered, "No Wolf." She touched his face lightly, her fingers trailing his beard. "We need to talk about this situation."

He grabbed her hand as it drifted from his beard. "What situation? You're here, we love each other. What else is there to talk about?"

"Dear Wolf," she began. "My marriage with Anthony was a disaster. Based on lies, deception, and misunderstandings. I feel guilty about his death, but at the same time am so angry about what he did."

"But that's all over now. The universe has made all things right again. You shouldn't dwell on the past," he said.

"I'm not dwelling on the past, Wolf. But I must be willing to learn from it. I cannot survive another mistake."

He pulled his hand from hers and stared at her. "What are you saying? We're a mistake?"

"No, but I need time. My mind must be clear of all that's happened. I can't stay at the Lodge. It's unseemly. I must rebuild my life on my own terms."

"The tea house? You can do that here. I'll build another cottage. I have the best chefs and staff..."

"No," she replied quickly. "It must be on my terms. I need to prove to myself I can do this." She turned to him with pleading in her eyes. "Don't you see?"

He leaned away from her. "No, I don't see. You trust Benson and your women to help you, but not me?"

"Oh, Wolf, please try to understand. I care so much about you, but right now I must cleanse myself from the past."

He stood, and Lobo jumped to his feet. "I did this all for you. I don't care about the past. It's over. This is our new beginning. How can you toss it away so casually? We've both suffered. We need each other more than ever."

She tugged his hand to force him to sit. "I'm not tossing anything aside. I want to build our relationship. To jump into this before I have a chance to put it all right in my mind is a mistake. One I couldn't recover from. Please, give me this time."

His back remained ridged; his jaw set in a hard line. Lobo whined. "I don't understand, but I can't say no to you. Take your time, I guess is all I can say."

He rose and walked away, back into the Lodge, Lobo at his heels.

She continued to sit, hands clasped in her lap. Finally, she stood and made her way around the corner to examine the gazebo. It was beautiful, white lattice, a glass table in the center, green vines intertwined through the open framework. Tears came to her eyes.

I know I hurt him, but what else can I do? I need to find myself, know my worth before I commit completely to him.

She climbed the short steps and entered, choosing a white, padded bench to sit upon.

Wolf marched back inside the Lodge, his heart beating so hard he thought it might burst from his chest. *She's rejecting me! After all this, she wants a tea house. Maybe I have the wrong perception of her.*

He slammed the door to the office, Lobo scurrying out of the way. He threw himself into his chair behind the desk while the wolfhound slunk stealthily to his normal spot.

Not sure how long he sat there, he put his face in his hands and wept. A knock on the door roused him. He wiped his eyes on his sleeve and said in a tremulous voice. "What is it?"

Pete opened the door slowly. "Wolf? You okay?"

"I'm busy, what do you want?" he barked.

The door closed softly, and Pete sat across from him.

"I saw Martha in the gazebo. She's crying. I tip-toed away so I wouldn't disturb her. Care to talk about it?"

"None of your business," he spat.

"I think it is. I'm your best friend. You helped me when I needed it. It's my turn."

Wolf looked him in the eye. "She doesn't love me. I did all this for her, and she's rejected me."

"Just what did she say to make you come to that conclusion?" Pete asked.

"She wants to open a tea house. Wants to move to town. None of this made any impression on her. I think I misjudged her. I fell in love with a myth."

"She's been through a lot, Wolf. The death of a cheating, despicable husband has clouded her judgement of herself. If she was blinded by this guy who she knew much longer than you, then..."

"I don't care about that."

"But she does."

Wolf looked up at Pete. "Are saying I'm being a bully?"

Pete's face broke into a lop-sided grin. "You said that—I didn't."

Wolf blinked, stared at his friend, then chuckled. "I *am* being a bully, aren't I? It's just... I've waited so long. I want it all now." His shoulders sagged and he issued a deep sigh. "I need to give her the time she needs, don't I?"

Pete rose and went to the bar, poured a shot of whiskey for Wolf and one for himself. "You know, you counseled me, remember, I needed to rush headlong into my relationship with Victoria, but in your case, you need to pull back and give it the time it deserves."

Wolf accepted the shot glass and knocked it back. "Relationships are hard."

CHAPTER TWENTY-ONE

THE HEART TREMBLES; WITH ONE SHADOW GONE ANOTHER FALLS ~

Benson found Martha in the gazebo, started to turn around and leave her alone, but thought better of it. "May I join you?" he asked.

She wiped her eyes with a quick swipe and nodded.

He stood on the edge of the wooden floor. "Is something wrong, ma'am?"

She sighed and motioned for him to sit down. "A misunderstanding, is all."

While he settled across from her on a matching bench, he asked, "Something I can do? I'm here to help. All this upheaval with the move is bound to throw things off kilter. Just say the word. I am at your service."

A smile changed the sadness on her face to one of a calmer demeanor. "Thank you, Benson. I'm sure it will iron itself out. Wolf wants me to stay here at the Lodge. Open my tea house here. I told him I must cleanse the past from my mind and do this on my own. It's a matter of trusting myself again. He took offense and stormed off. He thinks I don't care about him."

"I see," Benson murmured. "Surely, he will come to understand you need time."

"I hope so. I've hurt him so much already."

He cleared his throat, then smiled. "On a lighter note, I have an appointment with a realtor in the morning to look at buildings. It's an early appointment, but you are welcome to come along. After all, you need the final say."

She shook her head. "No, I gave you the task. I trust your appraisal. I'd rather stay here and try to reason with Wolf. If it comes down to a choice of buildings, I will make the trip into town, but for now, I leave it in your hands. You know what I am looking for."

"Very well, Lady Buford. I'll do my best."

They chatted a while about Agnes and the Lodge chef until Ivy interrupted them.

"Agnes sent me to find you. Lunch will be served in thirty minutes," the young woman announced.

"Thank you, Ivy." Martha stood. "I must repair my makeup. I'll be along shortly."

When she entered the Lodge, she prepared herself to face Wolf, but he wasn't there. A glance at the closed office door convinced her he'd taken refuge inside.

For a moment she contemplated barging in and confronting him, but decided he needed time, so she made her way upstairs.

A glance in the mirror showed a reddened nose and smeared mascara. She quickly repaired the mess and changed to a smart, white linen day dress adorned with blue piping.

A quick pat to her hair finished the task.

She sat on the bed and replayed the conversation with Wolf in her mind. *Surely he will come to understand the need to take a little time to know we are a good fit, and to let the past fade away like a bad dream. We can't let these things hang over our heads. We deserve a clean slate.*

The mantle clock struck twelve. She heaved a deep sigh and prepared to face Wolf at lunch.

The stairs gave a homey creak as she descended. Halfway down she paused to look over the banister but didn't see him. She continued down.

Benson stood at the foot of the stairs. "The chef has prepared the staff's lunch in the kitchen, ma'am. The dining room table is set for three. I'm not sure who else will be joining you."

She drew back. "Why aren't you and the others lunching with the rest of us? I need your company just now."

"It's custom, ma'am. The chef wants all the staff to dine together," he said.

"Oh, I see, well…"

Wolf came out of the office, Lobo close behind. "I'll take it from here, Benson." He took Martha's hand, gave a tentative smile, and wound her arm through his. "May I escort you to lunch, Martha? I have much to make up for." He squeezed her hand. "We'll talk a bit later. We have company."

Benson gave a short bow and disappeared toward the kitchen.

Martha chanced a glance at Wolf. Her mood lightened at the prospect of coming to an understanding. "I'd be delighted, kind sir."

"My best friend, Pete, will be joining us. You haven't met him yet, and he's eager to make your acquaintance."

Pete appeared from Wolf's office, his long, blond hair a bit ruffled, his beard disheveled and uncombed, his red flannel shirt half untucked, and reached for her free hand. "Delighted to meet you, Lady Buford. You are as beautiful as Wolf described."

She blushed and assessed his unorthodox appearance but warmed to him instantly. "Why thank you, Mister…?'

"Oh, it's Pete Grayson, but please call me Pete. I wouldn't know how to answer any other way." He looked down at his attire, and tried to stuff his shirt into his jeans, run a hand through his unruly hair and smooth his beard. "Seems I'm underdressed. I apologize. Didn't know Wolf was going to invite me to lunch."

She smiled graciously. "Pete it is, then. I'm not here to set a fashion statement. You're just fine."

They entered the dining room, and Wolf pulled out her chair, then sat beside her.

As she settled in she asked, "Do you work at the Lodge with Wolf?"

Pete sat across from her. "Part time. I assist with the excursions. I own a business in town."

Wolf offered more information. "He's a mechanic and is also about to marry the best realtor in town, Victoria Jackson. I'm honored to be his Best Man."

Pete rolled his eyes at his friend. "She's the *only* realtor in town."

Wolf chuckled. "Well, that makes her the best."

"Oh," Martha remarked. "I believe Benson has an appointment with her tomorrow morning. So, congratulations are in order, Pete. When is the wedding?"

Before Pete could answer, the kitchen's swinging door opened with a clatter, and Chef Otis entered carrying a tray. He set it down and placed a steaming bowl of soup topped with shredded cheese in front of each of them.

"What's this, Otis?" Wolf asked.

"One of Lady Buford's favorites, Potato and Leek Soup."

Martha beamed. "How wonderful. My staff must have whispered in your ear."

"They did, indeed, ma'am. Many more favorites to follow!" Otis hurried back to the kitchen.

Martha watched with amusement as Wolf stared into the bowl. "Aren't you going to taste it, Wolf?"

"Of course. What about you, Pete?" he answered.

Pete looked down at his bowl, lifted his spoon, and delved into the savory brew. He tasted it lightly. His eyes lit up. "This is wonderful!" He dove in and devoured the whole thing before the others even took a bite.

Martha laughed, delighted at his reaction. "Your turn, Wolf."

He dipped his spoon and sampled the new dish cautiously. "Not bad, in fact it's delicious."

No one spoke for a few minutes as they all enjoyed the soup.

Martha glanced at each of them and relished the fact a favorite of hers was such a hit with these two mountain men.

Otis returned with a platter of beer-battered fish and chips, placing a plate in front of each of them.

"Now this is something I recognize," Wolf said.

Otis waited until his boss took the first bite.

Wolf gave his chef a thumbs up.

Otis beamed a smile and returned to the kitchen.

The meal progressed with little conversation until the dessert.

Steamed plum pudding.

Pete leaned back in his chair. "Excellent lunch! I'm loving the influence you are having on the cuisine at the Lodge, Lady Buford."

Wolf nodded as he finished the pudding.

"Please, call me Martha. And I'm afraid you will have to thank my staff. They put a bug in the chef's ear."

"Well, however it came about, it's a welcome change of pace," Pete said. "I hate to eat and run, but I have an appointment with a client in town." He stood and said, "Lovely, to meet you, Martha. I hope we see each other soon. Oh, and of course, you will come to the wedding, right?"

"I wouldn't miss it, Pete."

"Good. Wolf will give you all the details. Right, friend?"

"Absolutely. I'll be escorting her," Wolf exclaimed.

As Pete rose to leave a commotion sounded in the main foyer and the door to the dining room burst open.

A large man wearing a black cowboy hat stormed into the room. "Where's that scoundrel, Pete Grayson?"

Martha gasped at the violent intrusion.

"Whoa, Nash. What's the meaning of this? There's a lady present." Wolf interrupted the angry man.

Pete stepped between Nash and Martha. "I'm right here. No need to shout."

Nash took a breath, then swept off his Stetson and bowed slightly to Martha. "Sorry, ma'am. My annoyance got the better of me. Nash Nelson at your service."

Martha took in the intruder. The man was exceptionally handsome. Shiny black hair with eyes to match. Tall, and dressed in a white dress shirt and perfectly creased jeans. His alligator boots, obviously expensive, were polished to perfection. "No problem at all," she replied.

"What do you want, Nash?" Pete asked, his fists curled at his sides.

"This conversation is best discussed in private," Nash answered.

"Let's take it outside," Pete suggested.

Nash nodded and followed Pete into the foyer.

Wolf turned to Martha. "Sorry about that."

"He seemed very angry," she replied.

"I'll tell you all about it. Can we talk in the garden?" He pulled out her chair and extended his hand. "Shall we?"

She nodded and took his arm as he steered her through the main hall and into the garden.

CHAPTER TWENTY-TWO

WHAT'S LIFE WITHOUT A LITTLE GLORIOUS RUIN ~

Pete led Nash through the front door and turned the corner of the building for more privacy. "Now, what in the world is wrong this time?"

Nash slapped his hat back on his head. "You know what's wrong, Pete. That son of mine. You keep letting him go up to the lake fishing instead of showing up for work."

"Nash, Jr. is a grown man. I don't *let* him do anything."

Nash waved his hand at the answer. "You and Wolf encourage him. He wants to sign on with the excursions. I need him at the office."

"Just because he looks like you, doesn't mean he *is* like you. Neither of us has encouraged him. The lake is public domain. We can't stop him from going fishing. Maybe you should let him find his own way."

Nash's initial anger subsided. "I want him in the family business. It's my dream to have my son partner with me."

"*Your* dream. Not his," Pete stated.

"I know, it's just he's my only son..."

"You have a daughter, too. And...have you considered the fact you are a bully? Because plenty of people think so."

Nash stood quietly looking at the ground before he finally raised his gaze to face Pete, a defiant gleam in his eyes. "But Meg is a...a *girl*."

Pete said flatly, "She wants in the business. Your son doesn't"

"I suppose, but..."

"Talk to her," Pete suggested. "Think of it this way. She's beautiful, smart, and will be a great asset to the business. How can your son compete when his mind is on fishing all the time. He'll come into his own eventually. Give him space."

"Yeah, I guess...say, who was the pretty woman in the dining room? I've never seen her before."

"Lady Martha Buford from England. Stay away, Nash. She's with Wolf."

His dark eyes twinkled. "So you say. How did that come about? I never see Wolf with a woman."

"Met her in the Air Force. Long time ago. They're rekindling the relationship. I'm warning you, Nash. Don't get any ideas. She's taken." Pete wagged his finger at him.

"A woman is fair game until she's actually married. But don't worry. I'll keep my distance...for now."

$$\sim\sim\sim*\sim\sim\sim$$

Wolf guided Martha to the gazebo. "How do you like this part of the garden?"

"It's wonderful. But let's talk about what happened this morning. I'm afraid you misunderstood..."

He interrupted her. "I totally got it wrong this morning. Pete set me straight. I brought you out here to apologize."

"Pete, huh? You two are very close, I take it."

"He's my best friend, has been for years. I know you thought Polecat was, and he is, but I haven't known him as long as Pete. I guess a guy can have two best friends, can't he?"

Martha smiled. "Of course." She shifted on the bench to face him better. "So you are okay with me finding lodging in town? We'll still see each other often. I want the tea house.

Something completely my own, not given by a man. Do you understand?"

"Certainly, Martha. I was selfish. Just to know you are in close proximity is enough. Please forgive my attitude this morning."

She patted his hand. "All is forgiven. Since we straightened out the misunderstanding, tell me about this man who interrupted our lunch."

His face twisted into a frown. "Oh Nash. He owns half the town. Wealthy, arrogant, a pain in the a..., er, rearend. Stay away from him. He's bad news."

"What does he own in a small town like Murphy?"

"The newspaper, the print shop, the real estate office. Probably others I don't know about." He looked imploringly at her. "I mean it. Don't engage him. If your tea house takes off, he'll try to take it too."

She laughed, "Give me a little credit. I know now what a man like him can do. I'll be watchful."

Wolf placed an arm around her and snuggled close.

She didn't resist.

<div align="center">~~~*~~~</div>

The evening dinner consisted of only the two of them. The staff settled in their routine of eating in the kitchen. Martha missed the camaraderie of her crew but also savored the time with Wolf.

"Are you up to a short hike to the lake tomorrow?" he asked. "The weather will be perfect."

She chuckled. "Wolf, look at me. Do I look like the type who would don hiking boots and trudge up a mountain?"

"No more than I would wrap my meat hook hands around a teacup. But I'd be willing to try." His blue eyes shimmered with a challenging gaze.

She studied him. "You're serious aren't you?"

"I am. We need to explore our interests together. Be willing to compromise. There's a strong attraction, but are we compatible?"

The chuckle disappeared from her reply. "That's a loaded question, Wolf. I mean, look at us. You can't find a more *in*compatible couple. I'm a proper lady from England. You are a rough and tough mountain man. Can we really make it work?"

His voice, a mere whisper now, was sincere. "We can try, Martha. We owe it to ourselves after all this time. Will you?"

A tremulous smile appeared on her lips. "Well, I suppose, but I have nothing to wear. I can't hike in these shoes." She indicated her black, patent pumps.

He straightened his back in a hopeful posture. "No worries there. We have a shop at the Lodge where you can find anything you might need. My clients are always forgetting something. After dinner, we'll go shopping."

A flicker of fear made her heart beat faster. *Oh no, he's serious. I suppose I owe it to him. I can do this!*

She picked up her fork, ducked her head and agreed. "As you say then, Wolf. As long as it's not too far. I'm not use to this, you know."

"I'll take good care of you, my dear. I do this for a living, remember?"

$$\sim\sim\sim*\sim\sim\sim$$

The next morning, Benson rose early and headed to the kitchen for his morning coffee. The realtor said she'd send a car, and he wanted to be prompt. He carried the cup of fortification out to the foyer to watch for the transport vehicle after a brief conversation with Otis.

He was stunned at what he saw coming down the stairs.

"Lady Buford? Is that you?" he asked.

Martha smiled. "In the flesh, Benson. I'm going hiking with Wolf today."

He caught his jaw hanging open and closed his mouth with a perfunctory click. "Hiking? You?"

"Is it so improbable? I may not get far, but I'm going to try." Her eyes danced with amusement.

"I'm sorry, I didn't mean…"

"I know what you mean. This is the new me. Let's hope I can keep up." She landed on the bottom stairs with a clump of her hiking boots. "Are you going to Murphy to meet with the realtor?"

"Yes. She is sending a car for me." He peered out the window. "That must be it now." He glanced furtively around the room holding his cup tentatively.

"Let me take that for you. I'm hoping to hear good news on my return." She retrieved the cup from Benson and whisked him out of the door.

"Mr. Benson?" the driver poked his head out the window of the car.

"Please, just Benson. Yes. You must be my driver."

"Miss Vickie sent me. Are you ready?"

He climbed into the back seat and settled in for the long ride.

The driver chatted amiably during the journey, glancing in the rearview mirror regularly, his rustic brown hair almost obscuring his eyes.

He nodded and answered in one-word syllables wishing the man would simply concentrate on the road.

At long last, they arrived in front of a building with the title Realtor on the front. He tried to pay the driver, but the man refused, said it was on Miss Vickie.

The front door flew open and a chattering woman with an abundance of blond hair, too much red lipstick and piercing green eyes greeted him.

"You must be Benson. Come on in, I have coffee ready, we can have a bagel before we start out. I've looked forward to this. My aren't you the well-dressed man."

He tried to answer, but to no avail.

The loquacious Miss Vickie didn't give him a chance to interject.

Inside, she shoved a mug of hot coffee into one hand and a bagel into the other. He stood in the center of the room with both hands full.

She swept a flurry of papers at him. "I have several buildings to look at today." When he didn't take the papers, she apologized, "Oh, so sorry, your hands are full. No matter, I'll tell you about them."

She began the repertoire of each building while he stood helpless.

After the last page, she asked, "Are you finished with your coffee? Ready to get started?"

He put the bagel and coffee down on her desk and nodded.

"Let's go then!"

CHAPTER TWENTY-THREE

IN NATURE'S HUSH, MY HEART STOOD STILL ~

Martha thoroughly enjoyed shopping with Wolf the night before. When she leaned toward fashionable, he quickly pointed out practicality. She watched him blossom as he shared his expertise in all things mountaineering. In the end, she acquiesced when it came to comfort and endurance but drew the line at the hat. A class V Brimmer hat in Blue Moss. It matched the flannel shirt Wolf talked her into.

He suggested another, but she insisted and on that point he gave in.

She waited for him at the bottom of the staircase anticipating his reaction. Benson was on his way to town, Mac hadn't made an appearance yet, and the staff enjoyed breakfast with Otis in the kitchen.

Will he still think I'm beautiful dressed like a mountain woman?

She tingled with anticipation as the office door opened, and Wolf emerged.

He stopped. Stared. Opened his mouth to speak, closed it again while his face flushed bright red. "Sweet Jesus, you look amazing!"

She gave a quick awkward curtsy, the hiking boots making it difficult. "I'm glad you approve."

Wolf continued to stare.

Uncomfortable at his piercing gaze, she began to doubt her clothing choice. "Are we going to go hiking or are you going to stare at me all day? I told you this isn't me."

He recovered and hurried toward her. "I'm sorry, it's, well, you look so beautiful. I guess I never imagined you in such attire before. You're stunning."

"Oh come now, Wolf. This is not exactly my style. I look like a hobo."

"Trust me. You do *not* look like a hobo." He reached for her hand. "Shall we go into breakfast?"

Inside the dining room, Ivy wrestled with the coffee pot. She turned as they entered and stood stock still when she saw Martha. "Lady Buford, I...

She laughed at the 'lost for words' Ivy. "I know, it's a bit much isn't it? This is the new me! All ready to go hiking. Bet you thought you'd never see the day, huh?"

The young woman finally found her voice. "Your outfit is perfect. It suits you to a tee, ma'am."

"Thank you, dear. I appreciate the compliment. Is the coffee ready?"

"Yes, finally. I had to get used to this coffee pot, but it's working now. May I pour you a cup?"

Wolf stepped in. "I can handle it, Ivy. Thanks so much."

Ivy curtseyed and turned back to the kitchen.

Breakfast was spread out on the table, and he drew out a chair for Martha. "Ah, perfect. Just as I ordered. Bagels and jam. A light breakfast for the journey."

They ate in silence. After a second cup of coffee, he said, "Time to go. Are you ready?"

She nodded, wiped her mouth with the napkin and stood. "Whenever you are."

In the foyer he grabbed the backpack leaning against the banister, and gave it a quick pat. "All set. I packed sandwiches and bottled water for the trail."

An overwhelming feeling of inadequacy created a furrow on her brow. "Where's *my* pack? I'm not totally helpless, you know."

"This is your first time up the mountain. Trust me, you'll be sore enough without adding a backpack to the mix. This trip is on me. I want you to thoroughly enjoy it." His face lit up in a huge grin. "Maybe next time we can add the pack. Let's see how you like it today."

"If there *is* a next time," she said softly. "I'm bringing a camera." She indicated the Olympus OM2 hanging around her neck. "Is that allowed?"

"Certainly," he exclaimed. "I'll make a bird watcher out of you."

"I figure there will be plenty of opportunities to shoot the scenery." She held out her hand. "Shall we go?"

Wolf took her outstretched hand and squeezed it gently. "Thank you for doing this. I know it's out of your comfort zone. It means so much to me."

A vision of him holding a fragile China teacup in one hand and a crumpet in the other made her smile. "Just remember, turnabout is fair play."

"Care to explain?" he asked, his brow lined with deep furrows.

She pulled him toward the door. "You'll see, Wolf, you'll see."

The sun radiated warmth, even though the temperature didn't quite agree. The nip in the air only heightened her enthusiasm as she watched Wolf hoist the weathered backpack to its familiar place.

Hand in hand they headed toward the trail which led to the smaller lake a few miles up the mountain.

Martha's heart, light with anticipation as they hiked, filled with wonder at the beauty of the terrain. Every once in a while Wolf pointed out a bird and she adjusted the camera to snap a shot. "Maybe I'll start a scrapbook about birds," she declared.

Wolf's smile spread across his face, white teeth gleaming in the morning sun. "I think that's an excellent idea. If they are good, you could sell them to the nature magazines."

"Are you trying to talk me into a different career?" she teased.

"No, just pointing out your talent and creativity. Might as well make a few bucks while you're enjoying the outdoors."

"I'll keep it in mind," she answered. *Actually, it might be a good idea. But I'll keep the plan to myself for now.*

They continued until she saw an open field come into view. The trees parted and before them spread a beautiful field of mountain grass. On the other side, a huge buck stood staring at them.

"He's beautiful." Martha exclaimed.

"Shh, don't click that camera. He'll hear it even though it's a mile away," Wolf said.

"You mean it's a mile across there? It doesn't seem that far."

"Your eyes play tricks on you out here. Isn't it gorgeous?"

"Yes,"

They watched the buck for several quiet minutes until the animal decided to move on.

As they started across the plain Martha glanced at Wolf. She noticed the smoothness of his face; a serene look erased the lines of tension. He seemed at peace with his surroundings. In that moment, she knew he belonged here. An ache filled her chest. Could she be satisfied with this mistress of his soul?

<div align="center">~~~*~~~</div>

Benson followed the chattering Vickie up and down the small-town streets of Murphy, making mental notes of each building.

None of them suited and discouragement settled in...until they turned off the main street and into a side street.

"I don't really recommend this one," Vickie said. "But thought I'd show it to you anyway. It's off the beaten path, you know."

He studied the impressive edifice and knew he found the perfect building. The antiquated brick front gave it an old-world look. English ivy twined up and around the brick adding to the ambience. He visualized the tea house sign hanging above the door. "This is it," he said softly.

Vickie tried to interrupt and discourage him. "But it's down a side street."

"Show me the inside," he demanded.

"Well, alright, if you insist." She fiddled with the keys in her hand and opened the door.

He stepped inside and gazed about. "Perfect," he whispered.

"But..."

"This is the one," he interrupted.

For once, Vickie remained quiet.

The room, dusty and in disarray, with overturned chairs, toppled tables, light fixtures askew, and cobwebs hanging about transformed in his mind to the tea house Martha envisioned.

"What was this before? How long has it been empty," he asked.

She stepped forward to stand alongside him. "A bistro. It didn't do well. Closed soon after it opened. I believe the location had a lot to do with it. It's tucked away, no exposure. It's been empty about a year."

As she talked, he envisioned the walls painted a rose color, dainty chandeliers, gleaming white tables with matching chairs. Waiters dressed in tuxedo-like uniforms. A profusion of flowers and green plants. *Yes, this has much potential.*

He glanced at her momentarily. "Mismanagement. This is a perfect location if you know how to market it. Who owns it?"

"Nash Nelson. He owns everything in this town."

"I will bring Lady Buford here tomorrow. I'm sure she will love this place."

"Shall I have lease papers ready for her."

He shook his head. "We won't be leasing. We'll be making a purchase."

Her jaw dropped. "Nash will never agree to that. He controls everything."

"Nevertheless, have purchase agreements prepared. Ms. Buford can be very persuasive."

They toured the back room and the kitchen. The appliances needed replacing.

A lot of cleaning is necessary, but Agnes and the crew will jump in with gusto.

For the first time, Benson noticed a frown on Vickie's face. "What's wrong, Miss Jackson?"

"Well, Nash isn't going to like this I'm afraid."

"Don't worry your head about it. We'll handle Mr. Nelson."

"Yes, sir."

CHAPTER TWENTY-FOUR

THE HEART DANCES ON THE WIND UNTIL TORN AGAIN ~

Wolf watched Martha take in the scenery, snapping pictures, studying the mountain flowers and wildlife. His heart swelled with hope. *Maybe after today, she'll decide to stay here. Share my passion for the mountain and make a life at the Lodge.*

They arrived at the lake, breaking through the dense forest of trees, and standing in awe of the beautiful painting of nature.

Martha stood still, drinking in the beauty of the water, the fish jumping high to catch a fly or two, the hawks swooping down to scope out their dinner. "It's gorgeous."

Wolf smiled. "I tried to tell you. Come, there's a flat rock a couple yards from here. We can enjoy our sandwiches and refresh ourselves."

The bench-like stone sat near the lake's edge, a backdrop of evergreens making the scene complete.

He spread a red and white checkered tablecloth on the flat surface, fished out the sandwiches, and produced two wine glasses along with a bottle of his best vintage.

"Wolf!" She stood open-mouthed. "How in the world did you get those glasses here without breaking them?"

He bowed with the elegance of a subject acknowledging his queen. "Every precaution was taken, my lady. I'm not some clumsy oaf, you know."

"Of course not, but glass?"

"Anything for you, Martha."

He arranged the sandwiches and opened the wine, enjoying her reaction, and indicating her place on the rustic platform. The wine was poured, and he raised his glass in a toast. "To us, may we always be able to enjoy days like this."

She lifted her glass in acknowledgement and drank. "This is all such a surprise. So romantic, and I want you to know how much I appreciate your effort."

He accepted her praise with a nod of his head.

For a while they ate in silence as the birds twittered in the trees, the fish splashed, the wind whistled rustling the leaves and soaked up the bright sunshine.

Wolf dreamed of this day and never thought it would actually happen. The woman he loved, up here in this picturesque mountain lake. He always knew she was a beautiful woman, always stylish, perfectly dressed, perfectly coifed, impeccable manners, a true lady, but to see her in this setting dressed as a hiker, to him, her beauty shone even brighter.

"What are you thinking, Wolf? You keep staring at me."

"How gorgeous you look. You take my breath away."

"Oh Wolf, please stop. You're making me blush."

He jerked suddenly; his attention captured by movement on the other side of the lake. "Be very still, Martha. No quick movements."

"What is it?" she whispered.

"Turn slowly, look across the lake on the other shore."

She did as he directed, and gasped.

A mother black bear with two cubs observed them by the water's edge.

"Are we in danger?" she asked tremulously.

"I don't think so, but we must remain still. Nothing more dangerous than a mama bear with her babes. If we don't act threateningly, they should go back into the woods."

Her voice remained low. "Can I take a picture?"

"Not a good idea. She'll pick up the sound of the camera. It's an unfamiliar noise; she might react in a protective way. We'll watch them closely." He patted his pack. "I have bear spray and a horn if she approaches."

"No gun?" she asked.

"Not allowed in this neck of the woods. But don't worry. I've had these encounters many times. She's all the way across the lake. I predict she'll return to the safety of the trees."

Minutes passed.

They remained as statues as the cubs frolicked in the water. As predicted the mother turned around and disappeared into the woods, her cubs followed immediately. And then, they were swallowed up by the dense timber.

Wolf relaxed but turned to Martha. "We should pack up and head back."

"Why? They're gone," she declared.

"Might be they'll double back, maybe come this way. I can't take a chance. There are only two of us. Usually when I come up here, there are ten or more. The numbers alone will deter a bear. Believe me, she is aware of our vulnerability. It's about a two-hour trek back, so I suggest we head out. Next time we'll bring a tent and spend the night with a group."

"I wish I'd gotten a picture."

He wrapped the glasses, tucked away the remainder of the sandwiches, and stowed the wine bottle back in the pack. "There'll be other opportunities, I promise. You snapped a lot of wildlife today. I'd count the day a huge success."

She glanced back at the other shore and sighed. "Okay, but I'm not sure I'll be as brave next time after the bear sighting."

"Don't worry, I'll always protect you."

The hike back, though uneventful, garnered very little conversation, with Martha in front of Wolf.

He kept his head on a swivel, ever vigilant, protecting the love of his life. Every once in a while she looked back at him and smiled. His heart warmed as she looked to him for protection.

The Lodge came into view about four o'clock according to Wolf as he studied the sun.

He stopped her before they arrived at the main entrance. "Thank you for coming with me today. I hope you enjoyed it."

The look she gave him smoldered with desire. In a split second, she slipped one hand around the back of his head and pulled him in for a kiss. She withdrew, then said, "Does that tell you how much I enjoyed it?"

"I'm not quite convinced." He pulled her back in, and the kiss grew more intense.

Breathless, they slowly drew apart, savoring the intimate moment.

Without a word between them, he twined his arm through hers and headed for the door.

Benson stood in front of the main desk talking to Mac. He turned at the sound of the welcoming bell. "Ah, you're back! I trust you enjoyed the excursion."

"Very much," Martha answered. She disengaged her arm from Wolf's and hurried toward the butler. "Did you find a building for the tea house?"

Wolf's heart dropped at the eagerness on her face. The intimate moment shattered; their day alone faded into the background. He watched Benson and Martha in animated conversation and felt like an outsider in his own lodge. Martha's face, alight with excitement, listened intently to Benson's description of the building he found; no mention of the day she and Wolf spent together.

He waited a moment realizing he was not going to be included in the discussion, turned toward his office, and closed the door softly.

Lobo perked up his ears and leaped out of his bed to greet him. He didn't take the wolfhound on purpose so he wouldn't be distracted by the dog pursuing every animal he came across. The day was Martha's day, and he'd wanted no distractions.

"Well boy, at least you put me first. You're a good and faithful companion."

Lobo's tail beat a rhythm against the desk as Wolf scratched his ears.

The sun shone through the window making light dance against the decanter on the sideboard. He rose and decided to pour himself a drink, glancing back at Lobo. "She wants me to be patient, to try to understand. But I tell you, boy, it's hard. I thought we made progress today, but apparently I'm not a priority. What shall I do?"

The dog whined and moved to stand by his master, his tail wagging furiously.

"Ah, you don't have the answers, do ya boy?" He returned to his chair and knocked back the whiskey in one swallow.

<div align="center">~~~*~~~</div>

Martha concentrated on Benson's description of the building he considered appropriate for the tea house. Her heart beat faster as he described the ivy covering the brick walls, the intimacy of the side street, and the ideas he entertained for the interior. She could picture it, and her mind kicked in with ideas of her own.

"I can't wait to see it. When can we go?" she asked.

"Tomorrow, if you like."

"Oh yes, the sooner the better." She turned expecting Wolf to be at her elbow, but the hall was empty. "Where'd he go?"

Benson looked around. "He must have gone to his office."

A frown creased her brow. "I'll meet you down here at nine a.m." A glance at Wolf's closed office door planted a seed of uneasiness in her mind. *What now? Is he upset about something? I thought after today we were on the same page.*

The tea house forgotten for the moment as she reached to knock on his door. She didn't wait for him to answer but opened the door. "Wolf?"

Lobo offered a soft woof.

Wolf sat in the chair with his back to the door, studying the mountain through the window. He turned slowly to face her, the Hi-ball glass still clasped in his hand.

He didn't say a word, just went to the sideboard and poured himself another whiskey.

CHAPTER TWENTY-FIVE

IN LOVE AND IN BUSINESS SHE CHOSE BOLDLY WITH FIRE AND GRACE ~

"Is something wrong? Why are you drinking so early?" she said.

"Just trying to stay out of your way."

"Out of my way? I turned around to ask if you'd come with me tomorrow and you were gone." She moved toward the desk and sat across from him. "If something is wrong you need to tell me, not stalk off with an attitude."

He turned, glass in hand, and went to the window, his back to her. "I didn't stalk off. I felt awkward, like I was quickly forgotten and dismissed."

"Dismissed? After the wonderful day we enjoyed? After the...kiss? I truly don't understand you, Wolf. One minute you're loving and kind. The next you sulk like a recalcitrant child. These moods swings are concerning. And alcohol won't solve the root cause. "

She rose quickly, swiveled on her heel to leave but looked back at him. "I won't be down for dinner. I'm not hungry and I'm very tired."

The door slammed and she winced. Tears filled her eyes as she rushed upstairs noticing Benson and Mac watching with surprise etched on their faces.

In her bath, she let the tears fall. *I didn't mean to slam the door. I don't know what to do. Is he just insecure or is there more to it than that?*

Wrapped in her pink fluffy, floor-length robe, she sat at the mirror and contemplated the day. The warmth between them, the camaraderie, the laughter. The thoughts kept coming, *Is it me? Do I expect too much? Have I been selfish?*

Then it became clear. She addressed her reflection. "I left him standing alone in the hall, too excited to grab his hand and pull him along. He felt left out. I'm so stupid. The tea house isn't his dream; he wants me to stay here. Fear...he's afraid he'll lose me. Of course that's it. The loss he experienced when I married Anthony had a devastating effect on him."

Enlightened, she jumped up to dress, to hurry downstairs and repair the damage.

Before she could throw off the warm robe, a knock startled her. She clutched the bathrobe tighter and opened the door a crack. "Yes?"

Wolf stood in the hallway, his eyes seeking hers, a stricken look etched on his face. "Martha, please, I'm sorry. Can we talk?"

She opened the door wide, forgetting she was only in her robe. "Certainly! I'm so sorry, I was wrong..."

"No, love. It's my fault. My disgusting jealousy. It's childish and I apologize." He stopped unable to continue as he took in the state of her undress.

She stepped around him and closed the door.

Neither spoke.

Wolf wrapped his arms around her.

She didn't resist.

The next morning they descended the stairs together, hand in hand.

Martha noticed the controlled look on her butler's face, but surprise glittered in his eyes. "Good morning, Benson. Have you had breakfast? We'll be ready to leave after we eat a bite."

"Yes, I've eaten. I'm ready whenever you are."

"We'll be taking the four-by-four," Wolf announced. "Will you ask Mac to have it ready?"

Benson nodded his head.

Martha and Wolf strolled into the dining room where Otis already laid breakfast. Bacon and eggs with wheat toast, and very hot coffee.

They ate in silence but exchanged loving glances throughout the meal.

Benson poked his head into the room. "Mac pulled the truck up to the front door. He says it's all gassed and ready to go."

Martha daintily wiped her mouth with a red linen napkin, took another sip of coffee, and acknowledged the information. "That's perfect. I think we're ready. Right, Wolf?"

"Yep." He swallowed the last of the bacon, stood, reached for the coffee cup and took a swig. "All set."

$$\sim\sim\sim^*\sim\sim\sim$$

The trip to Murphy worried Benson after Martha's tearful exit from Wolf's office and the tears streaming down her face the night before. She sat up front; Benson occupied the back seat. As the trip progressed, he relaxed while observing them laughing and joking with each other. *They must have made up. Obviously since they came downstairs together. It's a good thing since any strain between them will only make the day more difficult.*

Wolf indicated certain points of interest and added pertinent information to each one. Old bridges, popular hiking trails, historical markers, and tourist businesses.

Benson soaked it in with interest. *He certainly knows this mountain.*

As they approached the town, Benson explained how Ms. Jackson promised the papers would be ready to sign once she receives Martha's approval. "Remember, Lady Buford, if you don't like it we can look at other properties. There are one or two she showed me which could suffice."

"From what you've described, I think I will love it." She turned to Wolf. "Do you know the building?"

"Yes, as a matter of fact, I do. Some kind of bistro, I think. A young couple opened it, but the food wasn't good, and they couldn't retain help. It didn't last long. It's been empty for quite a while."

Benson nodded. "Miss Vickie told me the exact same thing. By the look of it they didn't know what they were doing. I feel sure you can make a go of the tea house with your flare for style and knowledge of the proper food, pastries, and of course, tea."

In the mirror he saw Wolf's eyes flicker toward Martha and a frown crease his brow. *I certainly hope he won't try to throw a wrench in this transaction. Lady Buford wants this so much. However, they seem very compatible today. Surely they've worked through whatever happened yesterday.*

Wolf pulled the truck in front of Vickie's office, went around to open the door for Martha, and said, "Well, let's see what you think, my dear."

Benson followed them inside as he listened to Vickie's high-pitched voice greeting the couple. And then he heard another voice. Nash Nelson. His heart sank. *Mac said there is bad blood between Wolf and Nash. God help us if these two egos collide!*

He watched as Nash swept off his cowboy hat, gave a slight bow, and kissed her hand.

Benson noticed Wolf's face twitch with obvious irritation.

Nash acknowledged his adversary with one word and a nod. "Wolf."

"Nash," Wolf said, minus the nod.

"Well," Vickie interrupted, "Shall we go and see the building? We can actually walk from here. It's right around the corner."

Martha's face lit up. "The sooner the better. Let's go."

Nash beat Wolf to the door and opened it. "After you, Lady Buford."

"Please, call me Martha. No need for English formality."

Wolf grabbed her arm and muscled them through the door giving Nash a slight bump as they went through.

Nash grinned mischievously but followed them without a word.

Benson offered Vickie his arm and escorted her after the others.

She gave a little giggle as she grasped his elbow. "How gallant of you, Benson. You must teach Pete these English ways."

He thought it best not to reply.

As they turned the corner, he heard Martha exclaim with joy.

"It's perfect! I can tell already." She gazed up and down the brick walls, the prolific ivy snaking over the masonry, and the tall, arched spring line windows. "I knew I was right to send you, Benson. You've a great eye." She turned to Wolf. "Ready to go inside?"

"Whenever you are, Martha," he replied.

Vickie pulled out the keys and unlocked the door.

Martha's expression didn't reflect the same joy as it had when she saw the outside, but she was still smiling.

"Now, Lady Buford, if you will imagine small white tables, with red rose bud vases, white lace curtains, and the walls painted a spring rose, I think you will overlook the disarray you see right now. I envision multi-colored hanging baskets placed all around. The waiters must be dressed appropriately, also. You have a definite eye for fashion, so I leave that to you. Thoughts so far?"

"Oh, yes, I can see it very clearly. What about the kitchen?"

"Follow me," Vickie said.

As they trailed after her, Benson noticed Nash's silence and wondered what he was thinking.

"The appliances need replacing," Vickie continued. "With a little clean up and modernization, it will be a very functional kitchen."

Nash stepped up beside Martha. "I'll help you in any way I can, Martha. All you have to do is ask."

"I appreciate it, Mr. Nelson, but I think we need to talk about the financing first."

"Please call me Nash. Everyone does. The rent will be reasonable. I'll allow for upgrades and the like."

"Oh, no. You don't understand. I don't intend to rent it. I want to buy it outright." she said.

Benson observed Vickie squirm as money was discussed.

"Not possible, I'm afraid. I don't sell; I rent my property. Always have," Nash answered.

"Then we don't have a deal." She turned on her heel and headed for the front door..

"Now wait, Martha. Surely, you can see I need to maintain my business investments. I haven't gotten to where I am by selling off my property."

She ignored Nash's remark and addressed Wolf who couldn't hide the grin on his face. "What's the next town over, Wolf? I imagine they will be in need of a tea house. I might as well take my business there."

"Well, Bad Axe is about twenty miles east of here. It's small, but the people are friendly."

Nash stepped in front of Martha and interrupted. "Let's not be hasty. We can work this out. I won't sell but you can have carte blanche with whatever you want to do with it. I won't interfere. I give you my word."

"Sorry, I won't negotiate with you about this. I want it to be mine outright." She turned to Vickie. "I'm sorry Ms. Jackson, I hate to deny you the commission, but I'm firm on this. Let's go, gentlemen."

Benson looked at Wolf and the two smiled at each other. *Martha is proving a tough business lady. Good for her.*

The three hurried out the door and walked around to the corner to the four-by-four.

Wolf rushed to open the door for her before Nash caught up.

Benson scrambled into the back seat

Wolf revved the engine and roared off leaving Nash and Ms. Vickie staring open-mouthed on the sidewalk.

No one said a word for a mile or so as Wolf steered the truck toward the town of Bad Axe. Almost in unison the three burst out laughing.

When they caught their collective breaths, Wolf glanced at Martha. "First time I've seen Nash at a loss for words! You were magnificent. I'm so proud of you. I might have doubted just a tiny bit you could handle Nash Nelson, but you put me to shame. I have every confidence in your business ability."

Martha grinned at him. "I learned one thing while married to Anthony. I will never be a push over again."

Benson leaned toward the front seat. "Are you actually thinking of putting the tea house in Bad Axe?"

"Depends on Wolf's advice. He knows the town. What say you, my dear?"

He directed his gaze at Wolf's reflection in the rearview mirror, observed the squint and the frown. His heart dropped.

CHAPTER TWENTY-SIX

WITH QUIET GRACE, SHE CONQUERED ~

Nash Nelson raged with clenched fists at Vickie Jackson. dumping all his frustration on the hapless real estate agent. "Why didn't you make it clear to her I don't relinquish any of my properties. You know I insist on complete control. You're incompetent. I should fire you on the spot."

Vickie stuttered trying to reply. "I, I told Benson that very thing. Over and over. I assumed he relayed the information to Lady Buford."

He marched toward the office and called back to her. "Go lock the building. Looks like I'll have to take care of this myself."

He slammed the door behind him in the office, plopped down in Vickie's chair, and pulled out his cell phone. "John Sinclair! Just the man I need to talk to. How come you're answering your own phone? What happened to the receptionist?"

Nash cut off the man on the other end of the line. "Yeah, yeah, I get it. Anyway, I have a favor to ask. Three people are on their way to your office. A lady from England wanting to open a tea house." He paused as he listened to

Sinclair. "You heard me right. A tea house. I want you to turn them down. I've almost convinced her to take my building here in Murphy. I don't want anything to upset the negotiation. Got it?"

Again he paused. "I don't give a rat's ass about your problems, Sinclair. I want this woman to rent from me. I own the most profitable business in your town. Don't make me pull out. You'll do this or suffer my wrath." He hit the end button on his phone and slammed it down on the desk as Vickie came through the door.

"You're going to block her from opening the business in Bad Axe?" she asked, eyebrows raised.

"None of your business, Ms. Jackson. You'll keep your mouth shut or believe me you won't like the consequences. Understand?"

"Yes sir."

He rose and kicked the chair back. "I've got things to do. I trust you know enough to let me know when and if you hear back from Martha."

She ducked her head and whispered once more, "Yes sir."

$$\sim\sim\sim*\sim\sim\sim$$

Wolf didn't answer right away as they drove along, thinking of how to put it to Martha.

"Well, I'm waiting for an answer to the question," Martha said.

"Bad Axe isn't right for a tea house, Martha. It's small, rough, full of loggers and tough characters." He reached for her hand.

"So why did you bring it up?"

"First thing I could think of."

"Okay, are there any other towns around suitable for a tea house?" she asked.

"Not really. Smaller ones than Bad Axe. Biggest town outside of Murphy is seventy-five miles away." He squeezed her hand. "I wouldn't like to be so far from you."

She sighed. "Okay, so I will simply need to convince Nash to sell me the building."

Wolf smiled. "I have no doubt you can do it. He's a tough businessman, but if anyone can persuade him, it's you. Just be careful."

"Thank you, Wolf. Shall we head home? There's no point in going to Bad Axe now."

$$\sim\sim\sim*\sim\sim\sim$$

A couple of days passed without a word from Nash Nelson. Martha began to think he wasn't going to take the bait. *Maybe I need to reconsider Wolf's offer to open the business here at the Lodge.* As she came down for lunch on the third day since the trip to Murphy, she noticed Benson accepting a bouquet of yellow tulips mixed with greenery and tiny white freesias from a delivery man at the front door.

"Who's sending you flowers, Benson?"

"No one, they're for you, ma'am." He placed the offering on the desk. "There's a card."

"Oh, sweet Wolf. He knows how disappointed I am. He's trying to cheer me up." She reached for the card. "What do you think, Benson? Should I just open the tea house here at the Lodge?"

Before he could answer, she let out an unladylike whoop. "It's from Nash Nelson!"

Benson's bushy brows raised; and his eyes widened. "Oh my. Does he say anything?"

"He apologizes for his bad manners and wants to meet again." She tucked the card back into the envelope and said, "It's a victory! I must show Wolf." She rushed toward his office.

She knocked, but couldn't wait for him to answer, and pushed the door open only to find an empty room. Lobo wasn't in his normal space, either.

The note still clutched in her hand she turned back to Benson. "He's not here. Where can he be?"

Mac spoke up from behind the desk. "He's on a day excursion with a couple of clients. He'll be back this afternoon in time for dinner. Left early this morning. Last minute thing."

"Thank you, Mac. I was sure he hadn't mentioned the trip to me last night."

"You've a gleam in your eye, ma'am. What are you thinking?" Benson asked.

She didn't answer him but turned to Mac. "Is the truck available?"

Mac hesitated but nodded his head. "Gassed it up myself this morning. Wolf said he wanted to take you to Murphy for dinner tonight."

"May I borrow the keys?"

Benson piped up. "Not a good idea, ma'am."

"How about you drive, Benson, so I am properly chaperoned."

Benson and Mac exchanged glances.

Mac shrugged and tossed Benson the keys.

"Get the worried look off your face. We'll be back before Wolf returns." She turned to the stairs. "Let me get my pocketbook and we'll be off."

~~~*~~~

Martha returned to find Mac and Benson hovering over the bar, deep in conversation. "Okay, I know you both think this is a mistake, but trust me, I know what I'm doing. Those flowers prove he is willing to negotiate. I'll have the deal signed, sealed, and delivered by the time Wolf comes back."

Mac's smile didn't reach his eyes. "He'll skin me, ma'am, but can't say I wouldn't like to see you pull one over on the likes of Nash Nelson."

"Don't worry, I won't let him skin you. And thanks, you're a peach." She watched the blush spread across Mac's face and blew him a kiss, which made him turn a deep shade of scarlet. "Are you ready, Benson?"

"Yes, ma'am."
~~~

The trip to Murphy was uneventful. Benson concentrated on driving, only asking one question. "Do you have a plan, ma'am?"

"I don't need a plan. Old smarmy Nash will be gob smacked after I am through with him."

"Even so, I pray you will be careful. He's a wily one." Benson said.

$$\sim\sim\sim^*\sim\sim\sim$$

They arrived at Vickie's office. Martha didn't wait for Benson to come around for the car door but hopped out eager to face Nelson down.

As Martha burst through the door, Vickie turned with a start.

The real estate agent held a coffee pot, a surprised look making her green eyes glitter with apprehension. "Oh, Lady Buford. I wasn't expecting you."

Martha waved her off. "Sorry I didn't call first. Where can I find Nash?"

"Why he's in his office down the street." Still clutching the coffee pot, Vickie peeked around Martha to greet Benson. "Good morning, Benson. Anyone care for coffee this morning? I have bagels, too."

Martha shook her head. "Thank you, no. Just tell me where the office is."

"Two blocks down on the opposite side of the street. I can ..."

"Thank you," Martha said and left quickly, followed by Benson who hadn't uttered a word. She saw Vickie through the window pick up the phone. *Ever the faithful employee, warning Nash I'm coming.*

They walked the two blocks until they found a fancy sign in front of a pristine building. The sign read Nelson Enterprises in large black letters.

She opened the door and went in.

The receptionist looked up as the bell rang out to alert a new arrival. "Good morning," she said, peeking over large black framed reading glasses. "May I help you?"

"Good morning," Martha answered. "Yes, you can tell Mr. Nelson I am here. Martha Buford." She turned and gestured toward the butler. "This is Benson."

"I'm sorry, but Mr. Nelson doesn't see anyone without an appointment." She looked at the computer screen, brushing a strand of bleached blonde hair from her face. "I don't see your name on the list. I..."

"He'll see me. Just tell him I'm here." Martha interrupted.

The receptionist's face puckered into a frown as she continued to stare at the pair.

"Now." Martha demanded.

"Never mind, Liz." Nash entered from the left hallway. "She's right. I'll see her without an appointment." He strode forward, hand out-stretched. "Welcome, Martha." He grasped her hand with both of his in a much too intimate way. "Benson," he said with a nod of his head.

Martha withdrew her hand promptly. "We're here about the building"

"Of course, come this way to my office." Without looking toward Liz, he ordered. "Bring coffee right away,"

Martha couldn't see Liz's reaction to his gruff tone as Nash guided her toward the elevator with his hand on her back. They remained silent until they reached the fifth floor.

Nash ushered them in with a gallant sweep of his arm. "Please, have a seat. Make yourself comfortable."

The office exuded luxury, prominence, strength, and absolute power. The focal point, high curtainless windows, revealed a remarkable view of the city. His desk sat directly in front of the windows, a dark mahogany with a plush dark leather chair. Artwork abounded on the walls.

"Impressive, Nash." Martha said, as she gazed around. "I know you didn't see us coming, so I assume Ms. Jackson called."

"As a matter of fact, yes, she did," he answered.

"You have your staff trained well," Martha replied. She was still standing and intended to remain so.

Nash went around to his chair, but before he sat down, he gestured again for them to sit. "Please, let's get comfortable."

She shook her head. "No thank you. I am only here to see if you've changed your mind about selling me the building. We have other business to attend to in town."

Benson stood quietly behind her and only moved slightly when Liz entered the room with a tray of coffee and cups.

Nash sat down anyway. "We can talk about this over a friendly cup of coffee."

Her back remained rigid. "It's either a yes or a no, Nash." She turned her head toward Liz. "Thank you, but no coffee for me."

Liz's face turned red, and she looked a bit panicked as she turned toward Nash for instructions.

He waved her away. "The answer is still no, but I would like to negotiate with you."

Liz left the room with the cups rattling on the tray.

"Fine, then we will seek a place elsewhere." She turned to leave.

Nash stood. "Wait. Now don't be so rash, Martha. We can work this out."

"Did you think flowers would soften me up? I see you aren't used to strong independent women."

His complexion turned dark; his eyes flashed. "You say you will find a building elsewhere, well I'm afraid you will be disappointed. I've talked to the surrounding towns, including Bad Axe. They won't accommodate you. You see, I am the primary influence in this area. They do my bidding. If you want a tea house you'll have to go through me."

"That's where you're wrong. I'll open the tea house at the Lodge. You have no jurisdiction there. Good day." She turned on her heel and made her exit, Benson right behind her.

Nash didn't follow them.

She didn't see Liz as they left. Once outside, they walked to the car at a fast clip. Benson ushered her inside the vehicle and resumed his place behind the wheel.

He drove quietly for a time.

Martha chanced a glance at him.

They looked at each other, then burst out laughing hysterically.

"You were wonderful, Lady Buford! Did you see his face? I thought he was going to have an apoplexy."

Between gasps of laughter, she answered in spurts. "I thought he was going to bust a vein in his neck," She giggled a bit more. "He's not used to a woman standing up to him."

Tears ran down her face from laughing so hard. "I only hope Liz and Vickie don't suffer the fallout."

They continued back to the Lodge, chuckling and reliving the spectacular moment of putting Nash Nelson in his place.

But Martha was disappointed. She thought the flowers meant he'd reconsidered. "Well, Benson, I suppose we must open the tea house at the Lodge. Not what I wanted, but it's my only option."

CHAPTER TWENTY-SEVEN

HE CELEBRATED HER BRILLIANCE, JUST BEFORE THE SHADOW FELL ~

As Wolf broke through a stand of trees sheltering the Lodge, he noticed his truck parked in a different spot from this morning. "Has Mac been taking advantage of my absence again?" He chuckled as Lobo whined at his heels. "That boy. Always pushing the envelope."

His clients gathered around, thanking him for the day trip. "A pleasure to have you. I hope you all will come back and do an overnight sometime. Dinner is served in the dining hall in about an hour."

As they disbursed, he focused on the evening ahead. He planned to take Martha to the new steak house in Murphy. Not exactly his cup of tea because the dress code didn't suit him. Jacket and tie, but a small sacrifice to please his lady love.

He eagerly pushed through the foyer door and stopped short. Gathered around the front desk stood Martha, Benson, and Mac. "What's going on here? A mutiny?" He smiled at the trio.

"Oh there you are, Wolf!" Martha hurried toward him. "I can't wait to tell you what happened."

His gaze fell on the flowers at the end of the desk. "Those for you?"

"Yes," she said. "Nash sent them."

He didn't respond, but his smile turned to a frown.

"Listen, Wolf. I went to see him. I borrowed your truck." She held out both hands before he could interrupt. "Don't worry, Benson went with me. And don't blame Mac. I gave him little choice."

Wolf simply stared at her. "You went to see him?"

"Yes, I thought because he sent the flowers, he'd reconsidered my proposal." She rummaged through her purse and produced the note. "See, here's the card.

He read it silently, then handed it back to her, his heart pounding, his head swirling, but he maintained control. "And did he?"

"No. He insists he won't sell."

His shoulders relaxed and he took a breath. "So now what? There's no place else to open the tea house."

"We were discussing the possibilities. I might as well open it here. It's your idea anyway. I think once word gets around, I can draw in a good clientele."

His smile returned. "Excellent!" He turned toward Benson. "Thank you for accompanying Martha today. Even though I know she is capable of handling Nash, I feel better knowing you were with her."

"Of course, Mr. Kelley. I could never leave her alone."

"Then a celebration is in order." Wolf said, "I'm taking you to the new steak house in Murphy tonight anyway. Benson, you're welcome to come, too."

"Oh, no sir. This night is for you and m'lady. I have obligations elsewhere."

"As you wish, then. Martha give me time to shower, and we'll head back to Murphy." He faced his desk clerk. "Mac, we'll talk of this later."

"Don't you dare punish, Mac." Martha set her jaw ready to argue with Wolf as they drove toward Murphy. "It was all my doing. I didn't give him any other choice."

Wolf didn't answer, just kept his eyes on the road.

"I mean it. I'll never forgive you if you discipline him for something that's my fault," she continued.

In a mirth-filled voice, he kept staring at the road, but finally answered, "I have no intention of punishing him, Martha."

"But you told him..."

"I know what I told him. He'll think about it, worry, think of a dozen punishments I might give him. In the end, I'll never mention the incident. Punishment enough, I'd say. My little trick to keep order among my employees."

"Oh Wolf, sounds kind of cruel, making him anxious."

"It works, though. Makes them wonder when the other shoe will drop." He chuckled as he passed a slow-moving delivery truck.

"Well, I suppose."

"The more important topic is why you decided to take on Nash Nelson without me."

Her glance slid his way but then she looked away quickly. "I don't need you to fight all my battles, Wolf. I've learned a lot this past year. I think I handled him just fine."

"Of course you did, but it's not over. Nash won't take this lying down. He'll try to throw a monkey wrench in the whole thing. You don't know him like I do."

"I don't know what he can do if I open it at the Lodge. That's your domain."

"He can influence people in town not to come here. Believe me, he runs the show in these parts."

"He'd do that?"

"I'd bet the Lodge on it. He's done worse to people who don't see eye to eye with him."

She sat in silence wondering why some people are so evil.

The road curved back and forth, but Wolf executed the turns with precise expertise.

He's an excellent driver, but he's excellent at everything. He's a good man. I wonder if I'm doing the right thing with this tea house. Should I give it up and devote myself to Wolf and his way of life?

Again, she looked over at him, his eyes trained on the road, his hands strong on the wheel. She noted the effort he made with his attire. A white button-down shirt with a bolo tie. Pressed black slacks, and his best black boots. The last time she saw him in dress clothes was in Spain, in his dress blues. Since her arrival at the mountain a flannel shirt, and jeans was his preference. Anyway he dressed, however, he looked handsome and comfortable in his own skin. *Quite a man anyway you look at it.*

They rounded a curve, and the town came into view.

"Where are we dining, Wolf?"

"The newest restaurant in Murphy. A steak house called. Kettle and Brew. I hope that will be satisfactory."

"Of course, anything you choose will be fine."

$$\sim\sim\sim*\sim\sim\sim$$

Wolf pulled the truck into the parking lot of the restaurant, stepped out, and opened Martha's door. As she moved from the vehicle he again appraised the class she projected just by how she dressed, her posture, and the way she deliberated her movements.

The little black dress she chose for this evening took his breath away. He didn't know much about fashion, but he admired the form-fitting off the shoulder style which suited her so well. The material was foreign to him, but it didn't escape his notice as it clung to every curve. The neckline plunged slightly revealing just a hint of cleavage. The only jewelry she wore were small diamond stud earrings. Nothing else. She'd brought along a black lace shawl in case she got chilly. He didn't know how she walked in the toe-heeled black stilettoes, but she did it with grace.

"You look beautiful, Martha."

She smiled. "We match with all black, don't we? And we didn't even talk about it. You look handsome, as well. I hope I'm not over-dressed."

"You're perfect."

He opened the door and ushered her inside where they were met by the hostess.

"Do you have reservations, sir?"

"Yes, two for Wolf Kelley."

"Yes, I see your name. Please follow me."

The young hostess led them to a cozy table in the corner. "Your waitress will be with you shortly."

"Thank you," Wolf said as he pulled out Martha's chair.

As he settled in his own seat, he tensed.

A man walked briskly toward them.

Nash Nelson!

CHAPTER TWENTY-EIGHT

HE STIRS THE STORM, BUT HER QUIET FLAME STAND'S FIRM ~

Martha, about to remark on the ambience of the restaurant, caught sight of Nelson striding quickly toward them. She tensed. *This can't be good.*

He arrived at their table the same time as the waitress, impeccably dressed in pressed jeans, a pale blue long-sleeved shirt, and a smart denim jacket, not a hair out of place.

The server, a small, mousy thing, looked terrified at the sight of Nelson. Obviously tongue tied, she stood silently, as Nash took over.

"Come back in a minute, young lady. I won't be long," he ordered.

She nodded and scurried away.

"Good evening. I'm happy to see you at my new restaurant. If I may, I'd like to join you. I've decided about the building." Nash placed his well-manicured hand on the back of the chair to pull it out.

Wolf opened his mouth to protest, but Martha beat him to the punch.

She spoke firmly. "I'm sorry Nash, but this is a special night for me and Wolf. Whatever you want to talk about can wait until later." She noticed Wolf sit back in his chair, a twinkle in his eye, and at the same time observed a pink flush climb up Nash's neck.

"I see." Nash said. "A celebration. May I ask the occasion?"

"It's personal. None of your concern," she answered.

His neck turned a brighter shade of pink as the flush crept toward his face.

The tone of his voice turned cryptic. "I advise you to tread carefully, Martha. I can always change my mind. My benevolence only goes so far. Will it be possible for you to come to my office tomorrow?"

"And I don't respond to threats. I'll call in the morning after I check my calendar. Now if you'll excuse us."

"I'll look forward to hearing from you." He turned and stalked away, bumping into a waiter trying to serve food to the patrons.

The dining room went silent as he bullied his way through to the front door.

She watched until he disappeared. "Now, where did our waitress go?"

Wolf laughed out loud. "You were brilliant!" He motioned for the young waitress to return. "I see now, you can totally handle Nash Nelson."

"He's a blustering, egomaniacal, narcissist and I won't let him get the better of me," she said.

"Are you ready to order?" The waitress asked, her face red with embarrassment.

"What's your name, dear?" Martha asked.

"Lydia, ma'am."

"Well, Lydia. Stand your ground next time. You are here to do a job. You've kept us waiting because of Mr. Nelson. If that ever happens again, you should look at the customer for approval first. If they ask you to stay there is little he can do about it even if he is the owner. And if you get fired, you come to me. Understand?" She rummaged in her purse for one of her personal calling cards and handed it to her. "Time we stood up to bullies like him."

"Yes, ma'am, but I…"

"Who is the manager?" Martha continued.

"Mrs. Pulkin."

"After you take our order, ask her to come out here. I want to speak with her."

"Yes, ma'am. What can I get you?"

Martha changed tactics and turned to Wolf. "Why don't you order for us. You know my tastes. I trust you to get it right."

Wolf hesitated only briefly. "Very well. Filet Mignon, a baked potato, and a side salad. And will you bring each of us a glass of your best wine?"

Lydia wrote it all down and smiled at them both. "I'll get it right out."

After she left, Wolf spoke up. "You've taken quite an interest in Lydia. What are you planning?"

"Well, I suspect if she follows my direction and ultimately chooses to defer to the customer, Nash might have her fired. I plan on speaking to the manager to make sure that doesn't happen. And if they fire her anyway, I will make sure she has a job at the tea house."

"Ah, always looking out for everyone else. You're a marvel. But why did you defer to me to order our meal? I thought you were showing her a strong take charge kind of woman."

Martha smiled. "I want to show her there are times to stand your ground and times to defer. It's a balance I have been learning. You don't always need to be in charge. That goes for men, too."

Just as he let out a guffaw, the manager arrived at their table. A middle-aged, slightly stout woman with warm brown eyes and graying brown hair.

"Is there something wrong I can help with?" Mrs. Pulkin asked.

"It's about Lydia. I gave her some advice on how to handle Mr. Nelson the next time he intrudes on a customer's table. Even though he's the owner, he has no right to impose on a customer's privacy or interfere with the waitress's job. So if the incident happens again and Lydia stands her ground, I don't want her fired. Understood?" Martha cocked an eyebrow at Pulkin.

The manager blanched. "But he's the owner. It could mean my job, too."

"Bullies are everywhere and until we stand up to them, they will keep encroaching on our lives. I will personally see to it you don't lose your job either." Once again she pulled a card from her pocketbook and handed it to Mrs. Pulkin.

The manager stared at the card in her hand. "Very well. I'll see Lydia doesn't lose her job. Mr. Nelson is here frequently and used to intruding where he wants. So I expect this incident will soon be repeated. Thank you. I hope we see you in here again soon."

"Oh yes, we *will* be back, you can count on it. And remember, the customer is always right."

Lydia arrived with the wine and the salads. Mrs. Pulkin rested her hand on the girl's shoulder. "Good job, Lydia. Keep up the good work."

After Mrs. Pulkin left, Lydia smiled as if she'd just won a million dollars. "That's the first time she's complimented me."

"Wonderful. Remember you are of value. Don't let anyone put you down or treat you as inferior. You'll get over your shyness as time goes on."

The wine was poured, the salads were delicious, and Martha waited anxiously for the steak.

Wolf shook his head.

"What is it Wolf? Is the wine unsatisfactory?"

"No. I simply can't get over how you bolstered the poor little waitress. She actually glowed as she left. I'm going to leave her a big tip."

"I'm glad to hear it. Now, are you going to come with me tomorrow to see Nash?"

"So you want me to?"

"Yes, I think I do. I don't know what he is proposing, but I want to have back up when I tell him I'll open the tea house at the Lodge if he doesn't agree to my wishes."

His grin spread across his face showing his straight white teeth. "I'll be glad to watch you make mincemeat of Nash Nelson. I wouldn't miss it for the world!"

Heat flushed her face at his compliment. "I can't tell you how good it makes me feel to hear you say that. Your support means the world to me." She reached across the table and covered his hand with hers. "This is what it's all about, Wolf. Working together, having each other's backs. Our relationship can only grow stronger when we make an effort to do that."

He turned his hand to grasp hers. "It took me a long time to realize that. You've taught me so much about love and what it really means."

"You've taught me, as well. The whole experience with Anthony opened my eyes. I thought I knew him, but he deceived me with such finesse, I felt such a fool." She reached with her free hand for the glass of wine and lifted it for a toast. "To our partnership, our love, and whatever comes next."

He lifted his glass. "To our future together."

They sipped the wine, hands still touching on the table.

"Would you like another glass, Martha?"

She shook her head. "No, one is enough for me." The glass was empty, and with a quiver in her voice, she said, "I'd really like to go home now." A blush warmed her cheeks as she spoke.

"Then by all means, let's go." He motioned for Lydia. "I'll pay the tab, and we can be off."

Lydia brought the ticket, smiling broadly "I'm so glad to meet you Ms. Buford. Oh, and you too, sir."

He handed her the credit card. "Wolf Kelley, my dear. Call me Wolf. We'll be back soon and will request you as our waitress."

"Oh, thank you so very much!" she replied. "Can I get you anything else?"

"No, we're fine, thank you," he said.

She hurried away to ring up the ticket.

"You really made Lydia's day, Martha."

"It warms my heart to see a sparkle of confidence emerge. I hope Nash doesn't do something to destroy it."

Lydia returned. "Thank you both so much. I really enjoyed serving you."

Martha smiled up at the young woman. "We enjoyed meeting you, as well."

Lydia dipped a tiny curtsey and returned to the kitchen.

"Did you see that, Wolf?"

He was bent over the ticket, pen in hand. "No what?"

"She did a little curtsey. I wonder if it was my English accent." She laughed lightly.

"Your English manners have quite an effect on people. I hope we see her again." He put the pen down, returned the card to his pocket, and rose to pull out her chair.

As they made their way to the exit, Lydia came running after them. "Mr. Kelley, please wait. I think you made a mistake."

"A mistake, what mistake?" he answered.

She held out the ticket he'd left on the table. "It's too much money for the tip. I believe you added one too many zero's."

He waved her away. "No mistake, Lydia. You earned it. Spend it wisely."

She blushed red. "Oh my goodness, Mr. Kelley. Thank you so very much!"

Martha reached out and hugged the embarrassed waitress. "You deserve it, Lydia."

As they strolled arm in arm back to his truck, Martha remarked. "You are really quite a man, Wolf. What a generous thing to do."

"All because of you, Martha."

They held hands on the way back to the Lodge, neither saying much, Wolf's free hand firmly on the wheel as he negotiated the twists and turns.

When the Lodge came into view, she withdrew her hand and pulled the shawl over her shoulders. "It's a nice night for a walk."

"Your wish is my command." He parked the truck in front and led her around the building to the garden.

She gazed at the stars as they walked toward the gazebo. "It's a beautiful evening."

"Even more beautiful because you are here." He pulled her into the gazebo, took her in his arms, and kissed her gently.

She pulled him close and returned the kiss with a passion she hadn't experienced in a while. The shawl dropped to the floor.

He pulled away slightly and moved to pick it up.

She stopped him. "I don't need it. I'm quite warm enough."

They kissed again, this time longer, fervently.

She pulled away finally. "We should go in. The servants will talk."

"Let them."

She laughed. "You rogue!" She stooped to pick up the shawl. "I have something I want to show you in my room."

"You do? What can it be?"

"I guess you'll have to come up and find out for yourself."

He didn't hesitate but put an arm around her shoulders and together they went inside.

CHAPTER TWENTY-NINE

LOVE'S BOLD BLAZE STOOD UNSHAKEN AND BESTED THE VILLAIN'S WILL ~

Early the next morning, Martha tip-toed down the stairs headed for the dining room. The foyer was still, no one about. The sun's rays barely peeked through the front door spilling a sprinkling of light on the flagstone floor. Wolf's office door stood half open and she moved toward it, but a loud curse followed by a soft woof drew her attention back to the dining room.

She peeked in and found Wolf wiping up a spilled coffee cup, mumbling to himself, Lobo lapping at the spillage on the floor.

"I didn't hear you leave this morning," she said.

The pot almost fell from his grip as he replied, "Oh, you startled me. Dang coffee pot. Otis needs a new one. Anyway, you looked so peaceful I didn't want to wake you."

"Here, let me help." She took the pot from him and poured a fresh cup and filled one for herself.

They sat at the table and sipped in silence, basking in the glow of the previous evening.

The lightened sky lifted the darkness through the windows with a promise of a beautiful day. The morning singsong of the birds set the peaceful ambience begging not to be disturbed.

Wolf set his cup down. "Are you ready to face Nash?"

"Yes, but it's too early. He won't be in the office for a couple of hours. Besides, I want to make him wait a bit. Am I being boorish?"

"Not at all. It'll make him realize who he's dealing with."

The blissful atmosphere shattered as Otis blustered through the swinging door. "Mr. Kelley! You are about early this morning." He glanced at their coffee cups. "I see you made your own coffee. Please forgive my tardiness."

"You're not tardy. I'm early. That blasted coffee pot almost got the best of me. I think you need a new one," Wolf said.

"Oh, no, no. You must treat her as a fickle female. With a little tenderness she performs very well. Would you like breakfast now? I was about to whip up waffles with strawberries."

Martha interjected, "We'll be out in the gazebo this morning. Can you have one of the girls bring us breakfast there?"

"Certainly. It won't take long." Otis rushed back to the kitchen.

"Nice idea. I love the gazebo," Wolf said. "I built it with you in mind."

Martha rose, went to the sideboard, grabbed a tray, poured them each more coffee and headed for the back door.

"Wait, let me carry that." He hurried to retrieve the tray.

She held the door for him and giggled. "Such gallantry so early in the morning."

Sounds of the morning seemed to approve of their choice to come to the garden. The sun began to warm the chilly gazebo. She thought about running up to her room for a shawl. "It's still a bit cool this morning. I might need a sweater or something."

Wolf came around from the opposite side of the table and pulled a chair close to her. "No, you won't. I'm here. I have more than enough heat for both of us." He put his arm around her. "Better?"

"Much," she said.

Wolf nuzzled her neck. "Last night was so special, Martha."

She leaned back in his embrace. "Yes, it was."

Ivy came around the corner carrying a tray laden with waffles, a bowl of strawberries, real butter, and several small pitchers of syrup.

Martha pulled away from Wolf, sat up straight, and patted her hair, embarrassed to be caught in an intimate moment.

"Good morning, ma'am. Waffles are ready." The little maid nodded a greeting to Wolf. "Sir."

"How lovely, Ivy. Thank you so much. It's such a beautiful morning I couldn't resist the gazebo," Martha returned the greeting.

"Yes, ma'am." She curtsied. "Do you need anything else?"

Wolf spoke up. "Can you convey a message to Mac when he comes in?"

"He's here already. Loves waffle day. Sittin' in the kitchen having his fill." Ivy blushed as she offered the information. "I'll relay your message, sir."

"Hmm, I didn't know he came in early for breakfast," Wolf stated.

"Only on waffle day." Ivy informed him.

"I see. Well, tell him to have the truck ready to roll this morning. Not sure what time we're leaving. Just have it gassed and parked in the front as soon as he finishes his breakfast."

Ivy curtsied again and retreated back to the kitchen.

Martha chuckled. "Looks like a little romance is blossoming."

"Romance? What do you mean? Who?"

She punched him lightly in the arm and chided him, "Oh, Wolf. You can be so dense sometimes. Didn't you see the pink cheeks? The glimmer in her eyes when you mentioned Mac?"

Wolf searched her face as if trying to decipher her meaning. "Ivy and Mac?"

"Yes, the signs are all there. I think you are so wrapped up in your own interests you can't see what's going on."

"Well, I'll be." He snorted a small laugh. "You're right. All I can see is you."

She stabbed a waffle with the serving fork and settled it on her plate, then added butter, and strawberries. "I must get Otis's recipe. These waffles are so light and fluffy."

"He'll never share it with you. Very protective of those things. You know Nash tried to steal him from me," he added.

"No! Why did he choose you, if you don't mind me asking?"

"Nash didn't want to pay him enough. Wanted him to divulge his recipes as part of the deal. You should have seen Otis's face. Turned red as a beet at the insult and sputtered he'd never give up those recipes."

"I take it you don't care to know his recipes then?"

He followed her lead and slathered butter on his own waffles. "Of course not. What would I do with them?"

"I suppose Nash wanted to claim the rights to them. You give Otis free rein then?"

Wolf nodded as he stuffed another bite in his mouth. He chewed for a moment, then replied. "He's been with me since I returned from England. He loves to run the kitchen and he's darn good at it. Figure I shouldn't mess with a good thing."

"Good decision."

Mac appeared suddenly. "Phone call for you, ma'am. At the front desk."

"Who is it? Did you ask?"

"Sure, it's Nash Nelson."

She wiped her mouth with the white linen napkin and stood. "Thank you, Mac. I'll be right there."

Wolf rose as well. "This I gotta hear. Pretty early for the great Nash Nelson."

Martha led the way back to the foyer and picked up the phone. "This is Martha Buford."

She kept her gaze laser focused on Wolf's face as she spoke. "We had a lovely evening, thank you."

Moments passed as she listened. "Your office at eleven? Yes, we can be there." She cocked her head at Wolf and raised her eyebrows as a question.

He nodded.

Again she remained silent with the phone pressed to her ear. "Sorry, no. Wolf comes or I don't."

Wolf chuckled.

"Okay, eleven then." She hung up and turned to him. "He didn't want you there. Can you believe the man's audacity?"

"Typical Nash. Thinks he can persuade you with his so-called charm."

"There's only one man who can charm me." She walked to him and planted a kiss on his cheek.

Mac, who followed them inside, cleared his throat.

She turned to look at him. "Sorry, Mac. Too much?"

He smiled. "Not at all, ma'am. It's good to see Wolf so happy." His smile turned into an all-out grin as he turned to his boss. "Oh, the truck is ready to go when you are. Parked in the front."

"Well, I must change if we are to return to Murphy this morning. If you two will excuse me."

$$\sim\sim\sim^{*}\sim\sim\sim$$

Wolf planted a kiss on Martha's cheek as they stood at the front door of Nelson's office. "Go get 'em, tiger."

"Oh, Wolf, you silly thing," she said, "Come on, let's go in."

It didn't escape his notice her choice of attire. A conservative blue suit dress, a strand of pearls, sensible pumps. *Very professional. She's a wonder.*

Liz greeted them stiffly. "Good morning. Mr. Nelson is waiting for you. Please go in." She didn't rise to escort them in but turned her gaze back to the computer, leaving them on their own.

Ever the consummate person of manners, Martha nodded and said, "Thank you, Liz. You look very nice today."

The receptionist turned quickly toward Martha, said 'thank you', and returned to her work.

Wolf stole a kiss while they rode the elevator to the fifth floor.

Oh, stop," Martha giggled. "He might have cameras in here."

"I hope he does," Wolf declared with a grin.

Nash's office door stood open as they approached.

"Knock knock," Martha said.

"Come on in."

Nash stood as they entered. "Good to see you this morning. I hope the drive down was pleasant."

"Yes, thank you," she replied.

"Please, have a seat." He nodded at Wolf but didn't address him directly.

As they settled in their seats, Wolf noticed a tray of cups with a full pot of coffee in the middle. *Something must be up with Liz if he isn't enlisting her assistance. Poor thing, he must be a bear to work for.*

"Coffee?" Nash asked.

To Wolf's surprise, Martha agreed to a cup.

Nash poured, keeping his eyes on the task.

After handing them both a cup, offering cream and sugar, then pouring one for himself, he sat down, clasped his hands together, and began. "I've decided to sell you the building for the tea house."

Wolf fixed his gaze on Martha, waiting the see her response. He was pleased to see she wasn't giddy at the victory, but played it cool and calm.

"Just like that? No conditional caveats?" Martha placed her cup on the saucer holding Nelson's gaze.

"No conditions, Martha. I want you to have your tea house. I've been kind of a curmudgeon about it, I know. Will you accept my apologies?"

"Of course, but what brought about this sudden change of attitude?"

"Actually, my daughter, Meg. I ran it by her, and she thought I was unreasonable. In fact, she is very excited about the prospect of such a classy business in Murphy. I guess it's a girl thing." He took a sip of coffee. "You see, I'm bringing her into the business. This is one of her stipulations...that she have some say in the business."

"Smart girl. You're very lucky to have such an astute child coming into the fold."

Wolf watched Martha carefully. He hoped she wouldn't succumb to the fake charm of the man in front of him. Nash wasn't one to give in easily. Something more must be up his sleeve.

"What's your price?" she asked.

"You get right to the point, don't you?" Nash chuckled.

"The only way to do business, Mr. Nelson."

He wrote a figure on a sticky note and slid it across the desk.

She studied it for a moment, then handed it to Wolf.

After he glanced at it, he said, "Your decision, Martha."

She looked at Nash and slid the paper back to him. "Too high."

Nelson blinked at her. "Too high? But it's a perfectly good price for that piece of property."

Martha stood. "Then we don't have a deal. Good day, Mr. Nelson."

Wolf rose and moved toward the door.

Nelson kicked his chair behind him. "Wait. Will you give me a counteroffer?"

She hesitated but turned back. Without returning to her seat, she took the sticky note and scribbled something on it, shoved it back to him, and smiled.

He looked at it, a blush creeping up his face. "Why that's highway robbery."

"Take it or leave it." She waited a moment and when he didn't respond, she turned to the door.

"Wait, wait. Okay, you win. I'll have the contract typed up. We can meet again in a couple of days to seal the deal."

"Fine. Gives me time to contact a lawyer here to look it over before I sign."

"Now Martha, don't you trust me?"

"Not when it comes to business. I'm a cautious woman."

"You're a tough lady."

"Exactly. Good day, Mr. Nelson."

Outside, Wolf grabbed her and twirled her around. "You were magnificent."

"Put me down!" She wiggled out of his grasp. "People will see. How can I maintain my dignity if you act in such a manner?"

He laughed. "Sorry. I am so darn proud of you."

The light in her eyes reassured him. *She's pleased, as well.*

He opened the truck door for her, then ran around to the driver's side. As he slid into the seat, he gushed again. "Did you see his face? You had him on the ropes."

This time she giggled like a schoolgirl. "I did, didn't I?"

"Your dream is coming true, sweetheart. I'm so happy."

"I can't wait to tell Benson and the others. There's so much to do. Planning the décor, the menu, advertising, meeting the business owners in town." She stopped and settled into a thoughtful silence.

He noticed her brows knit together and asked, "What it is?"

"I was just thinking. How am I going to do all this from the Lodge? I mean, all that driving every day. Doesn't make sense. I probably should look for an apartment in town."

His heart dropped. *I was afraid of this. Just when we have gotten so close, am I going to lose her to a tea house?*

CHAPTER THIRTY

DREAMS COME TRUE. ALL IS RIGHT WITH THE WORLD ~

Martha wasted no time telling Benson and the others about the purchase. She gathered them in the dining room so all of them heard the news together.

The girls squealed with excitement, clasped hands, and did a little jump up and down jig.

While she tried to calm the ladies to give them their tasks, she noticed Otis peeking out of the kitchen doorway, listening. The door closed quickly when he saw her watching him.

Hmm. I wonder if he's going to miss Agnes. Another romance blossoming?

Benson spoke first, always the sensible one. "I'm so glad to hear it. Now, we can all roll up our sleeves with a purpose."

Her focus shifted as she studied the butler's face. "Have you been unhappy here, Benson?"

He shook his head. "No, no. Just not enough to do. Too much idle time, I guess."

She smiled. "Well, that's about to change. We'll have more work than you anticipated." Her focus turned to the women. "Ivy, I know you've gotten attached to this place, and

Agnes, you work well with Otis. I suspect he'll miss you. *But* each of you will take on jobs you are well suited for. This is why we made this trip to America."

Ivy blushed, while Agnes remained stoic.

She turned to Benson. "I've decided we need a house in town. It won't do to drive back and forth every day. We can find accommodation where we can co-exist in one house. Benson, again, I leave the task up to you."

"Of course, ma'am. I'll call Miss Jackson today."

"Ladies, I need a list of things we need to purchase for the dining area. Ivy, that's your task. Agnes, I need you to list what you need for the kitchen. When we get a comprehensive list, we'll figure out how to make our purchases."

Ivy and Anges both nodded, looking at each other then back to Martha.

"I'm giving you both large responsibilities. I know you can handle them, but Benson will have final approval in case something is overlooked." Her brow wrinkled as she studied the pair. "You don't have a problem with the arrangement I hope."

They spoke in unison. "Oh, no, perfectly fine."

"Alright then. You all know what to do. So on your way with the three of you," she said.

"One moment, ma'am. With your permission, may we use the gazebo to collaborate before we begin our assignments?" Benson asked.

"Absolutely. It gives me joy to see the three of you work together."

Her heart filled with pride as she watched them head outside. *I've got a great crew. Work ethic galore. The tea house will be amazing.*

After the three left, she turned to Ella and Elise.

"You two will not be left out. You will assist Agnes and Ivy in any capacity they need. When we acquire the house in town, I will turn over the running of the house to the two of you. Understand?"

Ella looked at Elise, then back at Martha. "Yes ma'am. We understand."

When they disappeared, she decided to talk with Otis.

The kitchen smelled of homemade bread, and spices hung in the air with something bubbling on the stove. Otis bent over a cutting board chopping with vigor.

"Smells wonderful in here, Otis. What's on the stove?" she asked.

"A special stew, ma'am. Agnes gave me a suggestion or two. For dinner. you know." Only then did he look up from the cutting board. "Is there something I can get you? Did you and Wolf have lunch in town? I'm afraid the staff already ate."

"Actually, I wanted to ask you if Wolf and I can have a sandwich. Not too much. I want to save my appetite for the wonderful stew this evening."

"Certainly. Shall I serve it in the dining room?"

"No. Wolf and I have much to talk about. I think in his office will be fine."

He nodded, put down his chopping knife and went to the refrigerator. "I have sliced ham or roast beef. Which do you prefer?"

She stepped toward him. "Roast beef will do fine. Easy on the mayo." Before he pulled the ingredients out of the frig, she asked, "Otis, will you miss Agnes? You probably heard we are going to move to town. I hope this won't inconvenience you."

He stopped, holding a platter of beef and looked at her. "I definitely will miss her. She's been a great help to me. I've also learned much from her, coming from England and all. But it is a wonderful opportunity for her."

She sat on one of the stools by the island. "I only plan on being open five days during the week to begin with. I want to make sure I don't overwork the staff. Weekends might be in the future, but I need to see how well the tea house goes over. I can send Agnes up here on the weekends if you like. You have bigger crowds then. She can help."

A twinkle replaced the bit of sadness in his eyes. "Why, that's an amazing idea." Then he frowned. "But won't it overwork her? She'd be working seven days a week."

"I think you know the answer to that question, Otis. Agnes is a powerhouse. I'm sure she'd jump at the chance to help you on the weekends. I'll speak with her."

Otis grinned. "Fine, ma'am, Thank you."

"I'll be in Wolf's office when you have the sandwiches ready."

Back in the dining room, she started toward Wolf's office but changed her mind and headed for the garden. Outside, she heard the excited conversation of her staff.

"I hate to break in, but Agnes, may I talk with you a minute?"

"Of course." Agnes rose and followed her to a private part of the garden.

"What is it ma'am? Is there a problem?"

"No problem. I spoke with Otis," she began. It didn't escape her attention how Agnes blushed at the mention of his name. "He seems a little overwhelmed because you are moving to town soon. It seems he's gotten used to your help in the kitchen."

"Oh," Agnes said.

"So I suggested you may come and help him on the weekends when they have the biggest crowds. I only plan to have the tea house open during the week to begin with. I told him I would talk to you about it. You'd be working seven days a week. Of course if you need personal days, that can be arranged. How do you feel about the extra load?"

The cook's face glowed with excitement, even though she tried to hide it. "Oh yes, I mean if he needs my help I will be glad to lend it. Thank you."

"You will be well compensated. Of course, I want your total concentration on the tea house, first and foremost."

Agnes nodded vigorously. "Absolutely, ma'am."

"Fine, now you can return to the others. I'll let you talk to Otis about our conversation."

Satisfied she handled the situation, the time to go over plans with Wolf took up her attention. The office was dim. Lobo woofed softly. "Wolf?" she said softly.

"Come in, Martha." He switched on the desk lamp.

"Why so dark in here? It's a beautiful day. You need to let the sun in."

"Guess, I feel a little gloomy," he answered.

"Gloomy? With all the excitement going on?"

"Well, you'll be moving to town. Can't say I like the idea."

She moved to the window and drew open the blinds. "Now, Wolf. It only makes sense. We talked about it, remember?"

He pulled a chair out for her to sit. "I know. Just got used to you being here."

As she eased into the chair, she looked up at him and clasped his hand. "I talked to Otis. He's bringing in a couple of roast beef sandwiches. We missed lunch, you know,"

"Hadn't thought about lunch. Only about you leaving." He slipped his hand free and went around the desk to his chair.

A knock sounded at the door.

"Come in," Wolf said.

The chef entered with a platter. "Roast beef, as you ordered, ma'am" He set it down on the desk. "Shall I bring coffee?"

"Yes, please," answered Martha.

As Otis disappeared, she handed a napkin to Wolf.

"I'm not hungry."

"Now Wolf, we've been over this. I can't have you moody like this. The tea house isn't going to come between us. In fact, that's why I'm here. I want you to help me choose a name. I also want your input on the dining room arrangement. I expect your help, not pouting."

"Am I pouting?" he asked.

"Yes, you are."

He continued to gaze at her, then grinned like a little boy with his hand in the cookie jar. "Well, you caught me alright. I guess I *am* pouting. Forgive me?"

"Certainly. Now let's eat and get down to business."

Otis brought the coffee and left quickly.

Martha handed out the sandwiches.

They ate in silence for a moment until she looked up and said, "So, any ideas about a name for the tea house?"

He chewed slowly as if pondering a great question. "Hmm. How about The Cozy Cuppa?"

She wrinkled her nose, then shook her head.

"Alright, The Kettle's Kettle.?

Again, another negative headshake. "Something more elegant, I think."

"Blissful Brews?"

She brushed that one off and said, "Maybe Scones & Sip?"

"Oh, I see, you want more of an English flare to it."

"Yes, I think I do. There's nothing like it in Murphy. It'll give the town some variety."

"Maybe Brew Ha Ha."

"Wolf, be serious."

"I *am* being serious. I think it's a great name."

"I'm thinking more along the lines of 'The Golden Scone'

Wolf smiled. "Now, I *like* that."

"We'll leave it for now. We have other things to discuss. Maybe I'll ask the others for some input."

"No, I like The Golden Scone. I want the choice to be ours. Please?" he asked.

"Of course. I love the name. It'll be our brainchild. Now, I want to discuss some business items with you."

They finished lunch in a companiable silence, then moved on to more serious matters.

CHAPTER THIRTY-ONE

SUCCESS DIMS THE COMING STORM ~

The days sped by as the plans for The Golden Scone unfurled. Martha checked off everything on her list; the tea house outfitted with the new décor, the kitchen completely installed, the pantry fully stocked, and the lawyers contracts were drawn up and signed. The day finally came for the Grand Opening.

Martha and Wolf stood by the staff as Benson turned the *Closed* sign around to read *Open.* Everyone clapped with enthusiasm.

Nash and Vickie stood by and joined in the festivities.

A line formed around the corner, and Martha found it difficult to hide her pleasure at the turnout.

Wolf clasped her hand as the first customers filed in.

Martha's taste resonated throughout the dining room. Small, square tables adorned with crisp white tablecloths, a single red carnation in a vase completed the look. The room, filled with fragrance, imbued a totally British atmosphere. Hanging baskets filled with seasonal flowers hung about the room giving the impression of an English garden.

Benson seated each guest, as Ivy took the orders.

Wolf remarked, "You're going to need to hire more staff if this keeps up."

"You're absolutely right. We at least need another waitress."

The crowd nodded and smiled at her; some making kind remarks as they stood near the door.

"I need to check on Agnes. I know she's capable, but I didn't expect this kind of crowd on the first day." She moved toward the kitchen.

"Sure," said Wolf. "I'll wait here and keep an eye on Benson and Ivy in case they need help."

"Thanks, I'll only be a moment." She made her way through the crowd to the kitchen, pushed open the door and stood rooted to the spot.

Agnes concentrated on arranging scones on individual plates, glancing at orders, and expertly plating each one.

The surprise was Otis. He stood at the refrigerator pulling out another batch of scones, ready to pop in the oven.

"Otis! What are you doing here?" she asked.

"Good morning, ma'am. I know how Opening Day is, so I decided to come and help Agnes. I hope you don't mind."

"Of course, I don't mind. What a kind thing to do. You're a peach, Otis." She turned to Agnes. "I see you have things in hand. I'll leave you to it."

The cook gave her a brusque nod and went about her business.

She found Wolf talking with Nash.

"You won't believe who's in the kitchen with Agnes," she addressed Wolf.

"Otis," he replied.

"You knew?"

Wolf grinned. "Yes, I wanted it to be a surprise. He came to me yesterday about the matter. I figured Agnes would welcome an extra pair of hands. Are you okay with our little scheme?"

"What a blessing. I am thrilled. Not because I don't believe in Agnes's ability, but Opening Day can be overwhelming."

Nash broke in. "I envy you, Martha. I've been trying to get Otis away from Wolf for a long time. Between you and Wolf's Lodge I need to be on my toes to compete with you both."

"Nash Nelson, stop it right now. There *is* no competition. Your restaurant is totally different from my tea house *and* Wolf's dining room. Can't we all simply enjoy the other's success and get along?"

"You're right, certainly, but I really, really wanted Otis," he replied.

"Well, you'd have a hard time pulling him away now. He and Agnes seem to have a thing going on," she informed Nash.

"Really? Sorry to hear it. One more obstacle for me to overcome."

She slapped him on the arm, playfully. "Oh, Nash, how you do go on."

Benson approached and asked, "Miss Vickie, Mr. Nelson, I have a table for you now."

"Thank you," Nash replied. "Can't wait to taste the cuisine."

As Benson led the pair to their table, Wolf turned to Martha. "Pretty chummy with Nelson, Martha. What's up with that?"

She frowned at him. "Do you think it will do any good to be rude to him? He owns everything else in town. I can't afford to make an enemy out of him. He can ruin me at a snap of his fingers."

He sighed. "I suppose you're right. Just a jealous streak, I guess."

"Never mind. Are you going to try one of Agnes's scones?"

"Will you sit with me?"

"Naturally."

When Benson returned he escorted them to a table.

Ivy took their order.

"I want the blueberry scones and Earl Grey tea." Martha said.

"Give me the same since I have no idea what any of this is," Wolf said.

They chuckled together and spent the rest of the day enjoying the flow of customers into The Golden Scone.

$$\sim \sim \sim ^* \sim \sim \sim$$

Wolf spent the entire day with Martha. After all, Opening Day is special, but he also knew he couldn't come tomorrow. Several clients booked a hike to the lake for a fishing expedition, so he must return to the Lodge. He dreaded leaving her.

Benson and Miss Vickie found a house for her and the staff to rent, so Martha committed to staying in town. Mac delivered her bags this morning, so he would return to the Lodge alone. A nagging fear settled into the pit of his stomach. *Foolish of me to feel this way, but I can't help it.*

The tea house stayed busy until closing. Martha's excitement radiated on her face, and he was pleased to see her so happy.

"You're a hit, sweetheart. The town really came out to support you," he remarked.

"Oh, Wolf. I couldn't have done it without you. They know you so it's because of you I garnered so much support," she replied.

Agnes came from the kitchen followed by Otis.

Martha hurried over to the pair. "Did you survive the rush? You look tired."

Agnes wiped her face with her apron, tucked a wayward strand of hair into her cap, and sighed. "Aye, tired, but so happy. I've never seen so many orders. I believe you are officially a success, ma'am." She turned to Otis. "I couldn't have done it without you."

The chef blushed. "Happy to help. But I am worried about the coming days. I won't be able to help, you know. Can't neglect my own duties."

"Naturally. However, I think I have the rhythm down now. So grateful you were here to kick it off." Agnes smiled and turned to Martha. "Permission to head to the house, ma'am. I want to be fresh for tomorrow."

"You don't need my permission. I am so proud of what you did today. Get a good rest."

Otis stepped forward and took her hand. "I'll walk you home. Make sure you're safe."

Wolf and Martha watched with a smile as the pair left together, Agnes's arm draped through Otis's elbow.

"Well, that beats all," Wolf said softly.

She squeezed his hand. "Romance is blossoming all around."

He shook his head. "I had no idea."

"Of course you didn't. You are blind to what's going on around you half the time. Turned out to be a pleasant surprise. They make a great couple."

Benson interrupted. "The kitchen is sparkling; the prep is all done for tomorrow. Ivy swept the floors, and the back door is locked. I believe Ivy and I are ready to go."

"Great job, Benson." She turned to the waitress. "And you, too, Ivy. Everything ran smoothly with the two of you at the helm. I'd say this first day was a complete success. Go on home, now. And thank you so much."

Benson nodded and offered his arm to Ivy. "May I escort you? Don't want you to get lost on the way."

"Thanks, Benson." Ivy grasped his arm and said, "Good night, ma'am and Mr. Kelley. See you tomorrow."

Wolf waited until the door closed behind them. "Is there a romance there, too?"

"No, I don't believe so. Remember, I told you about Ivy and Mac."

"Oh yes, now I remember. So what will happen to Benson? No love match for him?"

Martha laughed. "Benson can fend for himself in the romance department. I wouldn't worry."

"I guess that leaves us," Wolf said.

"Yes, I want to look around the place one more time before we go. Do you mind?"

He took her hand as they headed for the kitchen.

"It sparkles. You'd never know how busy they were today. Anges is a marvel. I'm lucky to have her." She checked the back door. "And Benson with his attention to detail."

They meandered through the dining area, Martha absent-mindedly straightening tablecloths and readjusting the vases on the table. "I hate to leave. I want this feeling to last for a long time."

"So do I, Martha, but you need your rest. You have four more days to get through before the weekend."

"You're right. Let's go."

She turned off the lights and locked the door, then headed for his car to say goodnight.

"Wait, I'm walking you to your door. Do you think I'd let you walk alone?" he said.

"I can walk alone, just fine."

"Of course you can, but not tonight."

She sighed and let him take her arm and tuck it inside his elbow.

They didn't talk as they strolled toward the house. The early evening was filled with birds chirping, cars heading home, and a police siren in the distance. Contentment filled her. She truly belonged here now.

At the door, she asked him if he'd like to come in.

"No," he said. "You need to rest, and I have a long day with clients at the mountain tomorrow, but I'll be back as soon as I can. Think of me while I'm gone?"

"Never doubt it, Wolf. Good luck with your expedition. Don't hurry back on my account. I think we have it well in hand. Concentrate on your expedition."

I'll miss you," he said.

"Are you going to stand there all night and talk or are you going to kiss me?" she teased.

The kiss was long, intense, and intimate contact created a fire within her, but she knew this wasn't the time to quench it.

They pulled apart and she opened the door but didn't go in until he turned the corner and disappeared.

Ah Wolf. You are a dear. Be patient, my love. We'll work this out in time.

CHAPTER THIRTY-TWO

THE EYES DECEIVE, THE HEART REBELS ~

But it *didn't* work out.

Days passed.

Wolf's expedition business grew bigger. Pete offered no help as the wedding approached, and Miss Vickie kept him busy with last-minute details. Without his friend, the workload fell on him alone. He called Martha, of course, but they never found time to talk...always something for her to take care of. Evenings proved inconvenient, as well, as she suffered from exhaustion.

The weekends booked up for him making it impossible to come to town for a dinner date. Frustration overwhelmed him. *This can't go on. I'll lose her.*

Finally, after two weeks, he found a break in his schedule and decided to surprise her.

Excitement and hope surged through him on the hour-long drive to Murphy. He whistled along with the tune playing on his car radio and enjoyed the sun shining through the windows.

Finally, he pulled up in front of The Golden Scone. Several cars took the available parking spaces on the street, and he hoped it meant customers for Martha. He found a space not quite a block away.

With a spring in his step he pulled the door open and entered but stopped mid-stride. The room was full of people, but the only ones he noticed were Martha and Nash Nelson at a table in the back. They shared a laugh and leaned toward each other in a very intimate way.

Benson spoke, "Good morning, Mr. Kelley. Would you like a table near the window?"

He couldn't speak, not able to see anything except Martha in conversation with Nash. He shook his head. "No," he croaked. "I've no time." He spun on his heel and left.

Back in his car, he tried to calm the pounding in his chest. Tried to make sense of what he witnessed. But no sense came. He turned the key; eyes clouded with tears and sped off. In the rear-view mirror, he glimpsed Martha hurrying toward the sidewalk trying to wave him down, but he drove on.

Just as I feared. Nash moving in, taking everything. He wanted Martha, now he has her. His plan all along. That's why he sold her the building. I'm such a fool.

Although he knew Martha was savvier than most women, he felt she became dazzled by Nash's 'savoir faire'. Most women fell for the fake charm. He could name several in the town used and abused by him.

I thought Martha would know better. Women, I'll never understand them. So back to the Lodge I go.

An hour later, he barged through the door of the Lodge, making Mac look up from whatever he was doing.

"Thought you were spending the day in town, boss."

Lobo trotted toward him.

"Never mind. Pack my gear. I'm heading to the lake. Don't want to be disturbed." He slammed the office door, took a deep breath, and went to the sideboard. After he poured a glass of whiskey, he took the glass and held it up to the light of the window.

Nash Nelson, my nemesis. Blast him!

He brought the glass to his lips, then paused. Aloud, he said, "What am I doing? Drinking in the middle of the day. Martha hates that. It's a weakness in me." He paused, then lifted the glass again. "Who cares, now, anyway?" He took a sip, then slammed the glass down. "I'm trying to be a better man, trying to meet her standards, but it's hopeless. I'm no match for Nash Nelson."

He flung himself into his chair leaving the glass on the sideboard.

A knock on the door jerked him back to reality. "Come in."

Mac poked his head in. "Your gear is ready, boss."

He grunted his response. "Close the door. I'll be right out."

The door closed silently.

He sat for a moment, then stood up, looked at the glass of whiskey and turned for the door.

His gear was piled by the front door, Lobo sitting anxiously beside the pack. "I'll be back tomorrow. Don't tell anyone where I am."

Mac nodded. "You got it."

"Oh, I'm not taking Lobo this time. See he's fed." He lifted the pack, settled it on his back, grabbed the fishing rod and headed outside, Lobo at his heels. "Not this time, pal. Stay."

Lobo whined but sat obediently.

Mac coaxed the dog inside and closed the door.

The hike was therapeutic, and he made sure the pace he set worked out all the anxiety of the situation rattling around in his head. At the half-way point he stopped to eat the sandwich Mac added to the necessities. *Ah, Mac. Always one step ahead of me. He's a good guy.*

When he picked up the pack again, the anxiety dissipated a bit. He felt better, more rational, so he slowed the pace and enjoyed the scenery ...and allowed the thoughts to simmer in his brain.

I jump to conclusions. My initial reaction to things is chaotic. Martha has pointed those things out to me numerous times. Driving off, going on this hike, both knee-jerk reactions. So what do I do about it? I should have walked over to the table and greeted the two of them like nothing was amiss. I'm sure their meeting was purely business. So why didn't I trust Martha?

A doe crossed the path ahead of him and skittered off in a hurry when she spied him. He smiled. The wildlife in these mountains calmed him, made him feel one with nature. *This is the life I wanted. Simple, uncomplicated. So why do I continue to try to change her? It's the city life she wants. A business of her own to run. Independence. Not the wild life I live. Should I let her go?*

He rounded the bend, and the lake came into view. The sunlight glinted off the water, the treetops swayed slightly in the breeze, the birds called back and forth to each other. *This is it. What it's all about. Solitude, peacefulness.*

The pack slid off his back with ease, and he set about making camp. The pup tent was easy enough. Finished with that, he gathered wood to make a fire. When the fire settled at a slow burn, he concentrated on baiting the hook on the rod. He wanted fresh trout for dinner.

The slight lapping of the lake water soothed his nerves, and almost with the first cast he caught a nice rainbow trout. Hungry, he cast again and waited. The next one took a little longer, but he finally reeled in a second fish.

The fire burned steadily, so he pulled out the frying pan and set about cleaning and preparing the fish for his meal.

Dinner sizzled in the pan as dusk settled over the camp. By now, calm returned to his soul. He put everything out of his mind, even Martha, and enjoyed watching the stars pop out one by one.

Ah, there's the Big Dipper. Very bright tonight.

As he studied the other constellations, a sudden noise caused him to sit upright and scan the tree line. When he heard nothing else, he settled back against the log and resumed the scan of the night sky.

A full stomach and tired muscles after the long hike made his eyes droop as the warm fire lulled him into a sleepy state.

He heard it again and bolted upright.

A growling grunt. Very close by.

He measured the distance between the bear and the tent. The bear spray was inside of his pack in the tent. The bear was close enough to charge. He couldn't make it in time.

Stupid mistake. You know better than that Wolf Kelley. Now you've done it.

~ ~ ~*~ ~ ~

Martha stood helplessly on the sidewalk as Wolf's car disappeared down the road. Benson told her about Wolf's entrance and quick departure, so she tried to catch him. She could only imagine what he thought when he discovered Nash at her table.

Back inside, she pulled Benson aside. "You know what he must have thought seeing Nash here. It's been hard to connect lately we've both been so busy." She looked imploringly at him. "I don't want to drag you into this, but I need a man's advice. What should I do?"

Before he could answer Nash interrupted. "There's nothing you can do, Martha. He's going to think what he wants to. Give him time. He'll come around."

"I wasn't asking you, Nash. In fact, you're the last person I'd ask. You two don't exactly mesh. Please go. I'll talk to Agnes about the private party you're planning and call Liz to give her the answer." She turned toward her table. "Benson, please follow me."

She waited for Nelson to leave before she took up the conversation. "So what do you suggest?"

Benson frowned. "I hate to intrude on such matters,"

"You're not intruding. I'm asking."

"Well, then, I suggest you make some time for him. I know how busy both of you are, but if you're to maintain this relationship, you must make time."

"You're right. But it'll be an hour before he'll be back at the Lodge. I might as well finish the afternoon. I'll call him after we close."

In a rare expression, Benson smiled and touched her arm. "Don't worry. He'll figure it out. Things will be fine."

"Thank you, Benson."

He nodded and went back to his duties.

She sat for a while, then looked at the clock. *He should be back by now.*

She went to her office and dialed the Lodge's number. Mac answered.

"Is Wolf back? I need to speak to him," she said. She listened to Mac for a moment, then hung up the phone.

When she found Benson, he was leading a couple to their seats. She motioned for him to come to her table when he finished.

He settled the couple and approached his boss. "What can I do for you?"

"He's gone to the mountain. Took his tent, so he intends to stay at least the night. Now what do I do?"

"He needs time. Give it to him. He'll come back to Murphy after he's thought about it for a while."

She nodded and he went to greet the next customer.

But a nagging fear troubled her. *He went alone. Mac said he didn't even take Lobo. Surely, it's not safe. He should have a buddy with him.*

An idea occurred to her. *Pete. I need to call Pete.*

She called Vickie for the number and dialed. "Pete, this is Martha Buford. I need to talk to you. It's about Wolf. Can you come to the tea house?"

Her mind eased after Pete agreed to meet her. Surely, he could help.

Fifteen minutes later, Peter strolled through the door.

"What can I help with, Martha?" he asked.

"It's Wolf. He saw me and Nash in a meeting and got the wrong idea. I tried to chase him down, but he sped off. I called the Lodge an hour later, but he'd already packed up and headed for the lake. Tent and all, *and* without Lobo. He plans to stay at least overnight. Pete, he's alone. You know that's not a good idea after the bear sightings lately."

"I see. You want me to go find him. Make sure he's okay," he answered.

"Well, basically, yes."

He looked at his watch. He's got about a two-hour head start on me. It'll be dark when I get there."

"Can't you take someone with you? Like Mac or at least the dog?"

"I can. Look, Wolf's smart. He's not going to put himself in danger. Can't this wait until morning? Give him time to process everything, see the light so to speak."

She vigorously shook her head. "No, I've a bad feeling. Please, Pete."

He sighed. "Okay, let me run by and tell Vickie. We were supposed to go cake tasting tomorrow. Then I'll head to the Lodge. See if I can beat nightfall."

"Thank you so much, Pete. And the thing with Nash. It was business, that's all."

He patted her hand. "I know, Martha, I know."

Chapter Thirty-Three

THE HEART CAN'T SEE WHAT THE MIND MISUNDERSTANDS ~

Wolf sat very still, knowing the bear would charge if he moved.

A stand-off. *What if it's rabid?* But because he didn't lunge toward him he dismissed the thought. *Maybe protecting cubs. Can't tell if it's a female. Wish I had a gun.*

Time passed at a snail's pace. He didn't move and neither did the bear.

Heart pounding, he slowly took stock of what he had around him. afraid any quick movement could trigger the bear. *The fire must be the reason it's not charged.*

The frying pan and spatula were the only 'weapons' within reach. *They don't like noise. I could bang the metal together, but it might charge quickly if I move. They always say to make yourself bigger, but I am sitting down. I hope the fire doesn't dwindle too fast. You're a stupid man, Wolf Kelley, to let yourself get in this position. I shouldn't have come alone.*

The fire continued to crackle, but he could see the wood burning quickly. He needed a plan, but all he could think of was to bang the frying pan and spatula together if he lost the fire.

So this is how it ends. Getting eaten by a bear. What a legacy. The great Wolf Kelley loses his life because of a stupid mistake.

As he worked up the courage to grab the pan and spatula an air horn sounded behind him. Then a flare lit up the sky.

Lobo raced toward him, barking.

The bear swiveled away and disappeared into the trees.

He jumped up. "Lobo? How...? Pete! Am I glad to see you!"

"Looks like I made it just in time. Where's your bear spray or your horn? Are you sitting out here without protection?"

A rush of heat crawled up his neck and face. "Stupid mistake. It's all in the tent. I caught some fish, was really hungry so I cooked up my dinner and sat back to relax when Mr. Bear decided to join me. Don't know if he wanted the fish or me for dinner."

"Not like you to be so careless Wolf. What's going on?"

He went to the tent, pulled out the spray and flare and returned to the fire where Pete dropped his pack.

"Well," Pete said. "You giving me the silent treatment?"

He settled beside his friend and asked, "Why are you here, Pete? I told Mac not to tell anyone. How did you know?"

"Martha called Mac. Yes, he told her. She was frantic." His face, stern, his eyes narrow. "He did the right thing, so don't punish him for it. You know how dangerous it is in this region. You shouldn't have come alone."

"I can handle myself."

"Oh sure. I saw how you outsmarted the bear. It's Martha, right? You've jumped to conclusions again."

"I saw it with my own eyes. Nash laughing; she leaning forward. Very cozy. I don't know, maybe he's more her style. I'm an old mountain man. Totally out of her realm. I simply can't compete."

"There's no competition, Wolf. She loves you. Nash is purely business. He's planning a private party, wanted Agnes's help. When are you going to stop this nonsense? For the life of me, if I were Martha I'd be so furious with you."

"You didn't see them together."

"Nonsense. I didn't have to. I took her word for it."

They sat quietly for a while, neither speaking, Lobo pressed tightly against Wolf's side. The flames licked the fresh pile of dried branches Pete put on the fire. Sparks flew toward the sky as the stars twinkled happily.

Wolf finally spoke. "I'm gonna break it off."

Pete's head jerked toward his friend. "You're what?"

"Gonna break it off. This won't work with her in town and me at the Lodge. She wants the tea house more than she does me."

"You're full of it, Wolf. You can make it work if you try. Your knee-jerk reactions are getting old. Why don't you try a little understanding?"

He stood up and stretched. "I think I have. What more can I do? I want to marry her, but this arrangement isn't conducive to marriage." He picked up the coffee pot from the fire, poured a cup for himself and offered to pour one for Pete.

"No thanks. I won't sleep as it is."

"Well, I haven't been sleeping much since the tea house opened, so won't make me any difference."

"You need to give this more thought. She's the only woman I've ever seen you get serious about. Don't throw this away, Wolf."

He settled back against the log. "Maybe just dating is better. Keep it casual, ya know?"

Pete shook his head. "I don't think she wants that. She's not the type of woman to settle for casual."

Wolf gulped down the coffee and stood abruptly. "I'm going to bed. I can't think about this anymore. I'm a loner and I think I should just stay a loner."

Pete stood and wrangled his own pup tent. "You've got it all wrong, Wolf. Besides, you agreed to escort her to the wedding. You know it's in a couple of weeks. What are you going to do about your promise?"

"Like I said, casual dating. Won't be a problem." He disappeared into his tent.

As he settled into his sleeping bag, the dog beside him, he heard Pete cussing and mumbling as he got ready for the night. The firelight filtered through the tent, so he knew his friend had stoked the fire. *Hopefully, the bear won't be back.*

~~~*~~~

The morning dawned a bit misty, the fire not much more than embers but no bear in sight.

Pete was gone.

He shrugged. *Must have headed out early.*

The first thing he did was retrieve the air horn and bear spray from the tent, hang the spray on his belt, and made sure the horn was within reach.

Hands on hips, he studied the lake, thought about catching a trout for breakfast, but gave up the idea for the hardtack in his pack. *Coffee, I just need coffee.*

After he revived the fire, he made the coffee and waited, sharing the hardtack with Lobo.

Finally, he settled back against the log, sipped the hot brew, and thought again about Martha. *She's gonna be real mad at me this time. I keep promising her I'll do better, then I pull a stunt like this. Geesh, Wolf, are you trying to run her off?*

~~~*~~~

Martha stood next to the main desk at the Lodge questioning Mac while tapping her foot impatiently. "So, you don't know how long he'll be gone?"

Mac popped a rubber band in his hand over and over. He kept glancing at the front door as if Wolf might walk through it at any moment. "No ma'am. He ran out of here in a hurry. Told me not to tell anyone where he was going. He's gonna skin me alive when he finds out I told you."

"I'll see he doesn't," she said.

"I don't see how…" Mac stopped in mid-sentence. "Oh, here's Pete. Maybe he can shed some light on this."

"Pete!" She noticed the pack on his back as he hurried through the door. "I take it you've been with Wolf?"

Pete shrugged the pack off his back, stretched, and with a sigh, answered. "Yeah, spent the night at the lake with him. Stubborn old..." He stopped. "Oh sorry, Martha. He's just so frustrating. Almost got eaten by a bear."

"What?!" she said.

Pete told her the story after which she asked, "Did he talk about me, er, us?"

"Matter of fact, he did. But I don't want to expound on that. It was man to man, if you know what I mean."

"Of course, I understand. You see, he got the wrong impression when he showed up at the tea house. He drove off before I could explain." She shook her head with a deep sigh. "I'm getting a little tired of stroking his ego about this."

Pete frowned, looked at Mac, and said, "We'll be in the dining room." Then to Martha he offered, "Want a cup of coffee?"

"Maybe tea, but yes, I'd like that."

Pete made the tea, poured himself a cup of coffee, and sat across from her.

"He loves you, Martha. I've never seen him so smitten with any woman before. He also hates Nash Nelson. It makes him crazy to see you with him. He was so distracted last night he forgot all the safety measures. He could've been killed by that bear if I hadn't showed up. I left very early this morning. I don't seem to be the one to talk sense into him. I don't know what it's going to take. The wedding is coming up soon and we really want you and Wolf to come together, but..."

"You left him alone up there, after the bear almost killed him?" She interrupted.

"I left him with Lobo. That dog is a vicious adversary when it comes to Wolf. He's got his air-horn and bear spray. He'll be fine. Like I said I'm not the one who needs to talk to him. I've done all I can."

"It's not your place, Pete. I'm sorry I involved you. Maybe Wolf and I are not meant to be. We're so different. Our lifestyles and all. Maybe..."

"Don't talk nonsense, Martha. Anyone can see the love between you. With a little understanding it will all work out. Give it time."

They chit-chatted about Pete and Vickie's upcoming wedding for a while. She assured him she would be there regardless, accompanied by Wolf or not.

He yawned.

"I can see you're tired. You need to get back to town and Vickie. Concentrate on your life. I'm sorry I asked you to intervene."

"You were worried. Frankly, I was too. Wolf's stubborn. He's prideful, but he's a good man. One of the best. I'm glad I went, although I don't know if I did any good. At least I scared off the bear. We'd be having a totally different conversation." He stood, pecked her on the cheek, and said, "You call me any time, Martha. Wolf's my best friend which means you are, too."

"Thank you, Pete. Do you think he'll be back soon?"

"I'd take that bet. I at least got him thinking about what a total jerk he's been. I figure he'll make his way back soon."

Pete waved as he disappeared through the dining room door.

She sat a while sipping her tea, mulling over the ups and downs of the relationship with Wolf.

Finally, she went to the foyer and told Mac. "I'll be in the gazebo for a while. If your boss comes back tell him where I am."

"Will do, ma'am."

Before she went out to the garden, she refilled her tea and snatched a biscuit from the sideboard.

The garden filled her with peace and calm. The birds twittered, and the fragrance of flowers filled her soul. *I can't keep doing this. If he's going to be jealous every time I talk to another man, then this won't work at all.*

She didn't know how long she sat there, but she did make a decision. *How will I tell him?*

The sun beat down from straight overhead now. Morning passed, and the heat of the afternoon crept in. She rose to tell Mac to prepare her old room, but as she stood Wolf suddenly appeared.

"Wolf," she whispered.

"Please, don't go, Martha. We need to talk."

CHAPTER THIRTY-FOUR

AN END TO A LOVE STORY? ~

Martha returned to her seat and waited for him to speak.

He didn't.

His head remained bowed, his breathing shallow.

Finally, she took the lead. "Wolf…"

He interrupted, "First, let me say I'm sorry. Second, I've come to a conclusion."

"So have I," she answered.

He blinked, studied her face a moment, then continued, "I think we need to take a break for a while. We don't seem to be on the same page with this relationship."

"According to you, obviously," she said. "But you're right. I can't keep explaining myself every time I have a conversation with someone. You keep promising you will be more understanding but go off in a huff if something doesn't suit you. It's a bit tiresome."

"I know." A blush darkened his face. "I apologize. It seems I have a lot to work on."

"So, you still want to take a break?"

He thought for a moment. "Maybe not an actual break. How about a slow down?"

"A slow down. Care to elaborate?"

"Well, we just date for a while. No commitment, no expectations. Simply enjoy one another's company."

She didn't respond.

"Well?"

"This is what you want?" She searched his face not quite understanding what he meant, not quite sure of her own feelings.

"No, not at all, but until we can make a solid commitment to each other, I think this might be best. The situation is difficult enough with you being in town and me here."

Anger stirred within her. "You're saying you want me to give up the tea house? It's the only way this relationship will work?"

He reached for her hand. "No Martha, not at all, but how can we build a relationship long distance?"

She withdrew her hand. "I think we can both make compromises, Wolf. You're simply not willing to try." Her temper got the best of her. She stood to leave.

"Please don't go. We need to talk this out," he pleaded.

"I certainly don't need to talk more to see it's *me* that is expected to change. You talk a good game, but you've missed the mark this time. We don't need to take a break. This just needs to end." The table wobbled as she brushed against it making her escape.

Wolf followed right behind her. "No Martha, please. I'm a fool, I give you that, but I certainly don't want to end it."

They burst into the foyer, still arguing, Martha headed for the door.

She flung a comment to Mac who stared at them in disbelief. "Cancel the room, Mac. I won't be staying."

Wolf followed her outside. "You planned to spend the night? How did you get here? I don't see a car."

For the first time, she stumbled with words. "I, uh, Benson brought me."

"Well, where is he?"

"I sent him home."

"So you came up here to spend the night?"

"Well, yes, but that's off the table now."

He caught up with her and took her hand. "You can still spend the night. I'll leave you alone. Please?"

"No. I want to go back to Murphy. I'll call Benson. He'll be happy to come and get me."

He let go of her hand. "If you are determined to go, I'll take you. It'll be an hour before he can get back up here."

She stopped and turned to him. "Well, I suppose."

"One minute while I tell Mac."

A curt nod was her answer.

He returned, opened the truck door for her, and waited for her to get in.

The ride to Murphy did little to lighten the mood.

Her heart raced, and thoughts of life without Wolf in it frightened her. In spite of the anger beating in her chest, she still loved him and didn't want to be parted. But the tea house loomed in her mind. She loved it, too. Business was good and growing. *I don't want to give up either of them.*

Wolf drove in silence, both hands on the wheel, eyes fixed on the road.

She saw his jaw working out of the corner of her eye and knew turmoil churned inside him. *He's really done it this time and doesn't know how to get out of it. Well, let him stew. He deserves it.*

When they entered Murphy, she spoke softly, "About the wedding..."

He turned abruptly to her as he parked on the street. "Please, don't say you don't want to go. Pete will be so hurt. I want to escort you. I don't want this to be over. Can you think about it for a bit before you answer me?"

Without a glance, she opened the door before he could get out of the car. "I'll think about it." She slammed the door shut and hurried down the little alleyway to the tea house.

Inside, she stopped to catch her breath and heard his truck pull away, grateful he didn't follow her.

Benson stared at her with eyes as big as saucers. "Martha, what are you doing here? I thought you were spending the night. Are you okay? How did you get here? You should have called me."

She patted her hair and smoothed her skirt trying to regroup. "It's fine, Benson. Wolf brought me. Change of plans." Somehow she knew Benson suspected what had happened by his next words.

"Agnes might need a little advice in the kitchen. I think she's trying a new recipe."

The room, full of patrons, grew silent when she'd blustered through the door, so she flashed a grateful smile at Benson, and headed for the refuge of the kitchen.

<div align="center">~~~*~~~</div>

The room, warm and inviting, proved to be exactly the escape she needed.

Agnes, with sleeves pushed up to her elbows, rolled out dough on the cutting board. She looked up briefly when Martha entered. "Mornin' ma'am."

"Good morning, Agnes. How's it going?"

"Very well, I'm keeping up with all the orders. I might want to talk to you sometime about adding a staff member. I can use a prep cook."

She grabbed a stool and sat to watch Agnes work her magic. "Of course. I'll start interviewing right away. You shouldn't have to do all this work by yourself. I wanted to see if the tea house could make it or not. Looks like we're doing alright according to the books. What about Ella? Do you think she would like the position? I don't want her to feel left out of the tea house."

The cook stopped rolling for a moment. "Oh no, ma'am. She's at the height of her glory running the town house. A complete control freak, that one. With the rest of us working here, she's top dog now at the house." She stopped, took a breath and ventured, "Might I have a say in who you hire? It's not a big kitchen. It's best to get along with whomever we hire."

"Naturally, Agnes. You may sit in on the interviews. You'll have the final say."

Agnes went back to her rolling.

Something about the simple back and forth of the rolling pin made her reflect on what happened with Wolf.

Back and forth. That's certainly how I would describe my relationship with Wolf. We can't seem to get on the same page. Will we ever or is it a pipe dream?

"Agnes, why have you never married?"

The cook stopped abruptly. "Marry? Well, I suppose because I haven't found the right man. There's not many of them who will put up with the likes of me, I guess."

She continued, "But have you actively looked? I mean, surely you wanted a family, a husband.

"Oh, aye. When I was but a lass, there was a young buck. Brody, they called him." The rolling pin remained suspended in the air as she looked wistfully into space.

"And? What happened to him? Why didn't you marry?" she pursued.

Agnes plopped the pin down on the dough and rolled with a vengeance. "Twas his mum. Said I wasn't good enough for her boy. Introduced him to another lassie, an aristocrat, so to speak. He listened to his mum and dropped me like a burnt biscuit."

She watched as Agnes attacked the dough, knowing the pain she probably endured over the incident. "My dear friend, if Brody was so quick to drop you, he wasn't worth having. You are worth more than all the uppity snobs in the world. You do see that, don't you?"

The rolling pin halted once more. "Aye, I do. Hurts, none the less."

"Of course it does. And you never found anyone else?"

She put down the rolling pin and wiped her hands on the apron tied around her ample waist. "No. Threw myself into my cookin'. I'd rather take pride in what I do well, than be tied to a man who doesn't appreciate me."

"You're a wise woman, Agnes. What about Otis?"

The cook swiped a stray curl from her brow, blushed like a schoolgirl, and picked up the pin again. "Otis is my friend. We understand each other, that's all there is to that, ma'am."

"I see. I didn't mean to pry."

"It's no matter." Agnes stopped rolling again, placed a hand on one hip, and looked directly at her. "And why would ye be asking me all these questions? I recall you were spending the night at the Lodge with Mr. Kelley, but here ye are. Somethin' happen, if I may be so bold?"

"You have every right to ask after I've grilled you on your love life. Something *did* happen. I need advice."

"Advice from me? I'd be the last person to be givin' advice, ma'am."

"You're exactly the right person. You have a level head."

In a bold move, the cook pulled a stool close and sat down. "Alright, tell me what's happened."

Martha recounted the story word for word, even acknowledging her part in the matter. At the end of the discourse, she told Agnes she still loved Wolf. "Am I being selfish to want The Golden Scone? Please be honest with me. I need another woman's point of view."

Agnes thought for a moment, placed her hand over Martha's and said, "You are not bein' a bit selfish. You've a right to want what you want. It's Mr. Kelley's duty to support you. But he's a man, God help us. We both know how childish they can be sometimes. I say give him the space he's asking for. He needs to think things through, decide what he wants, let him take the lead. You keep doing what you're doing, running The Golden Scone. He'll come around."

She patted Agnes's hand on top of her own. "Thank you. But what of Pete and Vickie's wedding? Shall I go with him or not?"

"If he calls and asks, yes I'd say go. If he doesn't, then go alone." She winked at her. "My money's on that phone call. He'll ask ye. Be patient."

"What if someone else asks me before Wolf does call?"

Her smile turned into a frown; her brows knit together. "Are ye talkin' about that Nash Nelson fellow? Ach, I'd steer clear of that one. Too sneaky, something shady about him. He's not half the man Wolf Kelley is."

"You don't know him like I do. He's not half bad once you get to know him."

Agnes drew back on her stool and eyed her boss. "Don't tell me you're fallin' for the scoundrel. His sole purpose is to break you and Mr. Kelley up so he can swoop in and save the day. I have eyes, ya know. Believe me, once he gets the prize, he'll move on to greener pastures. I hate to say it, but he reminds me of someone else."

"Are you talking about Anthony?"

"I'll not besmirch the name of the dead. You know well who I refer to."

Martha sighed and stood up. "I've wasted enough of your time. I'm sure you have orders to fill. You've given me a lot to think about. I appreciate your candor, Agnes."

CHAPTER THIRTY-FIVE

DARK THOUGHTS BLOOM BENEATH A BORROWED SMILE ~

Martha went out the back door, avoiding the dining area. She told Agnes to tell Benson she went to the townhouse. *Agnes made some valid points. Time to think things through.*

Her room was on the top floor. Benson and the rest of the staff took the first floor rooms for privacy. There was a separate bathroom, and a sitting room. The bedroom soothed her spirit with the decor of deep rose, a pitched roof, which she loved, and a window above the bed. She'd brought a bedspread embroidered by her mother. English flowers and multi-colored birds adorned the precious piece. If she closed her eyes she could almost picture England in this cozy environment.

She sat down in the rose-colored overstuffed chair and breathed in the fragrance of a spring candle. Her intent was to think the whole situation through to its conclusion.

Instead, she fell asleep.

Nash Nelson rocked his office chair reflecting on the scene he witnessed yesterday when Wolf saw him with

Martha. *He doesn't deserve a fine woman like Martha. She needs to be with someone of sophistication, like me. Well, I'm glad he saw us. Maybe she'll see through Wolf's barbaric ways, realize they'd never make it as a couple and break it off with him. Maybe I can help that along.*

He laughed out loud.

A knock stirred him out of his revelry. "Come in."

Liz came through the door with a handful of mail. "I've gone through the business correspondence, but there are a couple of personal items."

"Fine, you may go," he barked.

He tore open the top piece as Liz closed the door. An invitation to Vickie and Pete's wedding. *Ah, a couple of weeks from now.*

A plan formed in his mind. *Now, wouldn't it just be a shame if I got to Martha before Wolf. After he left so abruptly the other day, I figure things are a bit iffy between them. They do list a plus one if I so choose, why not ask her? First I need to find out their status. I don't like to be turned down, after all. But if they are on the outs, then she is fair game.*

He decided to have lunch at the tea house to sniff around, see what he could find out. The regular customers and staff must have knowledge of their relationship. *People do like to talk, and I am pretty good at pulling information out of the right people.*

The tea house buzzed with patrons as he entered. Benson greeted him with a polite nod. After he was seated, Ivy came to take his drink order.

"Have you seen Martha this afternoon?" he asked her. "I have a business question for her."

The waitress paused with a sigh, then said, "She's probably in the kitchen." Her pen poised over the order pad, she asked, "What do you want to drink?"

He bristled at her abrupt tone. "A lemon tea and a blueberry scone. When you go back there, ask her to come out here."

Ivy stared at him, but answered politely, "Yes, sir."

Nash motioned for Benson to approach his table.

"Yes, Mr. Nelson. What can I do for you?"

"Your waitress, what's her name? Ivy? Well, she was a bit rude just now."

Benson narrowed his eyes. "Oh, in what way?"

"She heaved a big sigh when I asked to speak with Ms. Buford. I found it rude."

"I see," Benson said. "As you can see, we are quite busy. I'm sure she is simply overwhelmed today. We are looking into hiring a second waitress. I will speak with her. Lunch is on the house."

Nash didn't see the need to say thank you. He gave his customary curt nod and dismissed him with a wave of his hand.

Benson went back to his post to greet the next customer.

Ivy returned with the tea. "Your scone will be along shortly."

Impatient, he barked at her. "What about Ms. Buford? Did you give her the message?"

"No sir, I did not. She isn't here. Left about a half hour ago. Sorry."

"Left? I should have known that before I ordered." Angry, he stood abruptly spilling tea on the white tablecloth. "Never mind the tea *or* the scone." He stalked out, elbowing Benson in the process.

"Incompetent fools," he muttered as he stormed down the sidewalk to his office. "Scones for lunch, how stupid. I wouldn't darken the door of the place if it weren't for Martha."

He burst through the office door and barked at Liz. "Get Ms. Buford on the phone and forward it to my office." Still fuming, he gave another order. "Have a burger delivered to my office. You know how I like it."

In his office, he plopped down in his chair, picked up a pencil. and drummed it on the top of his desk. The phone rang. "Yes?" he answered gruffly. "What? No answer? Well try again." He banged the phone down. *Where could she be?*

As he contemplated Martha's whereabouts, a light knock on the door disturbed his thoughts.

Before he could answer, his daughter opened the door and walked in, a smile lighting her face. "Hi Dad. I was decorating my new office and wanted your opinion."

His shoulders relaxed when he saw Meg. Although he loved all his children, Meg had a special place in his heart. Her bright personality accompanied by her no-nonsense style, and business acumen gave him a sense of pride, even if she *was* a girl.

"What in the world could I contribute to decorating a woman's office?"

She sat down in a chair opposite him.

"Not about color or anything. More about placement. I have a couple of college awards, my degree, that kind of thing. I'm not sure how I should display them. Or if I should display them at all."

"Of course you should. What nonsense. You earned them. Flaunt it."

She laughed. "Oh Dad. I'm not like you. I'm a bit more modest." She suppressed the laugh and looked intently at him. "So, what's going on? Liz said you're in a mood."

"Oh, nothing you need to worry about. Just that confounded tea house."

She raised her eyebrows. "The Golden Scone? Why it's a big hit. Everyone is going there. What's wrong with it?"

"Not the tea house exactly. The owner. Martha Buford."

"She's a lovely lady. What's the problem?" she asked.

"Wolf Kelley's the problem."

"Now Dad. You're not sticking your nose in their business are you? Everyone knows they are a couple. I know your reputation with the women. You better leave them alone. None of your schemes."

He picked up the pencil again and started drumming. "No scheme. There's trouble in paradise. I'm attracted to her. I'd like a shot. She's an attractive lady."

She frowned. "You didn't have anything to do with the trouble did you?"

"No." He paused, looked away, and then added. "Not yet."

"Dad."

"My personal life is none of your business."

She stood up and moved toward the door. "It is when it affects the business. Leave her alone; leave *them* alone." Before she closed the door, she said, "Never mind my office. I'll get Liz to help me."

After Meg left he whirled the chair around to face the window. He knew she was right, but years of imposing his will on others made it almost impossible for him to let it go. *I want what I want. Simple as that.*

They'd always been rivals. When Wolf came back from the military to start the Lodge, he tried everything to shut him down. But the mountain man always found a way to thwart him. But this time was different. He saw the crack in the relationship. *This* time might be the perfect time to chalk up a win against Wolf Kelley.

CHAPTER THIRTY-SIX

HIS WORDS, LIKE VELVET, MASK A VIPER'S STING, BUT AN UNEXPECTED ALLY APPEARS ~

Martha woke from her nap settled in what she must do about Wolf. We're too mismatched. How will this relationship work as a married couple? I know that's what he wants, but I'm afraid it will simply tear us apart. I think the best thing to do is keep it casual.

The mirror reflected the resolve on her face, but her eyes clouded with doubt. She spoke to her reflection, "I do love him. Maybe I will grow tired of the tea house in time. Sell it to the staff, move up to the Lodge and marry him. Maybe..."

After making herself presentable, she went downstairs to find Ella. She missed lunch and wanted a sandwich before she headed back to the tea house.

She found the head maid in the living area dusting.

"Good afternoon, Ella. I didn't see you when I came in earlier."

Ella put her cloth down and smiled at her employer. "I was probably out back. There's a little area I'd like to make into an herb garden. Do you remember we had one back in England?"

She nodded. "I do remember. The fragrance was always so soothing. Are you a bit homesick?"

"Oh no, ma'am. I like a bit of mint in my tea, and I thought it might be well to grow our own. The tea house can use it, as well."

She sat down and patted the chair next to her. "Please sit a moment."

Ella sat, a frown crumpling her face. "Is something wrong, ma'am"

"No, no. I just want to ask you something. Are you happy here? I mean, would you like a part in the tea house itself? A waitress or prep chef maybe? I know you do the laundry, the tablecloths, the towels and such, but you're stuck here alone all the time. I just thought you'd like to be with the others."

Ella chortled. "Oh no. This is a perfect place for me. Peace and quiet. I can do things my way. No. I will help if you need me, but I prefer it here."

Martha laughed. "Exactly what Agnes said." She rose from the chair. "I'm hungry. Think I'll go and make myself a sandwich."

Ellas jumped up. "I can make one for you, ma'am."

She waved her aside. "No need. I'm quite capable in the kitchen. Go about your work."

As Ella returned to her dusting, the phone rang.

"I'll get it, Ella." She picked up the receiver. "Hello." She listened carefully. "Nash." Her voice cooled. "I'm sorry. No. I won't accompany you to the wedding." Again, she listened. "I already have an escort." Another pause. "Not that it's any of your business, but you know it's Wolf. Now, if you will excuse me, I need to return to the tea house." She put the phone down with a bit more force than she intended.

Ella hurried into the hallway. "Anything wrong, ma'am?"

"Oh, only Nash Nelson. He tries his best to come between Wolf and me. We're having problems enough without him butting in." She took a breath. "Never mind, but if he ever calls the house again, I'm not here. Understand?"

Ella answered in a firm voice, "Of course. I'll see to it he doesn't bother you here, at least."

"Thank you. Now to make my sandwich and head back to work."

$$\sim\sim\sim^*\sim\sim\sim$$

Only a few customers remained at The Golden Scone when Martha finally arrived. Closing time was thirty minutes away. Enough time to give a pep talk to the staff and send them home.

To her dismay, when she entered, Nelson grinned at her from a table in the corner.

She tried to ignore him, but he called out as she walked toward the kitchen. "Come have a cup of tea with me, Martha."

"Why must you persist, Nash. I'm not interested. Ours is simply a business relationship. You don't need to patronize my business. You're a meat and potatoes kind of guy."

"This is a public place. You won't deny me a good scone will you?"

She turned without comment and headed for the kitchen.

Agnes looked up from her work and greeted her. "Good afternoon, ma'am. Just puttin' the kitchen to rights for the day." She did a double take. "Are you alright? You're flushed."

"It's Nash Nelson. He called me at home, now he's here. I can't escape him. He's so obnoxious. Thinks he can woo me away from Wolf."

"Aye, some men don't get the hint." She picked up her rolling pin. "Do ya want me to get rid of him for ya?"

She laughed. "No Agnes, nothing so drastic. I'll handle it."

Benson poked his head into the kitchen. "Ma'am, someone to see you."

"Okay, I'm coming."

When she returned to the dining area, she noticed Nash was gone, but in his place sat his daughter, Meg.

"Hello Miss Nelson. So good to see you again. Did you come for another blueberry scone?"

Meg smiled. "I'd love another one, yes." Her smile disappeared. "I've come for a different reason, however."

"Oh? One moment, let me get Ivy."

After the waitress took Meg's order, Martha sat down across from her. "Now what can I do for you?"

"It's Dad."

Her shoulders sagged. "I see. What has he done now?"

Meg frowned. "Don't get me wrong. I love my father, but I don't always approve of his ways. Especially toward women. We lost our mother when we were young, and it's been a parade of ladies ever since. Now he's after you."

She grunted a laugh. "Yes, he does try to worm his way in. I have a relationship with Wolf as everyone knows. Your father seems bound and determined to wedge himself in there."

"I've warned him to stay away from you, but he says you are fair game. I simply want to warn you. Don't let him destroy your relationship with Wolf."

Ivy brought the scone and a cup of tea.

Meg thanked her and continued, "He and Wolf go back a long way. There's always been a business rivalry between them. Dad is more aggressive about it. He can't stand to lose."

Martha nodded. "Yes, I've noticed. But don't worry. I have it all well in hand. I can take care of Nash Nelson."

Ivy returned with a cup of tea for Martha. "Agnes sent this out for you."

"Ah, perfect." Martha lifted the cup. "To strong women!"

She and Meg visited about the business.

"The tea house is perfect. I love it here. Gives this old mountain town some class.

"Thank you, Meg. It's good to have you in my corner. My English ways are a bit foreign to this area, I know. I've always believed everyone can benefit from learning something new. For those who can't travel to England, well they can get the feel of it by coming here. Maybe I'm naïve in thinking in such a way. What do you think?"

Meg nodded vigorously. "I totally agree. A sample of a different culture is a good thing. I was thrilled when I heard about it. These 'set in their ways' mountain folk can learn a thing or two. Has business been good?"

"Better than I ever expected. Of course, I have to credit Agnes. Her scones are the best and authentically English. This could never work if they weren't superb in every way."

Meg motioned for Ivy. "You're right. And I have to have another." She giggled. "Makes it hard to watch my weight, though." After she asked Ivy for another scone, she returned to the conversation with a serious note. "You need to take some credit, Martha. The tea house is absolutely gorgeous. That's from your touch. And the tea. I never knew there were so many different kinds. I always just bought what was in the grocery. Seems dull now."

"Well, thank you, Meg. It's always been a dream of mine. And with Wolf's help, it's come true." She paused and looked down at the teacup.

"What is it, Martha? You look sad."

"Nothing...only, well, it's Wolf. After all the help he's given me, he seems sad, upset, maybe even confused. It's changed our relationship. Not for the better, I'm afraid. Oh, I shouldn't be telling you this. We barely know each other, but it helps to confide in another woman."

"He loves you. Anyone can tell just by looking at you two. As much as he wanted to see you achieve your dream, it also took you away from him. I suppose there's a little green monster flitting around inside his brain." She smiled and said, "I consider us friends, so feel free to confide in me anytime. I'm on your side."

Martha sighed. "Yes, I've seen the little green monster. He wants me all to himself." She looked earnestly at Meg. "Somehow I feel a real connection to you, so I'm just going to say it. How can I be simply a milksop partner? Doesn't what I want count, too? I even spoke to Agnes and she doesn't think I'm selfish, but sometimes I feel as though this relationship is too complicated. Maybe it'll never work out."

"And Dad doesn't help, right?"

"Exactly."

Meg reached across the table and patted her hand. "I'll work on Dad. But at the same time, you'll have to work on Wolf. He should be confident in your relationship, not conflicted. Don't give up the tea house. You'd never be happy."

"Thank you, Meg. I feel as though we've become fast friends."

"Absolutely."

Chapter Thirty-Seven

A Wedding and time for reflection ~

Wolf was impressed with how Pete and Vickie's wedding turned into the event of the year in the small town of Murphy. Filled to capacity, the church celebrated the love of the popular couple.

The new Mrs. Pete Grayson flushed with happiness in her long sleeve almost sheer lace wedding dress, the A-line appliqued gown with a V-neckline and modest V-back, and court train, brought out an elegance few had seen in her before.

Pete also stunned in a simple black tuxedo and black tie, the long beard trimmed to perfection, his hair slicked back. He looked positively civilized.

The whispers among the guests revealed no one had ever seen Pete dressed so formally.

Wolf escorted Martha as planned. He kept his arm possessively around her, drawing her close until he was summoned to join the other groomsmen in the back. *I want to enjoy every moment I have with her.*

He noticed she didn't resist and smiled with love in her eyes as he departed to fulfill his duty to Pete.

Nash arrived, accompanied by Meg.

Martha had managed to steer him away from them throughout the festivities and heaved a sigh of relief when they left.

After everyone saw the couple off on their honeymoon, Wolf and Martha headed for the Lodge.

"The wedding was beautiful. Vicki made a gorgeous bride," Martha said as they traveled the winding road.

"Pete cleaned up pretty good, too," he agreed.

"Yes, he did. It was a wonderful ceremony."

He glanced away from the road for a moment then remarked, "You look beautiful today. I've never seen you so radiant. The peach looks so good on you."

"I'll have to return the compliment. Your suit makes me remember the days in England when you wore your Air Force blues."

"Can I ask you a question, Martha?"

"Certainly," she replied.

"Do you find me less attractive in my mountain attire? I mean, you seem to enjoy it when I dress up. Are you disappointed in me somehow?"

She looked across at him. "What a strange question, Wolf. No, I don't find you less attractive in your work clothes. You're a handsome man whatever you wear. Why are you asking such a question?"

He shrugged. "I don't know. Worried, I guess, that you find me less appealing now than when we were in England."

"How silly. We keep going back and forth with this. Can we just stop?"

He remained silent after her answer.

Finally, she said, "I'm sorry, Wolf. I guess I spoke harshly. I didn't mean to hurt your feelings. We need more time to settle into this relationship. We come from very different backgrounds. Suppose we enjoy what we have and take it a day at a time."

He reached across and took her hand. "Yes, perhaps you're right."

One day at a time...

For whatever reason Martha kept putting him off and couldn't put a finger on why. Months passed. They remained a couple, celebrating milestones together, enjoying special dinner dates, even a few trips away together.

But she remained aloof. Kept him at arm's length when he asked for commitment.

Nash Nelson continued his pursuit of her despite frequent rebuffs.

Nash's daughter, Meg, proved a blessing for her and the friendship they developed., and worked tirelessly to divert Nash from her path. Sometimes it worked, sometimes it didn't, but the two women remained in a secret pact to thwart Nelson.

Martha remained focused on The Golden Scone shying away from Wolf's proposals of marriage. She often asked herself why she couldn't make a commitment. The answer was always the same.

Fear.

Fear of failure, of disappointment, of not being worthy of Wolf's trust and devotion. Her own judgement came into question. *After all, look at the mess I made of my first marriage. How could I have been so wrong about Anthony? How can I trust myself to keep Wolf happy? No, it's best to keep things the way they are. Best not to destroy his happiness because of my failures.*

And so time passed.

And then Ricki Sheridan showed up on her doorstep to bring the news... Wolf had been shot.

Martha remembered the day she met Ricki and Kory. Ricki was the game warden in Dallas, here for a survivalist class at the Lodge. Kory hired on as Wolf's assistant guide. She saw him a time or two but never had the opportunity to meet him. They came together with the news of Wolf's gunshot wound and the horrific ordeal at the Lodge.

Wolf sent the two star-crossed lovers to her home to have a place to stay while he recovered. And she counseled them. Pleaded with them not to make the same mistake she'd made.

Of course, she went to see Wolf. And they'd reminisced...

"So much time has passed," she whispered.

Wolf's face clouded. "Why did we let that happen?"

For the life of her she couldn't form an answer.

He took her hand. "It's not too late. We can start again."

Her eyes glimmered with tears, and she looked away. "Maybe we're not the same people. Maybe time passed us by."

He shook his head. "No, I don't believe it for a minute. I know I'm a bit broken down after this shooting, but we simply can't waste any more time. Let's marry and enjoy our years together, loving each other. It's not too late to have a child." He sat up straighter in the bed. "I'll turn over the business to Kory. I built a cottage close to the Lodge. We can live there. I can help out when they need me."

Martha watched the twinkle grow in his eyes.

He continued, "You've made an absolute success of the tea house. What more is there to prove? Benson and Agnes are ready to retire. Ella can hardly get around to do the work you ask of her. It's time to turn over the business to someone else."

She studied his face. "A child?" she whispered. "You want a child?"

"Yes, I've always wanted a kid. Especially with you."

"You never said anything, Wolf. We never talked about children." Her voice turned wistful, almost with a grain of regret.

He fiddled with the sheets for a moment. "I didn't think about it at first, but as time went on, I thought about how my dad taught me the ways of the mountain, the love of nature. Well, I began to want those things, too. A son to take over the business, or a daughter to run the classes Kory and Ricki started." He looked intently at her. "Don't tell me you haven't thought about children."

She ducked her head; afraid he'd see the blush forming. "Yes, once in a while."

"Why didn't you mention it? We always talk about everything, but you never brought it up."

"Well, you never mentioned it either. I thought you didn't want them."

He shook his head. "Is this what held us back all this time? Children, not talking about them?"

The silence between them deepened until she stood and said, "No, I feel it's more than that. Our differences, my fears, your stubbornness. So many things."

"Other couples deal with things like this. We can work out all of them. That is what marriage is all about. Please, let's try."

She looked up at him, then down again at the handkerchief she twisted in her lap. "I don't know."

"You're putting me off again? You tell me I have to get over my jealousy. I've done that. Nash doesn't get to me anymore. Surely you've noticed." He stopped her hands from wrangling the handkerchief. "It's time for *you* to show good faith."

Trapped, she blurted out the bombshell she kept from him.

"I'm going home to England. Mother needs me."

CHAPTER THIRTY-EIGHT

THOUGH THE STORM HOWLED, THEIR HEARTS STOOD FAST ~

Martha's plane departed early a week after she told Wolf her mother summoned her. Ricki took her to the airport.

Benson and Agnes handled The Golden Scone to perfection. No worries there. Wolf settled back at the Lodge with a hired nurse keeping tabs on him.

"We'll look after him, too, Martha. Don't worry. Concentrate on your mother," Ricki assured her.

"Thank you both. I can't tell you how much I appreciate you."

She waved at Ricki through the small window on the plane as it took off even though she probably couldn't see her. *Ricki and Kory are lucky kids.* She laughed to herself. *Why I'm only a few years older than they are. I can't wait to get back to help with their classes.*

The long flight finally ended at Heathrow Airport. Dame Buford's butler picked her up.

Her stomach knotted as she approached the front door of her mother's house. So long since she last saw her. Often she tried to persuade her to come to the States, but the elder Mrs. Buford flatly refused. Before she knew it time rolled by and the promised visits to England stretched further and further apart.

Her mother's letters were cryptic, riddled with admonitions about her daughter's treatment of her. But every letter she received pushed her away from making the trip.

Now, guilt washed over her as the doorknob turned in her hand, and she steeled herself for the verbal onslaught.

The butler took her bags and informed her Mrs. Buford rested in her room upstairs.

"Thank you, Jenkins." She turned to go, but hesitated and asked, "How will I find her? I know she is ill, but has it taken a toll on her? Should I be prepared for the worst?"

He frowned. "Yes, she is ill, but not too frail. She's stronger than she lets on. This visit will bolster her considerably."

She nodded and climbed the stairs.

Mrs. Buford's feeble voice answered at her knock. "Come in."

She wasn't prepared for the tiny woman in the bed, surrounded by large pillows and a down comforter. Age took its toll. Her champagne-colored hair now streaked with gray peeked out in disarray from a lace morning cap.

"Mother, it's so good to see you," Martha began.

"It's about time," was the disapproving reply. "I must be on my deathbed before you come to visit?"

"Now Mother, please..."

Mrs. Buford interrupted, "Come, let me look at you."

She approached the bed, hands clenched. The time away from her mother changed her. Strength replaced meekness. Confidence replaced self-doubt. Maturity and success revealed to her how tied to her mother's apron strings she'd been. Now she found it difficult not to rebuke the demeaning comments.

"You look pale. I don't think America has done you any good," Dame Buford continued.

"The flight was long and grueling. I need to rest. I'm really fine."

"You can rest when I'm gone. I'm dying, you know."

Martha sighed. "I spoke to the doctor on the phone, Mother. You're not dying. Yes, you're ill, but it's nothing they can't treat at the hospital. That's why I'm here. To see you go."

Mrs. Buford shook her head vigorously. "No. No hospital for me. People die there."

"People also get well in the hospital. You need treatment."

"I absolutely refuse."

She prepared for the battle with her mother. "Alright then, there is nothing I can do. I'm going to call and make reservations for a flight back to the States."

"You wouldn't leave me to die alone!"

"You're not dying. All you need is a few days in the hospital so they can administer breathing treatments. I'll stay if you agree, otherwise I have responsibilities with the tea house."

The elder Buford remained silent, her head bowed, her hands fidgeting with the sleeve of her gown.

"Well, Mother?"

Her mother looked up. "How is The Golden Scone doing? I enjoyed the pictures you sent. I wish I could see it in person."

"The tea house is doing better than I ever expected. I've invited you several times. You always refuse." She placed her hands on her hips. "Now what about the hospital?"

Another short silence. "Well, if you're going to be a bully about it, I suppose I can go."

"Good, I'll call the doctor and set it up. "

In a very meek voice Mrs. Buford asked, "You will stay for a while then?"

"A week, no more. I must get back."

"But you have Benson and the others to watch over it." Her nose wrinkled as she spoke. "I don't suppose you are still chasing after that Wolf Kelley?"

"I'm not chasing after him." She took a breath. "I might as well tell you now. We're getting married."

Wolf groused around as he settled into his room at the Lodge. Kory and the nurse made sure he was comfortable as he complained. He wasn't happy at all. Martha was gone. She'd dropped a bomb on him. Her mother was ill, so she decided to fly to England and be with her. It rankled him a bit. Dame Buford had a way about her, a whining controlling demeanor that turned Martha into a sort of whipped puppy. Her mother always pressured her to give up the tea house, come back to England permanently and find a suitable husband. She wanted grandchildren. Even though the older lady took a shine to him in Spain at first, she didn't find him appropriate for her daughter now.

The nurse came in with a cup of hot tea. "You need to drink this to calm yourself."

"I don't need tea. I need a cup of strong coffee."

Kory stepped in. "Now, Wolf, no coffee for a while. It's too stimulating. You need rest. The tea will calm you down."

"I don't need calming down," he shouted. "I need to get back to work."

Kory took the tea from the nurse. "Drink it for Martha. It's her special brew. You know she'd want you to."

His face shed the angry demeanor and softened at the mention of her name. His mouth opened as if to issue a retort but closed promptly.

He took the cup from Kory and sat down on the bed. Finally, he gulped it down, handed it back to Kory, and said, "There. Satisfied?"

Kory grinned. "Perfectly satisfied. Now, stretch out on the bed and rest. The trip from the hospital took a lot out of you. Lunch is in about an hour."

Wolf protested, "But the office..."

"...will wait," Kory finished the sentence.

The nurse retrieved the teacup from Kory. "He's a stubborn one. The doctor gave strict orders for him to rest, no work for a week. I'm afraid following those orders will be difficult."

Kory issued a stern eye directly at his boss. "I'll be here to enforce them. Ricki will help. Between us we'll make sure he doesn't give you any trouble. Right, Wolf?"

Wolf's entire face crumpled into an irritated frown. "We'll see." He crossed his arms like a pouting child. "I'm hungry, where's Otis?"

Kory shook his head. "Don't you remember? He went to visit his mother about a month ago. Won't be back for another week. The replacement cook was a plant by Desmond. He's in custody. So, we're without a cook. I can make you a sandwich."

"Did I hear right? *You* are going to make a sandwich?" Ricki breezed into the room.

Wolf grunted. "I'd rather starve."

She came over to the bedside and planted a kiss on Wolf's cheek. "How about I make the sandwich?"

A light glistened in his eye. "Best idea I've heard all day."

"Good. Will roast beef be acceptable?"

"Absolutely." He paused. "Have you heard from Martha?"

"Yes, her plane landed safely, she's at her mother's." Ricki answered. "Don't worry, she'll be back in a week. Give you time to fully recover and be ready to greet her properly."

"*If* she comes back. You don't know Dame Buford. She digs her claws in and hangs on until she gets her way."

"Have a little faith, Wolf." Kory interjected. "From what you tell us Martha stands on her own two feet now. Spent enough time on her own running her business. My bet's on her."

"Yeah, well, it's been quite a battle trying to persuade her to marry me. I won't be comfortable until the final 'I do' is said."

"Let me go make your sandwich." Ricki smiled at the surly mountain man and left the room.

He looked at the nurse. "I don't need a babysitter. You can go until it's time for my meds."

She looked at Kory.

He nodded. "Yes, go have a cup of tea in the kitchen. Ricki will show you around. I'll stay and wrangle this one."

Finally alone, Kory asked, "So she agreed to marry you?"

"Yes, but after so many disappointments, I can hardly breathe thinking it will all fall through." He glanced at his assistant. "You know the cottage I built last year? I want you to make sure it's perfect. We're going to live there."

"I love that cottage. Of course I'll go through it with a fine-tooth comb. Make sure all is as you want it."

"And Kory," he continued.

"Yes?"

"I want you to take over the business. All of it."

Kory stared at him. "You what?"

"You heard me. I'm done. From now on I want to concentrate on Martha. If you need me I'll be around, but I want no part of the excursions from now on. And between you and Ricki, I am leaving the Lodge in good hands. You're partners."

"But Wolf, we have the couples retreat classes to conduct. How can we manage...?"

Wolf held his hand up. "There's Mac to run the day to day. Otis will be back to run the kitchen. I've done it all for years, I believe you and Ricki will do fine. And like I said, I'll be around."

"I don't know what to say."

"Say yes and get in touch with my lawyer. I want it all legal like."

Ricki strolled in holding a plate covered with a white linen napkin. "What's going to be all legal?"

Wolf laughed. "Always walking in at the tail end of a conversation aren't you?"

Kory explained, astonishment in his voice, "He wants to give us the Lodge. For us to take over. All of it."

"What?" she exclaimed. "But our classes..."

"He said we have Mac and Otis, and the others to help us. He and Martha will move into the new cottage."

Ricki stood rooted to the ground still holding the sandwich and glancing between the two men. "I don't understand."

Wolf picked up the explanation. "It's been a long road since I began to pursue the woman I love. She's agreed to marry me, and I intend to spend all my time with her. I'm done with the Lodge unless you need me. I want you and Kory to have it."

Ricki handed the plate of roast beef to Wolf, clasped Kory's hand and announced, "We'd be honored."

CHAPTER THIRTY-NINE

AS THE SERPENT SMILED, THE LION ARRIVED ~

Martha resisted the urge to laugh at the expression on Dame Buford's face when she blurted out she and Wolf's plans to marry. She held her tongue though and watched as her mother tried to speak.

"Marry? You mean...? But I thought you came back here to stay....to take care of me."

"No, Mother. I'm going back to the States and marry the man I love. What I should have done in the first place. I listened to you and your so-called logic instead of listening to my heart. I've wasted precious time and won't waste any more."

The older woman didn't speak for a time. Her face crumpled into despair.

"Now, I'm going to call the doctor and set up admitting you to the hospital." She placed a kiss on her mother's brow and straightened the bedclothes. "Be right back."

Jenkins met her at the bottom of the stairs. "How is she, Miss Martha?"

"Feeling sorry for herself, but I'm calling the doctor. She needs treatment at the hospital. If you will drive, I'll sit with her in the back seat."

"As you wish," Jenkins replied.

The doctor agreed to the hospitalization and arrangements ensued.

$$\sim\sim\sim^*\sim\sim\sim$$

The treatments took hold and Mrs. Buford improved, despite complaining about the food, the nursing staff, the uncomfortable bed and other various grievances.

After a few days passed the doctor suggested she return home and recuperate there.

To Martha's surprise, her mother resisted the idea and played the invalid.

She wants me to stay and will do everything to make sure I do.

"No, Mother. The doctor knows what's best and home is where you need to be. I'll hire a nurse to look after you."

"A nurse? I absolutely forbid it. I have Jenkins. Besides, strangers in my home invite thievery. I won't have it."

"You'll do as I say, or I'll catch the next plane back to America. The hospital provides a vetted nursing staff. Your possessions will be safe. Jenkins will oversee everything."

Mrs. Buford sighed with an exaggerated shoulder rise and fall. "Oh, the burden I bear to have such an ungrateful daughter."

"The guilt trip will do you no good, Mother. I leave the day after tomorrow. When you are stronger you may come visit us any time. I'll send you an invitation to the wedding. Jenkins can make all the arrangements."

She left her mother's room listening to accusations of betrayal. This time, she brushed it off knowing it was only a ruse to convince her to give up her own happiness for the sake of her mother's. Arrangements for Mrs. Buford's discharge were set for the next morning.

As Jenkins approached the house, Martha noticed a man at the front door. Dressed in a dark suit the man stirred something in her memory, but she couldn't quite put her finger on it. The way he stood, the way he held his hat. *I know him, but from where?*

As Jenkins opened the door of the automobile, she slid out. Instead of going through the garage, she made her way up the walk to greet the man.

"May I help you?" she asked.

He turned.

She gasped, "Polecat!"

A grin spread across his weathered face, lighting his eyes with obvious delight. "Hello, Martha. I heard of your arrival and took a chance of finding you here, I remembered you sold the Chadwick house."

"But you're dressed as a civilian. Have you made England your home?"

His feet shuffled on the porch. "No, I actually mustered out a week ago. Planned on making a career of it but changed my mind. I want to go home."

"Oh where are my manners? Please come in. Have a cup of tea. Let's catch up."

Jenkins, who parked the car and went through the back door, opened the door from inside.

"This is a dear friend of mine, Jenkins. He's come for a visit."

The butler nodded. "I'll instruct Cook to prepare tea and biscuits."

"Thank you, Jenkins." She turned to Polecat. "Please come this way."

When they settled in the parlor, she asked. "How did you know of my arrival? Only Mother knew I was coming."

He gave her another lopsided grin. "Oh I follow the gossip columns. Have since we last met. They seem to know when you come and when you leave. I even found out about your mother's illness from the columns."

She laughed. "Oh my. I forgot about those. I never pay any attention to them. It's tedious to keep up with all of it. And frankly, I don't care who does what or who goes where."

"Well, I only scan them to see news of you," he said.

"Why, I thought you and Wolf kept in touch. Come to think of it, he hasn't mentioned you in a while."

The grin left his face. "We kind of lost touch. My fault mostly. Can't say why exactly. Got wrapped up in my career, until I lost interest."

"Oh, Polecat. How sad. Do you have a girl? Surely you've found someone by now."

A sparkle returned to his eyes. "There is one lady. We've been dating, but she doesn't want commitment. Wants to keep it casual. Anyway, I hope I'm not intruding."

"Of course not. It's so good to see you. But tell me why you've stayed so long in England. Why not go home? You know Wolf's got a position just waiting for you."

The maid came in with a tray.

Martha poured the tea.

Polecat reached for a biscuit and stuffed it in his mouth whole. After dramatically swallowing he said, "I can't get enough of these English cookies."

She laughed and offered another. "Well, if that is what's kept you here, I hate to tell you my tea house offers all the tea and biscuits you can consume. You've wasted your time here."

He blushed. "That's not the only reason. I never heard you and Wolf married. I didn't want to interfere, so chose to stay in the Air Force."

"Oh, Polecat, you are a dear. But the good news is we *are* getting married. Finally. You'll be back in the States just in time."

"That's wonderful news!"

"And of course you will have a part in the ceremony."

He shook his head. "Oh no, ma'am. I couldn't."

"I won't stand for your refusal. Wolf will be delighted. You know he was shot, don't you?"

The surprise on his face stunned her. "Oh my goodness. You didn't know."

As she relayed the story to him, he sat in rapt silence.

"Now, you know why it's so important for you to be involved. He needs his friends around him. People he can trust. You're high on that list."

"When you put it that way, how can I refuse? But Wolf doesn't know I've mustered out. Maybe I won't fit in his plan, after all."

This time Martha shook her head. "No matter what plans we make you will always fit in. You were instrumental in getting us together. How can we not include you? When does your plane leave?"

"Tomorrow morning."

"Can you delay it, reschedule? I leave the day after. We can go together. It will bring Wolf so much joy to see you."

"I think so. Are you sure?" he asked.

"Certainly, I'm sure."

He stood. "Then I must go and make new arrangements."

"Nonsense. You can call from here. And we have plenty of room for you to stay."

As he started to protest, she raised her hand. "I won't hear it. It's settled." Then she winked at him. "You know absence makes the heart grow fonder. Maybe your girl will think twice about commitment once you leave for the States."

He blushed. "Well, maybe."

"If anyone should know about that scenario it's me. Trust me. Anyway, Mother is much better, and I am bringing her home tomorrow morning. I'll get her settled in before my flight. I will warn you she will protest, but it's of no consequence. It's only her way of trying to control me."

Doubt etched his face. "I don't want to be a source of discord."

"Leave it to me."

$$\sim \sim \sim * \sim \sim \sim$$

By ten the next morning, Dame Buford was settled in her room still complaining and causing a ruckus when she realized Martha invited Polecat to occupy a room.

"This is still my house, Martha. You should have asked me. To have that sort of man ensconced in my home is shocking."

Martha sighed. "It's only one night. We fly out together in the morning. He's a friend. *My* friend. So I expect you to treat him courteously. Besides, you won't see him. You are having your meals in your room."

Mrs. Buford flushed. "But the gossip columns! How will I ever live it down?"

"Maybe if you stopped reading them, you wouldn't be so bothered."

Her mother huffed and crossed her arms, then her face softened into a contrite childlike image. "So you are really leaving me tomorrow?"

"Yes. The doctor says you are completely over your problem and just need rest. You don't need me for that. I have a wedding to plan."

"A wedding...without your mother."

"I need at least a month to plan. You should be completely recovered by then. I'll even buy your plane ticket. Bring Jenkins. He can handle everything," she replied.

She left her mother still pouting as she quietly closed the door.

CHAPTER FORTY

WHEN HEARTS MEET ONCE MORE, FATE KNOCKS TWICE... ONCE AS FRIEND, ONCE AS FOE ~

Wolf paced the office trying hard to calm his anxiousness as he waited for news of Martha's arrival. More than relieved she decided to return, he still harbored doubt about the wedding. He understood too well Dame Buford's strong hold on her daughter. He'd witnessed the total power in action. *She probably talked her out of marriage.*

Kory put his foot down when he wanted to meet her at the airport. "Absolutely not. You're not fully recovered and a trip like that will set you back. You need to look healthy and refreshed when you see her. No, Ricki and I will see her home. You'll just have to be patient."

Wolf grumbled and threatened, but to no avail. Now he paced in agitation, glancing at the clock, watching the minute hand tick by at an infuriatingly slow rate. *I should have fought harder. By the time they get here, I'll be beside myself.*

Mac came in with a cup of tea, steam still rising in curls. "Thought this might calm you down. It's Martha's brew."

Wolf glared at him. "Take it away now! I don't need tea. I need a whiskey." He stopped pacing in front of the sidebar and put his hand on the whiskey decanter.

Mac deftly stepped in between and scooped it up. "Now, won't that be a nice greeting for Martha with whiskey on your breath."

Wolf knew his face was red with anger, but he couldn't argue with Mac's logic. He flopped down in his chair. "Why didn't they let me ride along? This waiting is taking more of a toll on me than if I'd gone with them."

"It won't be long now. It's really pretty in the garden right now. Why don't you pick her a bouquet of flowers? You know how much the gazebo means to her." He glanced at his watch. "In fact, I'll make sure lunch is ready for her when she arrives. Just drink the tea and I'll see to everything."

Wolf studied his clerk, then sighed begrudgingly. "Not a bad idea." Swiftly, he grabbed the cup and downed it in one gulp. He stood, shoved the empty cup toward Mac and slapped his leg. "Come on Lobo. We need to choose some flowers for Martha."

Honeysuckle emitted a strong sweet fragrance as he stood by the gazebo. Carnations and roses were her favorites, and those were in abundance. He held the bouquet in his hand trying to decide what to do with them when he heard a noise.

He turned.

Martha stood looking marvelous in a powder blue traveling suit, eyes sparkling with tears and both arms outstretched. "Are you going to hug me or what Wolf?"

He dropped the flowers on the table and rushed to her.

They both laughed, kissed, hugged, kissed again, and clung to each other for a full minute.

He whispered, "I didn't think you would come back."

She nuzzled his neck. "Nothing could keep me away." She pulled back. "I have a surprise for you."

"A surprise?"

She turned. "You can come out now."

From behind an ivy laced column, Polecat emerged with a grin on his face and an outstretched hand. "Hi, Wolf. Long time no see."

He dropped Martha's hand and gaped at his old friend, stunned to see him standing right in front of him, "Polecat, what...?"

"Thought I'd surprise you. Actually, it was Martha's idea. Hope you're not mad."

"Mad? Why would I be mad?" He reached out his hand and pulled his friend into a bear hug. "This is wonderful. But you're dressed in civvies. Did you muster out?"

"Yep, finally came to my senses. Military life is not what I want going forward. I needed to be back in the States. Find my niche, start a real life."

Wolf grinned even bigger. "Well, you've found it. You'll stay here. Work at the Lodge. They'll need you now more than ever."

Polecat looked at Martha, then back at him. "What do you mean they?" He glanced once more at Martha who merely shrugged and shook her head.

Lobo pressed himself as snuggly as he could to Wolf's side and whined.

They all laughed.

"Seems you've left Lobo out of the loop, too, dear," Martha said.

"Well, if you must know *now*, I'll tell you. I've signed the Lodge over to Ricki and Kory. I'm renovating the little cabin down by the creek where we'll live, Martha. I'm taking a step back. Gonna spend as much time with you as I can." He turned to Polecat. They'll need a foreman. You fit the bill."

Polecat gaped at his friend. "Foreman? I know nothing about this business."

Wolf shrugged. "You'll learn. Your military training will really come in handy. Now, let's get you settled. You're staying here, of course. Oh there's a wedding coming up." He grinned at Martha. "I expect you to be one of my groomsman. Mac!" he shouted.

When Mac appeared Wolf barked instructions. "See this man to his room. Lunch in half an hour."

"You got it, boss," Mac replied.

After the two men disappeared into the Lodge, he turned to Martha. "Now. Where were we?" Before she could answer he swooped her up in a tight embrace and kissed her soundly.

Breathless, she laughed as they parted. "I think you nailed it."

As he led her back to the gazebo, he asked, "How did you find Polecat?"

"I didn't, he found me. Showed up at Mother's door. I was so surprised to see him. Figured he'd left the military long ago."

"Well, I'm glad you convinced him to come home with you. It's a great surprise." He frowned. "So tell me. How is your mother and did she talk you out of marrying me?"

She laughed. "Mother hasn't changed at all. Still all about herself. And she tried to talk me out of the marriage, but I stood my ground. You would have been proud of me."

He leaned in and kissed her tenderly. "I'm always proud of you. You're an amazing woman."

She filled him in on the visit as they soaked up the sounds and fragrance of the garden. The background was filled with the happy chirping of birds, as if they welcomed her home. The perfume in the air surrounded them in an embrace and added to the intoxication of their reunion.

Mac tiptoed into view. "Sorry to interrupt. Polecat is settled and lunch is served in the dining room."

"Thanks, Mac. We'll be right along." He took her hand as Mac disappeared inside. "One more kiss, just to make sure this isn't a dream."

The kiss was sweet, long, tender, and he felt her sigh as they parted.

She squeezed his hand. "I am so happy, Wolf. I know now this is what should have happened a long time ago. We've wasted so much time. Or should I say, *I* have wasted so much time. I can't determine why I waited."

A robin trilled as she spoke as if to admonish her statement.

Wolf squeezed her hand in return. "Don't second guess yourself. What you went through with Anthony changed your outlook completely. You didn't trust yourself anymore. I admit my lack of patience didn't help matters any, but maybe we had to go through all this to find our own path. It doesn't matter now. We're together. Our life together is just beginning."

"I suppose so. Let's go to lunch. I know you want to catch up with Polecat. We can talk later, alone, without any interruptions."

Her seductive smile intrigued Wolf. "Alone? Promise?"

"Trust me, I mean every word." She winked.

"In that case, I'm not hungry and Polecat can wait."

She rose with a giggle on her lips. "Later, I haven't eaten since early this morning. I need my strength."

He laughed, grabbed her hand and together greeted the others in the dining room.

~ ~ ~ * ~ ~ ~

Kory and Ricki joined them along with Polecat for a lunch of trout and garden salad with Agnes gloating as she brought it out. "All of these veggies were grown in our lovely garden.

"You're a wonder, Agnes," praised Martha.

The cook blushed. "Thank you so much."

Everyone complimented her on the excellent mixture of greens and flavor.

Polecat changed the subject. "So the wedding is soon?"

Wolf beamed. "Two weeks!"

As the conversation progressed, a disturbance in the foyer captured their attention.

Wolf rose to investigate but froze when Nash burst through the door. "There won't be any wedding in two weeks, if ever."

Martha gasped. "Why not, for goodness sake?"

"Because I'm having Wolf arrested for arson."

CHAPTER FORTY-ONE

THE SERPENT STRIKES, BUT LOVE WILL NOT PERISH IN THE FLAME ~

Benson stood in the kitchen, or what was left of it. The charred remains of the stove, counters, cupboards, and refrigerator stood in ruins.

Ivy stepped forward. "How did this happen, Benson? We checked everything before closing last night."

He patted her shoulder. "Don't worry, Ivy. We both made sure all was secure before we left. I'm no expert, but if I had to guess, I'd say it was arson. Someone did this deliberately."

"But, who? Everyone loves Martha," she asked.

"I don't know. We'll have to let the police do their investigation."

A firm voice sounded from behind them. "You're right, sir, and you are compromising our investigation. How did you get past security? Please leave the room, so the investigation can begin."

Benson turned to the officer. "I'm sorry. I'm the manager. I have a key to the front door. It's so unbelievable. We'll get out of your way."

"First give me your cell number in case I have questions."

The two men exchanged numbers.

He led Ivy into the dining area. "Thankfully, only the kitchen was destroyed."

"Will she rebuild now she's getting married? I heard her talking about moving to the Lodge after the wedding. What about our jobs?"

"Lady Buford won't abandon us. I'm sure she'll have a solution."

The fire happened early in the morning. In the aftermath and with the perimeter taped off, the firemen waited for the investigators to arrive.

Smoke filled the air, and the acrid smell of the charred building enveloped the entire block and beyond. A crowd gathered in the alleyway as word spread of the disaster. Police held back the crowd and told everyone to go home. Hardly anyone complied.

"I suppose I need to call her. She's arrived from England by now. I'll call the Lodge. Maybe break the news to Wolf before we tell her. She'll be heartbroken."

They walked in silence to the house. When they entered the front door, Ella stood in the hallway wringing her hands, face contorted with worry. "Is it gone?"

"Only the kitchen. The dining area was spared thanks to the quick reaction of the firemen. But it will take a major overhaul to get The Golden Scone up and running again."

"Does she know?"

"Not yet. I'm just about to call her at the Lodge. Is there any tea made? I need something to calm me before I call."

Ella nodded. "Of course. I'll just fetch it."

"What shall I do now? Anything I can help with? I feel helpless," Ivy asked.

"Why don't you help Ella. I think a nice dinner tonight for Martha and Wolf will be just the thing. Something special. We need to show a united front, make sure she knows we will stand with her through all this."

Ella entered with the tea. "Yes, Ivy. I can use your help. I'll get in touch with Agnes. She'll lend a hand. Lady Buford does so much for us. We need to stand with her now."

Benson sipped the tea slowly until the cup was empty. "Then we have a plan. If you will both excuse me, I'll make the call now."

The women left and Benson heaved a huge sigh and picked up the telephone.

Mac answered.

"Mac, this is Benson. I'm afraid I have some bad news. I'd like to speak to Mr. Kelley first if possible. It concerns The Golden Scone."

He listened to Mac's reply, then said, "You already know?" Another pause. "Nash Nelson? He suspects Wolf? Oh my goodness. What can I do? Shall I come to the Lodge?" Another pause. "Yes, I'll remain here until they arrive. But if you need me, just call." He hung up the phone and hurried to the kitchen.

"There's news," he announced. "Nash Nelson is at the Lodge accusing Wolf of arson. I'm not sure there will be a dinner tonight."

"Wolf Kelley? Why that's absurd. He'd never do anything like that. He loves Martha. He knows it would break her heart." Ella stood in the middle of the room, hands on hips.

"We know that, but Nash has always been after Lady Buford. This might be his latest ploy to win her over. I asked Mac if I should come, but he said no. I feel helpless. What can we do?" He looked at the women imploringly.

No one spoke, only stood together staring at each other.

The head investigator, tall, lanky, forty something Captain Barry Simpson, pushed a shock of blond hair from his forehead and surveyed the kitchen, his eagle eye trained to detect patterns of arson. "Here's the culprit." He pointed to a charred piece of cord. "A faulty toaster cord. See? The wall is blackened just here. You can see the pattern as it spread. No arson here."

The stocky built fire marshal with piercing dark eyes, Dirk Martin, dressed in protective gear, sighed. "Well, that's good to know. I'd hate to think an arsonist is running around Murphy. I hate it's The Golden Scone. My wife loves this place. Brings all her friends here. She's always loved a bit of culture in her life. Hope Lady Buford will rebuild. I hear she's getting married."

Simpson shook his head. "I don't know about that. Shouldn't be too hard to renovate the kitchen. The rest of the place is okay except for some smoke damage. With the right professionals she should be back in business in a couple of months. I'll go file my report."

Simpson left.

Dirk Martin informed his crew he needed to let the manager know arson was ruled out. He called Benson right away.

After Benson hung up with the fire marshal, he turned to the women who stood by anxiously waiting. "Turns out it wasn't arson. The toaster cord was bad. The fire started there. I think we will go ahead with the dinner."

Ella nodded, grabbed Ivy's hand and pulled her toward the refrigerator. "We've got this."

CHAPTER FORTY-TWO

THE LIE IS DEAD, AND THE TRUTH STANDS BRIGHT ~

Wolf growled, "Arson. What do you mean?"

Nash continued with a sardonic grin on his face, "I always knew Wolf Kelley was a fraud. He never wanted you to have The Golden Scone, Martha. Now that you're back, he's making sure you never have it again. He burned it down."

A collective gasp echoed through the room; electricity palpable in the air as Nash delivered the edict.

Martha stumbled backwards and covered her mouth, eyes wide, staring at Nash.

Wolf stood. "Burned it down? You're crazy, Nash. I talked to Benson yesterday. What are you talking about?"

"You know very well what I'm talking about. The fire broke out early this morning. Looks like arson according to the fire marshal. I say it's you. Who else could do such a thing?" He pulled out his cell phone. "I'm calling the police."

"In case you've forgotten, I've been shot. I can't drive yet. Kory has kept me secured here. How in the world could I get to Murphy and set a fire?"

Martha finding her voice, whimpered in shock. "The Golden Scone? Gone?"

Nash hurried to her side and circled his arm around her shoulder. "Don't worry. We'll rebuild. And in the meantime, we'll put the perpetrator behind bars." He glared at Wolf.

Martha jerked free of his embrace. "You get away from me. Wolf didn't do this. You know that very well. In fact, if I didn't know better, I'd think *you* set the fire."

Nash issued a derisive laugh. "Now what reason do I have to burn it down? I have no stake in your business."

Before anyone answered the question, Mac burst into the room. "Phone call, Wolf. It's urgent."

Wolf tossed a glance at Kory and a nod toward Martha.

Kory went protectively to her side.

In the foyer, Wolf asked, "Who is it, Mac?"

"It's Benson again. He called earlier to inform us of the fire, but we already knew. He says he has news of how it started."

Wolf picked up the receiver. "Yes, Benson. Mac says you have news."

He listened and his face relaxed at the information Benson gave him. "Thanks, old friend. Yes, we'll be glad to come to dinner. Keep us informed in the meantime."

Back in the dining room, Wolf faced Nash. "Benson called with news of how the fire started. No arson, a bad toaster cord. The fire marshal made the official report."

Nash put his phone down. "That can't be right. I saw the kitchen myself. It looks like it was set. I'm calling my own investigator."

Anger flushed his face. "Get out of my lodge immediately. If you ever step foot on my property again, I'll have you arrested for trespassing."

Nash balled his fists.

Kory stepped to Wolf's side. "You can't fight the both of us. I suggest you leave."

Nash moved toward the door. "This isn't over. You're a fraud, Wolf Kelley and I'm going to prove it."

When Nash disappeared from the dining room, Wolf hurried to Martha's side. "Are you alright? This must be such a shock to you."

"I can't believe it," she said. "My dream, simply gone. Just like that."

"Now, Martha, we'll rebuild it. You'll see," he soothed.

Ricki spoke up. "Don't you worry. Everyone will help. It'll be up and running in no time."

Mac, who remained in the doorway, offered, "Benson says it's only the kitchen. The dining area is intact. Of course there's smoke damage."

"See there. It's not as bad as we thought," Wolf continued.

"Well, that's something, I suppose." She sighed deeply. "I surely never expected this as my homecoming." To Wolf, she said, "Why is Nash accusing you of arson?"

He shrugged. "Because he's a jerk. He's always wanted you, Martha. He sees the wedding coming up and thinks this is his chance to discredit me in your eyes."

"He's despicable. I'll never trust him again." Another deep sigh and she straightened her shoulders and said, "I don't want to waste any time. Take me to town, Wolf. I want to see this for myself." To Mac, she said, "Call Benson, tell him we are on our way and to meet us there."

Mac nodded. "On it."

Wolf argued, "Can't this wait until tomorrow? You just got home from a long trip. You must be exhausted."

"No, it can't wait. I have employees who depend on me. And I must see the damage before I decide to rebuild. We go now."

In the end, they all went. Kory, Ricki, Polecat, Agnes, Wolf and Martha.

~~~*~~~

Benson stood in what was left of the kitchen, beside Ivy and Ella.

No one spoke. Everyone held a handkerchief over their noses protecting themselves from the acrid smell of fire and smoke. The light, dimmed from soot-covered windows, made it hard to see any detail.
~~~

The atmosphere remained somber, the mood bleak as they surveyed the damage waiting for the arrival of their benefactor. The firemen, told it was not arson and making sure the fire was completely out, left, making sure the area around the tea house was taped off.

Fifteen minutes passed without a word spoken.

Ivy tugged at Benson's sleeve.

"What is it, Ivy?" he asked.

"The toaster," she answered.

"Yes, what about it? The fire marshal said the fire started there. A faulty cord. You can see the way it fanned out."

"It's just...well,"

"Speak up, girl. It's what?"

"It's not our toaster."

Benson opened his mouth to speak, closed it again and stared at the toaster. "Are you sure? I'm never back here so I can't identify it. This is serious, Ivy. You must be certain."

"I'm sure. That charred toaster is only a two-slot model. Ours was a four-slot."

Benson walked over for a closer look. "It's only a two-slot alright."

"Agnes can back me up when she gets here. I used the toaster all the time for orders. I know what I'm talking about."

Benson whispered in a disbelieving voice, "Then it *is* arson."

A commotion at the front door alerted the group to Martha's arrival.

Benson turned to greet her only to be surprised to see an entire group of employees from the Lodge pushing through the door.

Martha stood at the front staring at the destruction.

No one said much. Just gaped at the destroyed kitchen.

Ivy moved over by Agnes and whispered in her ear.

The cook glanced quickly at the toaster on the burned counter. She nodded at Ivy.

Benson went to Agnes's side and said something in a low voice to her.

Martha noticed the two with their heads together and asked, "What are you whispering about?"

Benson cleared his throat, then said, "I'm afraid we have some bad news."

"What could be worse than this?" Martha asked.

"It's the toaster, ma'am."

"The toaster? Yes, the fire marshal said it started there. A bad cord or something."

"Yes, it started there, but we've discovered something else."

"Well, spit it out Benson," Wolf growled.

"The toaster is not ours."

Everyone remained in stunned silence for a few minutes.

Martha finally found her voice. "Agnes, can you back this up?"

The cook nodded. "Ivy is the one who discovered it. Ours had four slots. This one only has two."

Martha glanced at Ivy. "This is true?"

"Yes, ma'am."

Wolf let out a long whistle. "Then it *is* arson. Someone switched the toasters."

Kory took charge. "Everyone out of the kitchen. Don't touch anything. We need to call the fire marshal back and get him down here."

Back in the dining room, Benson made the call.

"This is awful, Wolf," Martha said.

"Who could do such a thing?" she continued.

"I can only think of one person," Wolf responded.

"Nash?"

"Has to be. You saw how he acted. Trying to pin it on me. He knows we're getting married. He's tried all these years to win you over. This is his last straw. Get me arrested for arson so he has a clear path to you."

"I simply have a hard time believing anyone can be so vile."

"Anything is possible when it comes to Nash."

The fire marshal arrived, and Benson, Ivy, and Agnes circled around him while he asked them to identify the toaster.

When he finished with the employees, he approached Martha. "I'm sorry to tell you it does look like arson. Your staff claims the toaster was not the one in use before the fire. Someone switched it out. Probably hoping no one noticed, or it would be completely destroyed in the fire. This is now a full-fledged investigation, and I must ask you all to leave the premises."

Martha took charge. "Of course. We'll be down the street at my home if you have any questions."

"I've got Benson's number if I need anything. You will all be asked to recount your activities the night before the fire."

She nodded and led the group out the front door.

CHAPTER FORTY-THREE

THE MASK HAS SLIPPED, AND THE DEVIL WEARS HIS NAME ~

Nash entered his office and threw the car keys on the desk, kicked the chair and went to the sideboard. "Dirk Martin. What an idiot. My next move is to get him fired as fire marshal." He poured a whiskey, knocked it back, and banged the glass down. "I paid good money to get him elected and this is how he repays me. He's finished in this town."

He flung himself into his office chair, whirled it around to face the window and reflected out loud. "This is my town, and everyone here belongs to me, or they can leave. Martha belongs to me, too. She owes me. I made it possible for her to have The Golden Scone. All I have to do is get Wolf Kelley out of the way."

"Dad, what are you talking about? Get Wolf Kelley out of the way? What does that mean?"

Nash swiveled around to gaze at his daughter, surprised he didn't notice her entrance. His mind scrambled to recover as he tried to remember exactly what he'd muttered vociferously. "Oh, hey Meg. Didn't hear you come in. What about the fire at The Golden Scone? Simply awful. You know about it, right?"

She sat down across from him. "Yes, that's why I'm here. But hearing you just now saying you want to get Wolf out of the way makes me wonder. Did you have something to do with the fire?"

He feigned a hurt expression. "Don't be ridiculous, Meg. Of course I didn't. I was putting two and two together. It has to be Wolf who set the fire. He never wanted Martha to have the tea house in the first place. Now with it gone, he's free to have her move to the Lodge. Just what he always wanted."

"They're getting married, Dad. Of course she's moving to the Lodge. She has the staff to run the Scone. It doesn't make sense for him to burn it down now." She leaned forward. "Are you trying to frame him? Get him put away so you are free to pursue Martha?"

"I don't have to stoop so low to get Martha. I haven't really tried. I mean, she's so hell-bent on marrying Wolf. It's a pity she doesn't see him for what he is or recognize I'm the better man."

Meg stood. "You're really a piece of work. You always have to win, don't you? I better not find out you had anything to do with this. I can just tolerate so much. Wolf is a good man. They make a great couple, and you need to leave them alone." She spun on her heel and left the room.

He watched her leave and curled his lip. "It's so sad my own daughter doesn't believe in me."

~ ~ ~ * ~ ~ ~

Dirk Martin surveyed the counter where the misshapen toaster sat. A bit worse for wear, but clear it was a two-slot toaster not a four-slot. "Somebody got sloppy. Good thing the Ivy girl spoke up. An arsonist might have gotten away with a terrible crime."

As his team combed over the entire kitchen, he sent one of them to check the security cameras around the entire block including the alley.

"Maybe we'll get lucky and catch the idiot in the act."

One of his men approached. "Nothing left of the cord, but there is a bit of accelerant detected by the outlet."

"Good. Take pictures."

The man nodded and left to comply.

Dirk's boots crunched under his feet as he walked around the kitchen, pondering on the perpetrator. He had his suspicions but couldn't prove anything without hard evidence. When he was appointed fire marshal Nash Nelson made sure he knew what he expected in the way of loyalty. Nash ruled this town. But what Nash didn't know was Dirk himself. He was a newbie to the town. Only five years in residence. Came from the neighboring town of Bad Axe. For years, he watched corruption ruin the family atmosphere and decided he'd had enough. Everyone warned him of Nash Nelson, but he determined if he didn't cave to his demands he just might make a difference.

"Well, here's the ultimate test," he whispered to himself. "Everyone knows about Nash's reputation with women. What he wants he gets. He didn't get Martha." He scratched his head. "But did he go to these lengths to get his way? Well, the evidence doesn't lie. Nash is smart, but even he can make mistakes. I simply have to find it."

The investigator returned and informed Dirk the camera footage was ready to view.

"Good, I'll meet you back at the station." Dirk swallowed hard hoping his hunch proved wrong.

$$\sim\sim\sim*\sim\sim\sim$$

The station, recently outfitted with the newest technology, buzzed with talk of the fire. Evidently, everyone here now knew arson was suspected. Along with the newest equipment, security cameras were set up around the city.

"Time to put all this to the test," Dirk said.

One by one, each camera was remotely viewed. Nothing showed on any of the main cameras on the street, but when they got to the one in the alley, Dirk held up his hand to stop. There in the darkened alley was an unmistakable figure.

He carried an object under his arm.

When Dirk had the technician zoom in he saw the logo.

Clearly printed for all to see was the factory stamp. The same one now sitting on a charred counter in the burned-out kitchen of The Golden Scone.

"Let's see if we can zoom in on his face," Dirk ordered.

When the technician did so, the room went silent.

CHAPTER FORTY-FOUR

THE WAIT IS ENDLESS... UNTIL IT IS NOT ~

Wolf watched Martha carefully. He'd witnessed her incredible strength in times of crisis before, but The Golden Scone was her baby, a longed-for accomplishment. His heart broke for her. *Will she feel obligated to postpone the wedding to help the staff re-open? If so, I'll stand strong for her.*

She considered the employees her responsibility. After all, she brought them over from England to start a new life. And now their livelihood is threatened.

She sat at the table staring into space, a look of despair ravaged her otherwise beautiful face. The sun dipped low dimming the light through the window, casting shadows around the room, adding to the bleak atmosphere.

He whispered to her, "Do you need to lie down before dinner? You look absolutely exhausted. Everyone will understand if you feel the need for a little time to yourself."

She shook her head. "No, I need to be here...around my staff. They're all wondering what is to become of them. I won't abandon them now. I have to restore The Golden Scone. I owe it to them. I'll rest after dinner."

"Always looking out for everyone else. Time you looked after yourself, my dear," he answered.

Before she could reply, Ivy brought her a cup of a special tea, the one she always tried to get Wolf to drink to calm him down. "Here ma'am. You look as if you need this."

Wolf took the China cup and saucer from Ivy and placed it in front of Martha. "There now. Time for you to take your own medicine, so to speak."

"Thank you, Ivy. What a perfect thing to do. It's just what I need."

Ivy curtseyed and left the room.

Tendrils of steam still wafted above the cup, and she bent over the brew drawing a deep breath, then sipped delicately.

He watched her take a drink and noticed her shoulders relax and the hard line of her jaw soften.

"Better?" he asked.

"Much." She took another sip. "I wonder when we'll hear from the fire marshal."

"These things take time. Not like on television." He patted her hand. "I'm sure it will be several days before we know anything."

When she didn't answer, he asked. "What are you thinking?"

The air left the room as she turned toward him, a look he hadn't seen in her eyes before alarmed him.

"He did it, didn't he?" The venom in her trembling voice unmistakable.

The answer he held back was inappropriate. Instead he said, "Let's just wait and see what Dirk finds out. Don't jump to conclusions."

"You know he did, Wolf. Why else would he accuse you like that? It's a last-ditch effort to get you out of the picture." She stood, leaving the tea on the table and paced. "I knew he was an egotistical man. Has to have everything his way." Then in a whisper she continued. "But this is vile."

The room grew silent. He couldn't answer her because he knew she was right.

Benson entered quietly. "Dinner is ready."

"Yes, Benson. Please ask everyone to come in. I want you all around me tonight. We will enjoy dinner together this evening," Martha instructed.

"Yes, ma'am." Benson retreated to gather the staff.

~ ~ ~ * ~ ~ ~

At first the dining room, now darkened by the disappearance of the sun, resounded with the arrival of everyone. Agnes, Ivy, Benson, Ricki, Kory, Polecat, and Ella.

Benson adjusted the electric lighting to provide a soft glow, not too bright for tired eyes.

Agnes prepared some of Martha's favorite dishes. Succulent roast chicken, a garden salad, mashed potatoes, and Yorkshire pudding.

"Ah, Agnes, you outdid yourself. Thank you for being so thoughtful." Martha praised the cook.

But while the others ate and tried to make normal conversation, Wolf noticed she only picked at the food. He poured her a glass of Pinot Noir hoping it's light taste would take up where the tea left off to relax her.

No one spoke of the fire, or the fact it was arson. The room crackled with clattering silverware and light conversation.

Halfway through the meal, Martha finally spoke, "You don't have to protect me. Do not continue to avoid the conversation. We have an arsonist to ferret out. I'd like to know what all of you think."

Kory took the lead. "I think we all know who the number one suspect is."

Agnes and Ivy nodded.

Benson sat silent.

Ella looked around the room with eyes wide as saucers.

Ricki offered her opinion, "I think we need to wait for the fire marshal to finish the investigation." She turned to Martha. "I know this is eating you up, dear. I hope we can focus on reconstruction and let the authorities do their jobs."

"He accused Wolf." Martha' s voice trembled. "You all know who I'm speaking of."

The conversation lagged for a moment and then came a knock on the door.

Benson rose to answer, but Martha stopped him. "Let me."

Wolf followed her.

She opened the door to Dirk Martin. "You have news, I presume?"

Shed of his protective gear, now clad in dark slacks and a buttoned-down shirt, he nodded. "We know who set the fire."

She paused for only a second. "Please, do come in. We're all gathered in the dining room. Would you like a cup of coffee or something to eat?"

He shook his head. "No, thanks. I only want to get this over with."

They led Dirk into the dining room.

He raked his curly dark hair back with a nervous swoop. "I won't beat around the bush. We have camera footage. The arsonist is Nash Nelson. I've informed the proper law enforcement. It's in their hands now."

Martha's voice broke. "Why? It makes no sense."

Dirk sighed. "Who can explain what goes on in a man's mind."

"What will happen to him?" Benson asked.

"They'll file formal charges. A trial probably unless he pleads guilty. I think we all know the answer to that. At any rate, he'll be off the streets."

"Poor Meg. This is going to hit her hard," Martha whispered.

Dirk turned to go. "If you need anything from me, please give me a call."

"Thank you," she said. "I'll see you out."

Wolf slouched in his chair and muttered in a low voice, "I'd like to be a fly on the wall when they arrest him."

CHAPTER FORTY-FIVE

AN ENEMY CAGED ALLOWS FOR A BRIGHTER DAY ~

Nash studied Meg through the jail cell bars, observing the black business suit she wore. "So, you don't believe me... that I had nothing to do with the fire."

"Dad, they have you on camera. I've viewed the footage myself. It's you carrying a toaster. Why do you continue to deny it?"

"Can't a guy bring a friend a gift? That's all I did. I figure they could use a second toaster. Geesh, Meg. Have a little faith in your old dad."

"Okay, if that's so, then where is the other toaster?"

He pushed away from the bars and sat down hard on the bunk behind him. "How should I know? I set the new one on the counter and left. They need to view the footage again."

"Dad. You replaced a four-slot toaster with a two-slot. That's pretty sloppy even for you. And why did you come in the middle of the night? Why would you have a key? You don't own that building anymore. I'm sure Martha didn't give you a key."

"I didn't know what kind they had. I was just doing a good deed. Give me a little credit. I came at night because I wanted it to be a surprise. I have a master key to every building in this town, even The Golden Scone."

She stood back from the gray iron bars and said, "I don't believe you."

He sprang from the bunk and grabbed the bars. "Meg. I need you to be on my side here. What is it going to look like if my own daughter doesn't stand beside me? I swear I didn't do this."

She shook her head. "I can't stand by you this time. You've gone too far."

He reached through the bars and snatched her hand, his voice hoarse with emotion. "Please. I need you. By the way, where's Junior? He hasn't come to see me. I need him, too."

She wrenched her hand from his. "Sorry. He's in the mountains. Refuses to come down until this is all over. He's through with you."

Nash's hand dropped to his side. "My own children? How can this be? Don't think I didn't notice how you are dressed. Taking over are you?"

"You did it to yourself, Dad." She turned abruptly and walked away,

The cold cell closed around him. He grabbed the bars with both hands again and tried to rattle them back and forth.

To no avail.

He tried a different tactic and bellowed, "Guard!"

When finally someone appeared, he spat out, "I need my lawyer. Now!"

Disinterested, the guard looked him up and down. "I'll see what I can do."

Alone again, he said in a low, angry voice, "I'll have his badge."

While he waited his thoughts turned to money, and he grinned to himself. *I can buy anyone in this town. I won't be here long.*

As the days rolled on, Martha's staff rolled up their sleeves and began the arduous task of clean-up. Thanks to Martha's excellent forethought, the insurance paid off quickly giving her the means to start fresh.

Wolf, Polecat, Pete, and Kory did the heavy lifting, assisted intermittently by Mac, who didn't want to be stuck running the Lodge the entire time. The men rotated out giving him a break from the reservation desk.

Martha hired professionals to deal with the smoke and the women concentrated on the dining area.

She insisted on a new look, however. Nicer tables, stylish padded chairs, more plants, Chandeliers. One wall was dedicated to special soaps, exotic cosmetics, special teas, and books. Something for everyone. Even new and improved uniforms for the staff were on the agenda.

"If I'm going to do this, I want to go big," she declared.

The wedding was also on track.

Wolf never asked her directly and kept his silence during the discussions about The Golden Scone's renovations.

Martha decided to test the water with him. "The wedding is still on schedule, right Wolf?" Martha asked.

She watched his face turn from startled to jubilant.

A grin spread across his face. "Of course, Martha. I was afraid to bring it up with everything going on. You mean, you still want to go through with it? Not postpone?"

She kissed him on the cheek. "I want to marry you, Wolf. Nothing is going to stop us this time. I have a little secret to tell you."

The grin faded. "A secret?"

"Yes. While everyone else is pitching in to get the tea house up and running, Ricki took on the task of wedding planner. This way we can stay on schedule with the wedding."

"Well, I'll be. I wondered what she's been up to. Haven't seen her around here to help. Figured she must be busy with those classes or something. Remind me to give her a big hug next time I see her."

She laughed. "Will do. Now will you help unload the order of books I had delivered?"

He bowed dramatically. "At your service, madame."

While they placed the special edition books, Wolf paused and asked. "We're still getting married at the church, right?"

She straightened from the box she bent over. "Actually, no."

"Oh? Then where? Here?"

"No, the Lodge. I want to get married there and always be surrounded by the most important event of my life. On your turf, not mine."

He held a classic leather-bound book of poetry in his hand as he gazed at her face in disbelief. "The Lodge? Oh Martha. What a wonderful gesture."

She pecked him on the cheek again and continued with the task at hand.

While Wolf whistled a happy tune as he continued the assignment, Meg Nelson walked through the front door.

Martha stopped dusting the shelves. "Meg. What a nice surprise."

"Hello, friend. I hope you don't mind my stopping by unannounced. We haven't seen each other since, well…"

She dropped the cloth and moved to give Meg a hug. "It's alright, dear. You can say it. Since the fire."

Wolf put down the book he held and slipped out of the room, leaving the two women alone.

After a heart-felt embrace, Meg pulled away. "I came to apologize."

"For what? You didn't set the fire."

"But my father…"

She took Meg's hand. "Come, sit down."

When they settled at the new marble topped table with leather tufted chairs, Martha gazed at Meg. "We're friends. Have been for quite a while now. If you think for one minute I blame you in any way you can just think again."

Meg shook her head. "I should have kept a closer eye on him. Should have known he'd pull something when you announced your wedding. I feel partly responsible for this."

"You're not your father's keeper. It's not up to you to monitor him." She swept her hand around the room. "Let's concentrate on the positive. Look at this place. It's been upgraded and I love it. I can leave it in Benson's hands now. They are starting fresh, and I can move to the Lodge knowing my baby is in good hands. Don't you worry one bit. Everything is working out."

"It's beautiful, Martha. You've outdone yourself."

She frowned. "Meg, you *are* coming to the wedding, aren't you?"

Meg sighed. "I don't think it's appropriate. Your friends won't feel comfortable with Nash Nelson's daughter there."

"Nonsense. You're my friend. Everyone knows that. You'll be accepted with open arms. Of course you're coming. We're having it at the Lodge."

"Oh, that's wonderful. In the main room?"

"No, in the garden. Wolf made the garden for me and it's gorgeous. Ricki is taking care of all the arrangements and décor. I'll be as surprised as anyone else when the wedding takes place."

Meg reached for her hand. "How delicious. Ricki really has an eye for that sort of thing. I don't know her well, but I've seen her work with the classes. She makes everything very inviting."

"So, you've been to one of her classes?" Martha asked.

"No, only heard about them. I'll be happy to see the Lodge again. I haven't been up there in a long time."

Wolf interrupted carrying two cups of tea. "Thought you gals could use some refreshment."

"Hello, Wolf," Meg said. "How lovely of you. Listen, I want to..."

"Nope. Don't you even try, my girl. We're good."

Meg blushed and in a low voice, said, "Thanks, Wolf."

"Enjoy your tea. Benson is having a hard time with a screwdriver, think I'll go assist." He turned and headed back to the kitchen.

"You've got a winner there, for sure, Martha," Meg said.

"You don't have to tell me. I can't think for the life of me why I waited so long."

Meg shrugged. "Life is funny, isn't it? But don't dwell on that. You're doing it now, so the future is in front of you."

"And you, Meg? What about your future? I never hear you talk of a boyfriend. Anyone you're interested in?"

Meg put her cup down. "I'm too busy. Now with dad...well, I really have my hands full. No time for a personal life."

"But surely you'll bring a plus one to the wedding," Martha said.

"I don't think so. Don't know who that would be."

"Well, leave it open for now. Maybe someone will come to mind. Just know it's an option."

"Where are you going on your honeymoon? Somewhere exotic?"

The room echoed with Martha's amused laughter. "Oh dear, we haven't gotten that far yet. I have no idea if we will even go on a honeymoon. To get to this threshold, the actual wedding is a milestone for us. One step at a time, I think."

Meg joined in the laughter. "Well, you should think of it at some point. What's a wedding without a honeymoon?"

"It's something to think about for sure. Any suggestions?"

"Maybe back to where you met?"

A look of nostalgia passed over her. "Spain," she whispered.

"Ah, that sounds romantic. You'll have to tell me that story someday," Meg said.

Distracted, she didn't answer at first as the memory of their first kiss on the back of the train overtook her. "What dear? Oh yes, I'd love to tell you all about that day."

Meg stood. "Not today, though. You have a tea house to finish, and I have an office to run. I'll get out of your way."

"Come back for the grand opening, okay?"

"I wouldn't miss it," Meg replied.

She walked her friend to the door. "By the way. I hate to ask, but have they set a date for the trial?"

Meg frowned and shook her head. "Not that I know of. Could be a while. It'll do my dad good to cool his heels in a jail cell for a while. Make him think."

"Or make him want revenge," Martha added.

CHAPTER FORTY-SIX

A DARK SHADOW THREATENS THE NEWFOUND JOY WHILE AN ALLY PLEDGES FEALTY ~

The grand opening for The Golden Scone was set for two days before the wedding. The forecast was perfect, the weather divine. Martha, however, was dizzy with the swirl of activity.

Ricki came by the tea house one day, with a few questions to finish off the wedding planning.

"I don't know if I can do this," Martha told her. "It's too much all at once."

"How can you say that? The staff did an amazing job; the tea house is better than before and ready to open. The wedding details are complete. All you have to do is walk down the aisle. Your dress is at the Lodge; Wolf's tuxedo is too. There's nothing left to do," Ricki smiled at Martha. "You're a worry wart, and I think you've just got the jitters. Perfectly understandable for a new bride."

"You're right. I *am* a bit anxious. With all that's happened, I feel as though something is going to ruin it all at the last minute."

"Not with Kory and me at the helm of everything. We've planned for every scenario. You're covered."

The two women clasped hands.

"I don't know what I'd do without you, Ricki. You're a godsend."

"Happy to help. I've had a blast."

Wolf walked through the front door making the little bell ring merrily and smiled at Ricki. "Good to see you, girl. Everything under control?"

"Yes, sir. Had a few little last-minute questions for the bride. Everything is checked off my list now. We're ready."

"Glad to hear it. I can't believe tomorrow is the day for the opening, then two days later I marry the love of my life." A broad grin spread across his face as he beamed at Martha. Then suddenly, the light in his eyes dimmed. "One thing I think you both should know. Nash is out of jail on bond."

Martha gasped. "Out of jail? How..."

"Someone from Bad Axe posted his bond. He's out until the trial next month," he continued.

Ricki's face hardened as she spoke, "I suppose he bribed someone with money. His children wouldn't bail him out. I'll tell Kory. We need to keep an eye on him."

Martha's knees gave way.

Wolf caught her and settled her in a chair. "Please don't worry. He'll have twenty-four-hour surveillance. I'll make sure of that. He's not going to ruin the opening *or* the wedding."

She brushed a lock of hair from her eyes. "I just know how angry he must be. Meg says he swears he didn't do it even with all the evidence. His own children don't believe him. If he can burn my tea house what else is he capable of?"

Ricki looked at Wolf. "I think it's time for a rest. I'll take her to the house."

"No," Martha said. "I want to go the Lodge." She looked pleadingly to Wolf. "Will you drive me? I'll feel safer there."

"Of course. It's more peaceful in the mountains. You'll rest better."

Ricki chimed in, "Just don't peek at the garden."

A weak smile was all she could manage. "I promise."

His arm wound protectively around her shoulders as Wolf led her outside to the car.

She pecked him on the cheek, and whispered, "I always feel safe with you. I can't wait to move to the Lodge permanently."

$$\sim\sim\sim*\sim\sim\sim$$

Ricki watched them drive off; relieved Martha made the call to go to the Lodge. "No better place for her to be right now."

"Who are you talking about?"

Ricki jumped at the sound of Kory's voice behind her. "Oh, I didn't hear you come in. It's Martha. Wolf is taking her to the Lodge to get some rest. She's pretty upset."

He frowned but kissed her cheek softly. "What's happened now?"

"Bad news. I was just coming to tell you. Did the refrigerator fit in the space? I know Benson worried it was too big."

"Yes, yes, it fit fine. What bad news?"

"Nash is out on bond."

He let out a long slow whistle. "That *is* bad news. How did he manage that?"

"Someone in Bad Axe is the word on the street. I'm sure it was a bribe."

"No doubt."

"I offered to take Martha to the house, but she wanted to go to the Lodge. Actually, I think it's the best idea. Harder for Nash to get to her there."

Kory swung his leg over a chair and leaned on the back of it. "We need more security. From what I've heard about his anger issues he might try something at the opening or even the wedding."

"I'm afraid of that, too. Think I'll walk down the block and talk to Meg. Get her take on the situation." She started towards the door.

Kory jumped from the chair and intercepted her. "Hold on. Not a good idea. Nash might be there. You know he's not going to let go of his business easily. It's too dangerous."

"I know, but Meg has a front row seat to his demeanor right now."

"Why not call her. Ask her to meet you here. I'd feel better. I'll be in the kitchen with the other guys if you need us."

Ricki thought a moment then nodded. "You're right, it will be better here. I hope she's open to talking with me. We've only met once." She pulled out her cell, googled the office number and pressed call.

The receptionist answered reciting the standard greeting.

Ricki asked for Meg and waited for the receptionist to connect them.

She glanced at Kory when Meg answered. "Hi, Meg. This is Ricki Sheridan. We've met once before. I hope you remember me. I'm planning Martha's wedding." After Meg acknowledged their meeting, Ricki continued. "I wonder if we could talk. I'd
love to treat you to a special tea and scone if you could break away."

She glanced again at Kory and nodded to him. "Great! Thirty minutes, then?"

Kory smiled as she hung up the phone. "See? That was easy enough. I'll tell Agnes to prepare an order. You can pick out a table, maybe over in the corner. I'll keep everyone out."

"Thanks, Kory."

The minutes passed quickly and soon Meg arrived. She didn't smile but was pleasant as Ricki shook her hand.

"Thanks for meeting with me. I know we don't know each other well, but we have a friend in common. Martha."

Meg sat down where Ricki indicated. "Is this about her?"

"In a way, yes."

Ivy came through the kitchen door with a tray, placed the cups and scones and left.

"This is lovely, thanks so much," Meg said as she reached for a scone. "I love this place and come here as often as I can."

Ricki took a sip of tea and set the cup down gingerly. "Martha has done wonders with this place. But now, Benson is taking over after the wedding. She and Wolf want time together. In fact, it's kind of what I wanted to talk to you about. Wolf took Martha back to the Lodge a little while ago. She heard the news that your father is out on bond. It upset her greatly. She fears he'll try to sabotage the opening or even the wedding. I wanted your opinion."

Meg paused, then said, "You get right to the point, don't you?"

"She's my friend, Meg. She deserves to be happy. I don't want this hanging over her head. Can you tell me what your father's demeanor is at this point?"

Meg sat back with the teacup in her hand. "I'm concerned, too. He's in a black mood. I've taken over his office and he's not happy about it. He's brooding. Has a look of hate in his eyes. I can't get my brother to come down from the mountain to help me out. I'm worried he'll do something stupid."

Ricki took up the conversation, "I will share this with you. Kory and Wolf have put in motion a team of security people. We're not taking any chances on him ruining the opening or the wedding. I wanted to give you a heads up. I hope you aren't angry."

"No, not at all. In fact, I'm relieved. Martha asked me to come to the wedding. I hesitated because I didn't want everyone to worry us Nelson's would cause trouble."

Ricki waved her hand. "No need to worry about that. We trust you. It's just your father..."

"No need to explain. I know only too well."

"So you're coming to the wedding then?"

Meg nodded. "Yes, I'll be there."

"What about the opening tomorrow? You are coming, right?"

Meg sighed. "That's kind of a different story. After all, my dad set the fire."

"We all want you there, Meg. Everyone knows this is completely on him."

Neither woman spoke for a moment and continued to enjoy the scones and tea.

Meg looked around the room. "Martha has outdone herself this time. It's better than it was before. I especially like the wall of books, soaps, and teas. It's a great addition."

Ricki agreed, "She has a flare for elegance for sure. So, can we count on you for tomorrow?"

"Yes, I'll come. Thank you."

CHAPTER FORTY-SEVEN

SHE COMES ARMED WITH SIGHS AND SIDE-EYES ~

Martha noticed Mac's surprised expression as she and Wolf walked through the front door. She laughed at his frantic look as if she'd walked in on a secret. "Don't worry, Mac. I'm not going to peek. I only came here to rest up in my room."

His face relaxed as she reassured him. "Oh. Good. I've been told to guard the garden with my life. Are you ill?"

Wolf answered, "No, just got some bad news. You might as well know, too. Nash bonded out of jail. He's on the loose. So be extra vigilant."

"Will do, boss. Need more security?" Mac asked.

"Let me get her settled, then we'll talk." He guided Martha up the stairs.

Relaxed in his embrace she voiced her guilt, "You know, I should have stayed in town. This was a lot of trouble for you and I'm feeling better. Probably shouldn't have jumped the gun. I'm sorry."

He took the room key from her hand and unlocked the door. "Nonsense. This is the perfect idea. Peace and quiet. We have a hectic few days ahead of us. Rest is what you need."

The scent of roses filled the air as they entered the room. Wolf made sure fresh roses arrived every day even if she wasn't there to enjoy them.

She drank in the aroma. "You're so good to me, Wolf. I don't deserve you."

"It's the other way around, my dear." The curtains stood open letting the sunshine fill the room. He closed them, settled her on the bed, pulled her pumps off and gently laid her back on the plump pillows. "Now, is there anything else I can do before I leave you to rest?"

The darkened room, the calming perfume of roses, and Wolf's gentle touch made her sigh with contentment. "Just the quilt, please. I might get chilly."

He reached for the soft pink, hand quilted comforter, but drew back when she popped straight up from the bed.

"Oh no! I forgot. I can't rest. Mother is due to arrive today. We have to get to the airport," she exclaimed.

He picked up the quilt, gently nudged her back down on the pillows, and said, "I'll go. You stay here and rest. After all, you will need your strength to deal with your mother on top of everything else. I've got the flight information, so don't worry."

"Oh Wolf, I can't ask you to do all that alone. It's not fair. You should be getting rest as well."

"Happy to do it. Dame Buford liked me once. I'll use all my charm and woo her back. Just wait and see."

She giggled, yawned, and closed her eyes as he tiptoed out of the room.

$$\sim\sim\sim*\sim\sim\sim$$

Wolf turned into the airport, confident Mac secured the necessary security for the next few days, and Martha rested comfortably at the Lodge. Now the only thing left to conquer was Dame Buford.

After parking, he marched toward the terminal and spotted her instantly. The plane had landed ahead of time. She stood looking around, eyes big, a panicked look etched on her face. A man dressed as a butler was beside her with a very confused look on his face.

He waved as he hurried forward. "Here, Mrs. Buford. I'm here."

The stricken look disappeared only to be replaced by disappointment. "Where's Martha? I expressly asked her to pick me up," disapproval dripped from her voice.

"She intended to, but a situation arose. So here I am." He decided to ignore her snub.

"Is she alright? She's not ill, I hope. This climate isn't..."

He cut her off. "She's fine. Resting at the Lodge. She'll be fine by the time we arrive. Let's get your bags. The sooner we get out of here, the sooner you can see her." He took her elbow. "Do you have your baggage claim.?"

She looked toward the properly dressed man who produced it. "This is Jenkins, by butler. I couldn't have made this trip without him. I hope you have accommodations for him, as well."

Wolf took charge, gave Jenkins a nod, and said, "Of course." He took the baggage claim from him and led the way.

Minutes later, they were in the car headed home, Mrs. Buford in front, Jenkins in back.

He chitchatted with her on the long drive. At first she hesitated, gave short answers, and stared out the window with a frown on her face.

Jenkins sat in silence in the back seat.

Halfway home, he'd told a few jokes and noticed the icy demeanor fall away, and if not a smile, the frown had disappeared. *Ah, the old Wolf Kelley charm is working.*

By the time they reached the Lodge, her original approval of him returned. They'd talked of Spain, the train ride, and she admitted she'd like him right off.

He watched her take in the view of the Lodge as they approached and heard her whispered review.

"It's beautiful. I can see why Martha wanted to stay here."

"We have a beautiful room all ready for you. The wedding will be held here at the Lodge, so we arranged for you to stay here," he said.

"But I wanted to see the tea house. She has a house in town, doesn't she?"

"Yes. The opening is tomorrow, so you will see it then." He parked in front. "Let's go in. Mac will get your luggage."

He opened the car door and helped her out, then ushered her into the Lodge.

Jenkins hesitated and hung back as Wolf took over.

"Mac, will you retrieve Dame Buford's bags, please?"

"Yes, sir! Pleased to meet you ma'am. If there is anything you need, just call on me." He hurried out.

She nodded at him taking in the view of the magnificent great room. "It's breath-taking."

"Thank you," Wolf answered.

Mac introduced himself to Jenkins and together they wrangled the bags.

"Mother!" Martha hurried down the stairs.

Mrs. Buford swiveled. "Martha. There you are."

They embraced.

"How was your trip? I know you must be tired. Your room is ready for you."

"Actually, I was looking forward to some tea at your tea house, but here I am at the Lodge," she answered, sarcasm in her voice.

"Not to worry. I only have to snap my fingers, and you can have a sample from the tea house. Even down to the scones." She turned to Mac who settled the bags at the foot of the stairs. "Can you ask Otis to whip up afternoon tea?"

"Will do."

Martha took her arm and guided her to the dining room.

Jenkins followed behind.

"Lovely," Dame Burford approved.

Otis was prompt and even served everything with an Old English tea set.

Jenkins took the tray from him, set it on the table and guided his mistress to a chair, taking his position behind her.

"Ah, just like home," she observed.

"Tomorrow you'll see the real thing. It's the grand opening after the fire," Martha declared.

"Such a terrible thing to happen. What is the world coming to?"

"We won't try to solve that right now. Tell me about your trip."

After Dame Buford sufficiently complained about every aspect of the flight, Martha cut her off and asked, "Are you ready to see your room?"

Mac and Wolf carried her bags upstairs and Martha led her mother to the room at the end of the hall.

Dame Buford let out a little gasp as she surveyed the room.

Dark wood paneling set the tone of Old English. An ornate fireplace with a mantle- piece that exhibited an elegant clock served as the centerpiece. The large bed covered in a crisp white lace coverlet added charm and a homespun feel. Roses touched every part of the room in a very proper English way.

"Oh my. I feel as though I never left home. Really, it's gorgeous."

Wolf smiled. "I'm glad you like it. Martha outdid herself, I think."

A slight smile graced Dame Buford's face but quickly disappeared. "She knows me well. I will rest comfortably here. Now, if you don't mind, I'd like a moment alone with my daughter."

"Certainly. I'll show Jenkins to his room. And Mac, we've got things to do downstairs," Wolf ordered.

After the men left, the older woman turned to her daughter. "You don't expect me to live here, do you? You will see to it I return to my own home in England?"

CHAPTER FORTY-EIGHT

THE DEVIL PROWLS WHILE LOVE BEGINS TO WHISPER ~

Wolf motioned Mac to follow him into his office. He poured himself a whiskey and offered one to Mac, who declined. "Now, who can we reach out to for more security?"

Mac sat down across from his boss. "I know some guys. I can get on the phone. They won't do it for free, though."

"Naturally, I'll pay them, but I need to be sure they aren't some of Nash's stooges. You know he throws money around like nobody's business when he wants something. Can you be sure they'll do the job and not sabotage us?"

"These particular guys have been burned by Nash Nelson, so you don't have to worry about that." He stood and stretched.

"Hurt your back with those bags, Mac?" Wolf asked.

"No, didn't sleep all that well last night. I'm fine."

Wolf stayed in his office chair swirling his drink. "I'll get Kory to spell you tonight. I need you on top of your game for the next few days. Didn't mean to push you so hard. This Nelson thing has me spooked. Can't let him get the upper hand."

"Thanks, boss, but you don't have to worry about me. I'll be fine and won't let you down." He turned and left the room.

Wolf studied the scene out of the office window. When he built the Lodge he made sure the window in his office faced the mountains. The power of the scenery always rejuvenated him, kept him balanced and feeling strong. He felt it now. *Okay Nash Nelson, do your worst. I'm ready for you. Martha is mine and I won't let you ruin any of this for us.*

$$\sim\sim\sim^*\sim\sim\sim$$

Nash Nelson paced his office, fists clenching and unclenching, trying to restrain the anger building inside his head. His own children turned their backs on him. Meg took over the business, and his son wouldn't come down from the mountains.

The trial was set for a month from now. Plenty of time for him to figure out a way to exonerate himself. On his mind at the moment was revenge on Wolf and Martha. *I've got to sabotage the opening and the wedding.*

The door opened and Meg walked in. "Dad, what are you doing here? The court order says you can't be here until after your trial."

"I don't care what the court order says. This is my business and I'll be here any damn time I want to be."

"Do I have to call security?" she threatened.

"You'd do that on your own father?"

"In a heartbeat. You can't get out of this one, dad."

He dug into his right-hand pants pocket and pulled out his car keys. "Fine. I'm outta here." He pushed by her, knocking her into the wall.

Liz said nothing as he barreled past her and out the front door, got in his car and sped off.

He didn't know where he was headed. Just drove until the anger subsided to a dull roar in his ears. When he finally had control of his faculties an hour later, he realized where he'd ended up. Right in front of Wolf's Den Lodge.

He quickly turned the car around and headed down the hill to a seldom used side road, maneuvered the vehicle behind a stand of trees, and waited. The Lodge was visible from this vantage point, but he was sure no one could see him. *Now I wait and hatch my plan. Wolf Kelley isn't going to beat me.*

$$\sim\sim\sim*\sim\sim\sim$$

Meg took up pacing where her father left off. She decided to buzz Liz at the receptionist desk. "Did you see where he went?"

At the negative reply, she finally sat down. "What do I do now?" she said to the empty room.

After a few moments, she picked up the telephone and dialed the Lodge. "Yes, Mac, hi. This is Meg Nelson. Is Wolf around? I need to speak to him."

She only had to wait a moment.

"Hello, Wolf. Meg Nelson here." She hesitated, then continued. "It's my dad. He just stormed out of here. I don't know where he went, but I know he took the car. He might be headed in your direction. Or to Martha's house. I've never seen him so angry. He feels betrayed."

She listened a minute, then replied, "Thanks. Just thought I should give you a heads up."

After the conversation with Wolf, she decided to make a visit to the tea house. "Surely he didn't go there, but I can't take any chances."

Liz nodded to her as she explained where she was going. "Call me if he shows up here again."

She went around to the back of the tea house, figuring they'd be working there.

Kory greeted her. "Hi there, Meg. What brings you by? The opening is tomorrow."

"Yes, I know. I spoke to Wolf a minute ago and thought I should warn you, too. My dad stormed out of the office like he had a purpose and I'm afraid he might make more trouble."

He stopped what he was doing and gave her his full attention. "I haven't seen him. There's five of us working today. I think we can handle him."

"Wolf said Martha was at the Lodge, so I'm not worried about her. But some of the staff might be at the house. He could decide to make havoc there."

Kory nodded. "Benson is there. I'll call and make sure all is well. You say he stormed out? Did anyone see what direction he went?"

"No, Liz saw him get in his car but couldn't tell where he was headed."

"Well, you've warned Wolf. Martha is safe. I'll check on the house. You did good. Thanks for the warning. We truly appreciate it, Meg."

"Can I have a sneak peek at the dining room? The kitchen looks amazing," she said.

"Of course, right this way."

While she gushed over the décor Kory called Benson. "You're sure he's not lurking around somewhere?"

Assured Benson had everything under control, he turned back to Meg. "It's beautiful isn't it. Better than before."

"Absolutely. Martha is a wonder."

The front door swung open, and Polecat walked in hidden behind a huge bouquet of carnations. "Where do you want these, Kory? Wolf outdid himself this time."

"Oh, just put them down anywhere. I'll let Martha decide when she gets here in the morning."

Polecat said, "No. they're too heavy to move again. Let's choose now."

Kory looked at Meg and said, "Meg, give us a woman's point of view. Where is the best place?"

Polecat peeked around the bouquet. "Oh hello, Miss Nelson. I didn't see you there."

"Hi Polecat. I can't imagine you could see anything with that bunch of flowers in front of you." She turned to Kory. "Really, I don't think I'm qualified to choose a spot."

Kory laughed. "You're more qualified than me or Polecat. So pick a place before he drops from exhaustion."

She looked around. "Well, at first glance, over there by the bookcase on the table in the corner."

Polecat said, "I can't see where you're pointing. Someone guide me."

Meg took his arm and showed him where to set them down.

They all stood back to gaze at the display.

"Perfect," Kory said.

"I think you're right, Kory." Meg said. "It's just what that corner needed. I hope Martha approves."

"She'll love it," Kory answered. "Well, I need to finish in the kitchen. Time is running out. See you tomorrow, Meg?"

"I wouldn't miss it."

Kory hesitated, then asked, "Polecat, do you mind going to the hardware store? I need a couple of picture hangers. You know the ones that won't stick to the walls permanently."

"On it. Can I walk you out, Miss Nelson?"

Meg looked up at the tall, handsome man they called Polecat. "I'd like that. But only if you call me Meg."

"You got it. Meg," Polecat agreed. "I just remembered I don't know where the hardware store is. I'm new to this area."

"Oh, it's a couple of doors down from my office. I'll show you," she offered.

As they walked Meg conjured up the courage to ask about his name. "By the way, Polecat is an unusual name. Where did it come from?"

He laughed. "Well, it's not my real name, of course. Got the nickname in the Air Force. My buddies think I'm like a weasel. Getting' in and out of things by the skin of my teeth. I guess I have a knack for the behavior."

"Okay, so are you going to tell me your real name?"

He shrugged. "Do I have to?"

"Not if you don't want to. I promise, though, not to tell anyone."

He sighed. "You are the only one I would willingly tell it to. It's Alistair. My mother named me for her father. I hate it. I made everyone call me Al until Polecat stuck."

She repeated the name. "Alistair. It has a nice ring to it. Very distinguished. Like an aristocrat."

"You think so? I always thought it sounded nerdy."

She went on. "Alistair Robinson. Sounds like a poet or something. Do you write?"

His guffaw rang down the street. "You've got to be kidding. No, I don't have that talent."

This time she shrugged. "Too bad. Your name alone would sell."

They arrived at the hardware store.

"Here it is," Meg stated.

He looked up at the sign. "Hardware Store. Catchy name."

She laughed. "Well, Dave doesn't have much imagination. Anyway, this is where I leave you. My office is a couple of doors down. Nelson Enterprises. We don't get fancy in Murphy. Straight and to the point."

"Well, thanks for showing me where it is." He hesitated, ducked his head, and in a sort of stutter, asked, "Are you going to the wedding?"

"Why, yes, I am. I hear you are a groomsman."

"Yeah, not sure I know what to do but stand there. But I'd do anything for Wolf."

"You'll do fine." She turned to go. "See ya there, I guess."

"Wait. I was wondering. I don't have a date. I'd like it if you'd go with me." His eyes grew wide, and he flushed with embarrassment. "Unless, of course, you already have a date."

She turned back to him and smiled. "As a matter of fact I don't. I'd be happy to go with you, Alistair."

"You would?"

"Yes. Do you want to pick me up here at my office? My house is out of town in the opposite direction of the Lodge."

His shoulders relaxed and the blush faded. "Yes, I can do that."

They discussed the time and parted ways.

She stopped at her door and waved at him as he went inside the store.

"Well, now," she whispered to herself. "How about that?"

CHAPTER FORTY-NINE

VILLAINY SLEEPS AND JOY TAKES UP THE CROWN ~

Martha simply stared at her mother. "What do you mean will I see you get home to England? Do you think I'll hold you prisoner here?" She waved her hand around the room. "You said you love the décor, that it reminded you of home."

Dame Buford heaved a heavy sigh. "Daughter. You surprise me. Propriety demands I remain polite. Yes, this is all well and good. You made a splendid effort. I'll be very comfortable here, but it is not home. I don't intend to stay longer than necessary."

"I understand, but I hope you'll stay long enough for us to show you around Murphy and the surrounding places. There is so much to see, so much to do. The people are very friendly."

Another sigh from the older woman. "And what of your honeymoon? Do you want me around for that? You haven't said where you're going or for how long. I don't intend to stay until you return."

She lowered herself into a wing-back chair. "We're not going on a honeymoon right away. We'll go later when we have everything running smoothly. We plan to go back to Spain, where we met. We can stop and see you on the way back."

"I see."

"You still don't approve of Wolf. What have you got against him?"

Dame Buford sat gingerly on the edge of the chair near the bed, smoothing the pristine coverlet. "Nothing specific. It's just that he's taken you away from me. Lord knows I'm too old to make this trip again. So with you all the way over here, I'll probably die alone."

"Oh Mother, for pity sake. How you go on. You're a long way from dying. Wolf and I will make the trip at least once a year. I won't abandon you."

"You say that now, but your life will…"

The clock on the mantle sounded the hour with a charming tiny bell sound, reminding Martha her mother needed rest. "We'll talk of this after dinner. You need to rest. Come let me help you."

Her mother surrendered to her machinations.

When she was settled beneath a soft quilt, she smiled up at her daughter. "Thank you my dear. Will you call me when it's time for dinner?"

"Certainly. You need a good two hours of rest. I'll knock softly to let you know it's time to rise."

She tiptoed out of the room and closed the door gently. Her mother's eyes were closed, but something told her she wouldn't go gently into slumber.

Downstairs she found Mac and Wolf with heads together deep in conversation.

"What are you two cooking up now?" she asked.

Wolf greeted her with a cautious smile. "You might as well know."

"Know what?"

"Nash broke his court order. He showed up at his office which is a violation. Meg phoned to warn us he stormed out of his office when she threatened to call police. He got in his car and sped off, angry. I've talked to Kory and Benson. Kory is keeping watch at the tea house and Benson at the townhouse. Mac hired a few good men to keep watch on the Lodge and surrounding area. I think we have it covered."

She paled. "Will that man never cease?"

He crossed the room to peck her on the cheek. "I didn't want to tell you, but it wouldn't be fair. You need to be cautious. We've got it handled though." He brushed a strand of hair from her eyes. "Is your mother all settled in?"

"Yes, but she's worried we won't let her go home. This is all foreign to her. But I'll handle Mother."

One of Mac's henchmen barreled through the door.

Mac looked up and asked, "What is it? Did you spot something?"

The stocky man, gun in holster, nodded. "Yes, a car on that old side road to the right of the Lodge. Do you know it?"

Wolf and Mac answered unanimously, "Yes."

Wolf continued, "Describe the car. Is anyone inside?"

"Yes, a lone man. The car is a red sports car. I couldn't tell the make. Thought I'd better let you know before I confronted him. He's just sitting there."

"Sounds like Nash's Mazda RX-7. Don't do anything, just watch him. If he makes a move surround him and let me know. I'm gonna call the police. It'll take them about an hour to get here. Everyone on high alert." He headed for his office.

The man nodded at Wolf and went back outside.

Martha followed Wolf.

After he alerted the police, he settled back in his chair and looked at Martha. "Don't worry, we've enough men to handle everything."

"I know, but Mother is here. I hate putting her in danger."

He leaned forward. "Everything will be fine. The men will see to it. Let's call Kory and Benson and let them know."

She nodded.

"Kory is on his way up here and Benson is holding vigil at the house. Polecat stayed at the tea house. All bases are covered." He stood and went to his sideboard drawer, drew out a pistol, and strapped it on.

"No, Wolf!" Martha cried.

"Now, my dear. It's fine. I'm not going anywhere. The police will be here shortly, and the guys have the property covered. I can't in good conscious *not* prepare for the worst with you and your mother here. Nothing can make me leave you alone. But I must be prepared." He walked around the desk and circled his arm around her shoulders.

She relaxed a bit. "Oh, I thought you were going out there to confront him."

"No. I've been shot once. Don't want to go through that again. I'm here to protect my women." He gave a half-hearted laugh.

She chuckled. "You sound like something out of an old western."

Mac knocked on the door and opened it slowly, walkie-talkie in hand. "Just an update, boss. He's still sitting there. Hasn't moved. Hasn't gotten out of the car."

"Good. The police are on their way. So is Kory. We just need to keep an eye on him until they get here."

Mac glanced at the gun on his hip. "Want me to arm up?"

"Maybe just a gun under the registration desk. I don't think you need one on your hip. Might scare someone who happens to walk in."

"Got it."

When Mac left Martha looked at Wolf. "Do you really think he'll do something"

"Not really. He likes to make a big splash. If I read him right, he'll wait until tomorrow or the wedding. He's violating his court order by coming so close to the Lodge, so best case they will haul him in for that and we won't have to worry."

"Do we have to sit here and wait? Isn't there something else we can do?" she asked.

"Well, we can't go to the garden, but we can sit in the dining room and have coffee. Sound good?"

He led her out of the office and nodded at Mac. "Having coffee in the dining room."

"Gotcha. I'll let you know if something happens."

It wasn't easy waiting on something to happen. She watched the dining room door afraid Nash would bust in at any moment. The coffee didn't soother her. Actually made her more jittery. *Should have had tea.*

And then she heard it.

Pop, pop, pop.

Wolf stood abruptly.

"Is that gunfire?" she asked.

He nodded, placed a hand on her shoulder, placed another hand on the gun butt.

They waited.

More gunfire. More waiting.

Forty-five minutes later, Mac poked his head through the swinging door. "Police chief is here."

"Have him come in here. Never looks good to the guests to have cops in the main room."

The chief entered with a smile on his face. "We nabbed him, Wolf. He tried to shoot it out with our officers, but we have a couple of sharp shooters. Got him in the arm. He didn't put up much of a fight after that. He's back in custody for violating the court order, assault on officers, and weapons charges. Won't get out before the trial now."

Wolf stood and shook the chief's hand. "Thank goodness. You boys did a great job. What with the re-opening tomorrow and the wedding in two days, we sure didn't need this added worry."

Martha whispered her thanks, "Yes, thank you so much."

"Glad to be of service."

Wolf grinned at him. "You will be at the wedding, right?"

"Wouldn't miss it."

Kory came in breathing hard. "They caught him? Is that what I'm hearing?"

"Yep," said Wolf.

Kory's body relaxed. "Great day in the morning. Good work, Chief."

The two men shook hands.

Wolf offered the chief a cup of coffee.

"Thanks, but I have other business to attend to. Maybe next time."

Martha spoke up, "I hope there won't be a next time. Not this kind anyway."

After the chief left, they settled at the table for more coffee, but Otis bustled in and shooed them out.

"Dinner will be ready soon. I need to make sure all is prepared for Martha's mother for her enjoyment. Shoo. Shoo." He waved his hands at them.

$$\sim\sim\sim*\sim\sim\sim$$

An hour later, Martha tiptoed to her mother's room and knocked softly.

"I'm up. Come on in."

Dame Buford sat before her dressing table perfectly coifed and dressed in a lovely lavender frock.

"Did you get any rest at all, Mother?"

"Why, yes I did. However, I peeked outside a while ago and saw police cars all over the place. Do you want to tell me what's happened?"

"Nothing for you to worry about. Let's go down to dinner."

Otis out did himself. The main dining table was now covered in white laced tablecloth. Candelabra adorned the center of the table with candles lit. Fine China marked each place setting.

"Oh, how lovely," Dame Buford exclaimed. "But where is Jenkins?"

Otis stood to the side of the door, beaming. "He's happily ensconced in the kitchen with the others. I hope I have everything right. Agnes helped me as usual."

"It's perfect, Otis," Martha assured him.

Wolf seated the two women.

Ricki appeared at the last minute and Kory seated her.

Otis brought course after course of the finest English cuisine ever served at Wolf's Den Lodge.

They all settled into the ambience and enjoyed the company and the meal in a quiet. amiable atmosphere.

"This is just what the doctor ordered," Wolf said. "We won't have this luxury tomorrow!"

CHAPTER FIFTY

FORTUNE DID SHINE AND THE STARS ALIGNED ~

The day dawned with a promise of success and perfection in the air. A light breeze swayed the tops of the trees only slightly, giving relief to the expected high temperatures.

Martha stood in front of the window, dressed in a smart pink frock with a handkerchief hem, and watched the peaceful scene relaxed in the knowledge Nash Nelson could not wreak havoc on the grand opening of The Golden Scone. The halls bustled with the staff going about their morning chores and she smiled knowing at the tea house a similar scene played out.

A knock sounded.

Wolf filled the doorframe dressed in a white shirt and bolo tie, unruly black hair slicked back neatly.

His intake of breath convinced her she chose the right dress.

"You're beautiful." He offered his arm. "Ready?" he asked.

"Yes," she said, her breath catching in her throat.

Together they stopped at her mother's room.

Dame Buford, dressed in a smart blue suit, remarked, "Well, I must say you make a striking couple."

Wolf beamed.

"Thank you, Mother. Are you ready?"

The three descended the stairs where Mac greeted them with a tray of coffee cups.

"We plan to have breakfast at the tea house, Mac," said Martha.

"I know, but it's a long drive. I thought you could use the pick-me-up." He set the tray down on the rustic coffee table.

"How thoughtful," Martha replied. "We have a few minutes, so let's enjoy a little peace and quiet before we head out."

"Where's Kory and Ricki? I only see three cups here," Wolf asked.

"They left early. Wanted to make sure all was ready so you wouldn't have anything to worry about," Mac explained.

"Everyone is so nice," Dame Buford said in a soft voice.

"One of the reasons I like it here, Mother."

$$\sim\sim\sim*\sim\sim\sim$$

The ride to Murphy found everyone laughing, enjoying the scenery, and pointing out items of interest to Dame Buford.

All except Martha.

She sat silent in the second row of seats in the small van gazing out the window.

Wolf installed Martha's mother in the front seat with him, so she had a good view of everything.

Mac claimed the back seat.

The Lodge was shut down for the occasion. They'd made sure no guests were booked for the week.

Agnes and Otis followed behind the van in his not quite new Volkswagen Jetta.

This day, looked forward to by so many, left no one out.

They pulled up on the side street to the cheers of nearly the whole town, but made room as Wolf helped Mrs. Buford and Martha from the vehicle.

A new sign hung above the door, a surprise to Martha, a gift from the staff. Old English gold lettering surrounded by a dashing array of colorful flowers.

"It's stunning," Martha gasped.

Dame Buford nodded in agreement.

The crowd parted and she walked arm in arm with her mother on one side and Wolf on the other.

An array of flowers from well-wishers filled the room, and the perfume permeated the air.

Her gaze automatically landed on the colossal arrangement by the bookcase. "How did you ever get it in here?"

Ricki's laugh sounded beside her. "Polecat managed it. Meg was here yesterday and chose the perfect spot by the bookcase. I hope it meets with your satisfaction. If you want to move it I'm sure we can find a few brave men."

"Oh no. It's perfect right there. I wonder who sent it?" She lifted the card and read, "To the lady who stole my heart and amazes me with her brilliance every day. With all my love, Wolf."

Silence fell over the room as tears slipped down her cheeks. She turned to face him; his head ducked in embarrassment. "Thank you so much. You're wonderful," she whispered.

At that moment Agnes came through the kitchen door pushing a cart with a large cake. "Time for the celebrations to begin!"

The intimate moment interrupted, the room filled with conversation and slaps on the back, well-wishes, a bottle of champagne, and the crowd pushing through the front door.

The morning sped by and soon it was time for lunch. Folks came and went all day, and she felt the support full tilt from the community.

She glanced at her mother after they'd finished their lunch and noted how tired she looked. "Wolf, I think it's time for Mother to rest. I can take her to the townhouse. She can rest there. After all, we have another couple of busy days ahead of us."

He agreed but insisted on walking them down the block.

After a proper goodbye and thank you to her staff, they left with Dame Buford in tow.

As they sauntered slowly toward the townhouse, Martha observed, "It's been an exceptional day. I feel confident now leaving the staff in charge. I'll not worry one little bit about the tea house."

Wolf nodded.

Mrs. Buford spoke softly, "I must say, you have made a lot of friends here. They all seem very devoted to you and the business. Changes my perspective on things. I thought you were stuck in a wild country, but it comforts me to see the support you have."

"Mother, you will never know how much that means to me."

CHAPTER FIFTY-ONE

ONCE AGAIN, WITH STARS ALIGHT, FOREVER WE BEGIN ~

Two days later Martha's wedding day dawned with a pure blue cloudless sky. She sat alone in front of the dressing table trying to calm the butterflies dancing in her stomach. *It's here. The day I wed the man I've loved all this time.*

A quick glance out of the window reassured her the day was perfect for a garden wedding. *I can't wait to see the garden. I know Ricki did a splendid job.*

A whisper and a knock at the door caused the early morning daydream to vanish as reality surfaced.

"Martha, it's me Ricki. I'm here with your dress. Are you ready?"

She went to the door. "Come in, dear. I'm more than ready."

Ricki strolled into the room holding the dress sheathed in a cloth cover. "It was delivered yesterday. All the last-minute details are finished and it's ready for you to put on. I can't wait to see it on you."

"Did they include the short veil, as well? I know it's silly, but I want to feel as though this is my first marriage." She paused, and whispered, "I want Wolf to feel that, too."

"Yes, the veil is with the dress. I peeked. It's gorgeous. Let's try it on."

"Shouldn't I finish my hair first?"

Ricki nodded. "Anything you want, my friend." She hung the dress on the hook over the closet door.

While they worked together on her fancy updo, Ricki made conversation. "Wolf is going to be bowled over when he sees you in the dress. The off-white suits your complexion so well."

"I can't wait to see Wolf. He's so handsome when he dresses up. Not that he isn't handsome otherwise, but he's so shy about dress clothes it makes him even more appealing."

Ricki pinned the last pin. "Perfect, now let's get you in the dress." She pulled off the cover.

Martha stepped gingerly into the garment and pulled it up.

Ricki fastened the cloth-covered buttons one by one, then stepped back to observe her friend. "It fits perfectly."

"I must say, it's quite stunning," she remarked as she twisted and turned to see all sides in the mirror. "I simply love it. I only hope Wolf will approve."

Ricki laughed. "Oh my goodness, he'd have to be crazy not to love it."

The off-the-shoulder lace, elbow sleeved dress, garnished with sequins sparkled under the overhead lighting, giving an ethereal glow.

Ricki placed the silk flower circlet with the off-white veil attached on Martha's head. "Now the shoes."

She offered one foot, and Ricki slipped the lace-covered shoe on and did the same with the other.

"I think I'm complete now," said Martha.

"Not quite," Ricki announced. From her clutch bag she pulled out a small flat box and handed it to Martha.

"What's this?"

"Something old and something blue."

"How thoughtful, Ricki." She opened the box and gave a little gasp. "Oh my, it's lovely. Wherever did you find it?"

"It was my mother's. She gave it to me when I was a girl for my own wedding whenever that should happen."

Martha shoved the box back to Ricki. "I can't accept this. Your mother gave it to you."

Ricki gently pushed the box toward her friend. "And I'll have it for my wedding."

"What do you mean?"

"You'll give it back to me when that event occurs," Ricki explained.

"You mean, you and Kory are...?"

"We've put it off a bit. He's proposed, but with everything that's happened we've agreed to wait a few weeks more. I want you to have the handkerchief for your wedding. The lace dates back to my grandmother's wedding. And it's blue, so it covers all the bases. Both my grandmother and my mother had long marriages, so it's good luck. You can safeguard it for me and return it at our wedding."

Tears glistened in her eyes. "Oh Ricki, I am so appreciative of this gift. Of course, it will be my pleasure to present it to you at your wedding. Will you use the garden or go more traditional in a church?"

"We're talking about the mountain. We know just the place."

She winked. "I hope that is soon."

Ricki blushed. "Me, too. Now. I must go down and see if everything is ready. An eleven o'clock wedding is unusual, but the perfect time for the garden. I'm going to send Ivy up here to keep you company.

~~~*~~~

The time passed quickly with Ivy chattering away. Before she knew it Ricki was back with Kory by her side.

"Everyone is seated. We're ready for you," Ricki announced.

Martha looked at both of them with tears in her eyes and a smile on her lips. "I cannot thank you enough for all of this. Kory for walking me down the aisle, Ricki for being my Maid of Honor. It means the world to me."
~~~

Kory leaned in to kiss her cheek, then held out his arm. "We're honored to be asked to serve the two most special people in the world. Ready?"

She gave him a quick nod, held the handkerchief in one hand and took his arm with the other. "More than you'll ever know."

Ricki, wearing a simple lime green floral chiffon dress and holding a small nosegay of assorted pastel flowers, walked ahead of them down the stairs.

They didn't speak until they reached the door to the garden.

She looked at Ricki, eyes glistening. "I can't wait to see what you've done."

Ricki whispered, "I hope you like it."

Ricki opened the door and stepped through to the garden.

As Martha followed, she gasped at the scene before her. She'd never seen so many flowers and greenery. The guests stood and turned to look at her, everyone beaming with joy. Her mother stood to the side holding Martha's bouquet. A gorgeous cluster of red carnations and red roses, greenery, and baby's breath.

"Oh Mother, it's lovely. But I wasn't going to carry a bouquet. How did you know to choose carnations and roses?"

Tears danced in her mother's eyes as she handed her the flowers. "My gift to you, my daughter. And Wolf suggested them when I asked him about it. Every bride should carry a bouquet."

Martha accepted the offering and kissed her on the cheek. "Thank you. I love you so much."

Mac took Dame Buford's arm and escorted her to a seat in front of the gazebo.

"Kory, my make up is going to run all over the place if there are any more surprises. I can hardly see through the tears."

He squeezed her hand. "Not to worry. I've got my trusty hanky if such a thing happens. Now there's more to see."

They walked through an arch of flowers, guests murmuring words of love and friendship as they passed.

And then, as a violin played the wedding march, she stopped halfway.

The strains kept playing, but for Martha everything stopped, the music, the guests whispering, even the flowers faded away and she glimpsed Wolf standing inside the gazebo.

Time rolled away and once again she was back in Spain on the back of the train experiencing their first kiss. He'd been so handsome in his Air Force blue dress uniform.

And he still was.

For there, right in front of her, he stood dressed in that same uniform.

When she was able to walk again, Kory ushered her inside and stepped back.

"Wolf…" she whispered softly.

"Martha," he answered in a soft voice.

The music stopped.

Ricki took her place. Pete stood opposite her next to Wolf.

And then she looked past Wolf.

Polecat Robinson stood with Bible in hand.

She whispered to Wolf, "How?"

He replied, "He became ordained online, just for us."

Again tears threatened to spring forth. To see this man who encouraged her back in England, who cared so much about Wolf and his well-being, standing there ready to officiate their wedding overwhelmed her. It was almost too much.

Polecat performed flawlessly. When it was time for the vows, he nodded to Wolf.

Wolf began,

"Today, I vow what time could never steal.
In the quiet years we lost, not a day passed when your memory didn't breathe beside mine. We took different roads, but every path led me back to you—wiser, weathered, and certain.

I promise to honor not just who you are today,
But the woman I once loved, the soul I never forgot,
And the partner you've always been, even in absence.

With every scar we carry and every joy still ahead,
I vow to never take this second chance for granted.
You are my once, my always, and now, my forever."
		He placed a gold band on her ring finger.
		Now it was her turn.
"My Love,
Today, as I stand before you, I see not just the man I once loved... but the man I never stopped loving.
We lost time. We lost moments. But we never lost us.
Through silence, my heart still spoke your name. Through time, I carried you with me—in memory, in hope, in every unfinished dream.
Now, fate has brought us back. And I vow to honor this second chance completely.
I promise to cherish not only who we are today, but everything it took for us to find our way back.
I vow to be your peace when life is too loud, your strength when the past feels heavy, and your joy in the quiet, ordinary days we once only dreamed about.
And now, you are the one I will never let go.
This time, my love... we write forever."

The End

Acknowledgements

To my husband, Ron Wiseman—your unwavering support, constant encouragement, and belief in my writing mean more than words can say.

To my insightful beta readers, Nancy Hudgins and Ruth Buck—thank you for your sharp eyes, honest feedback, and dedication to helping me craft a stronger story.

And finally, to my wonderful publisher, Shannon Christensen of CS Publishing—your tireless efforts and commitment to excellence ensure each book shines at its best.

About the Author

Patty Wiseman, a native of the Seattle, Washington area, ventured to Bartlesville, Oklahoma after high school to attend The Wesleyan College. Following her college years, she settled in Northeast Texas, where she met and married her Texas-born husband, Ron.

Now the proud mother of two grown sons who are pursuing their own paths, Patty embraced a new chapter after a 25-year career as an administrative assistant in the financial industry. Upon retirement, she dove headfirst into her lifelong passion for writing—and hasn't looked back. With fourteen published books and more on the way, she continues to captivate readers.

An avid history enthusiast with a love for riddles, Patty's stories are known for their blend of mystery and romance, guaranteed to keep you turning the pages. She has received numerous awards for her work and finds great joy in mentoring aspiring writers.

A personal highlight in her writing journey is featuring her granddaughter, Savannah Cameron, on the covers of two of her books.

Her favorite quote beautifully reflects her philosophy:

"Find out who you are, then do it on purpose." – Dolly Parton